ROSES
IN THE
SAND

AGENT JAXSON LOCKE FBI MYSTERY THRILLER SERIES BOOK 3

MICHAEL MERSON

ROSES
IN THE
SAND

Prologue
Agent Carter

Agent James Carter sat naked in the wooden chair, trying to collect himself. His thoughts were confused, he was disoriented, and he was tied to a chair. But his biggest concern was the man who sat across from him. Carter briefly looked around the dimly lit room but couldn't find anything that would hint to his location. From what he could tell, there was no window, no door, and no sounds coming from outside the room. Cool air crossed over his body as the vent, which sat directly over his head, pulled the air from the room. As the air moved from the floor to the ceiling, he felt cold at first, but then he became warm as his body began to burn in different places along his arms and legs.

"Well, you got me here; now what?" Carter asked.

The man sitting across from him did not answer. He just sat there, observing his prey.

"Aren't you going to say something, or are you one of those serial killers who gets off on trying to scare your victims before you kill them? Because if that's the case, plan on being disappointed. I've accepted the choices I've made in my career, and I knew this situation was a possibility when I decided to join the task force to hunt you down. I came to terms with what could happen a long time ago. So I'm not screaming or begging just to entertain the likes of you," Carter explained as he tried to adjust his legs and hands. They had been tied tightly in place.

"I don't plan on trying to scare you, Agent Carter," the man answered, breaking his silence.

"So you're not going to kill me?" Carter asked suspiciously.

"Oh, I plan on killing you, Agent Carter. As a matter of fact, you're dying right there in that chair within the next few minutes," the killer remarked in a deep, clear, and confident voice. Agent Carter knew it was him. "Him" being SKO, the serial killer who had already killed two other agents before Agent Carter had been assigned to track him down. Agent Carter had spoken to SKO numerous times over the phone, and he thought he had gotten to know him. He also thought he had been closing in on the killer right before the killer captured him.

Agent James Carter had been tracking the infamous serial killer for six months. As he sat there, recalling the night's events, he shook his head, angry at himself. He knew he had let his guard down last night, and that was when SKO had made his move and got the drop on him. The liquor, the woman, and the atmosphere of the evening had been too much. They were going to be his downfall. SKO was the moniker the serial killer had given to himself some months back. The number of people SKO had killed was unknown, but it was over three, and three victims were all the FBI needed to label him as a serial killer.

"How are you going to do it? Are you going to cut my throat like you did to Agent Wilks, or are you going to bludgeon me to death like you did to Agent Bellows?" Agent Carter asked in a now dry, raspy voice. His throat was becoming hoarse, and his eyes started to burn, just like the other parts of his body.

"No on both assumptions. I have something special in

mind for you," SKO answered as he stood from the chair and moved closer to Agent Carter. When he was only a few feet away, Agent Carter noticed SKO was wearing a spit shield and rubber gloves. He was also covered from head to toe in what appeared to be a rubber suit.

"What are you wearing? Are you planning on stepping outside the box and killing me in one of the ways the drug cartels kill their enemies? Maybe you have a chainsaw somewhere behind you with my name on it. C'mon, when we getting started? I'm not begging. I won't give you the satisfaction! You crazy sick fuck!" Carter yelled from the confines of his chair.

"I've already started, Agent Carter," SKO answered calmly.

"What do you mean? What did you do to me?" Carter asked as the burning in his body worsened. Dark bruises were surfacing along his arms.

"I've given you something, Agent Carter, and it's starting to work." SKO moved closer to his victim for a better look.

"I was close to capturing you," Carter managed to say through the intense pain.

"You were never close! You followed the road I laid out before you. Now it's time for me to move on to another opponent," SKO advised the dying agent.

"What… What's happening to me?" Carter struggled to ask.

"The tissue in your body is eroding. In other words, you're bleeding from the inside out. When the chemical has run its course throughout your body, you'll be nothing more than a liquid mess on the floor while your bones will still be intact in that chair. Well, that's what I was told would happen by the man who sold it to me anyway. I'm actually excited to see if it really happens," SKO explained as he walked around the chair, observing the visibly melting man.

"Wait…" Carter said out loud.

"Wait? Are you begging? I thought you said you weren't

going to. Now I'm disappointed in you, Agent Carter," SKO admitted despairingly.

"I'm… I'm not begging. Where did this stuff come from?" Carter asked.

"Does it matter?" SKO asked back.

"To me, it does," Carter admitted right before his left eyeball slipped out of its socket and fell to the floor.

"Let's just say I got it from the man from Medan," SKO answered softly as he pushed a pencil into Agent Carter's leg.

"You'll never find anyone better than me," Carter managed to say as the skin on his face slowly slid downward.

"Very little pain, from what I gather. Very interesting," SKO said as he continued to observe the dying FBI agent. "By the way, I've already found someone else. I'm sending him to Pensacola, Florida. I'm interested in seeing how he performs on the case down there." SKO walked away just as Agent Carter's face completely slipped off the bone and slid down his chest and onto his lap.

POLICE LINE DO NOT CROSS
POLICE LINE

Chapter 1
Jerry

Pensacola Beach, one of the three small communities that make up Santa Rosa Island, had been evacuated two days prior to the arrival of Hurricane Jerry, a category three hurricane. Yesterday morning, three hours before Hurricane Jerry was predicted to make landfall, the National Weather Service downgraded Jerry to a category one. Deputy Brian Kennedy was assigned to patrol the residential and public areas along Pensacola Beach east and west on Via De Luna Drive from Fort Pickens Road to public parking Lot H. Deputy Kennedy had been awake for twenty-four hours, running from one call for service to another, assisting twenty to thirty citizens who had refused to evacuate the island after getting advanced notice to do so. During his shift, he broke up one hurricane party at the high-rise condominiums on the west side of the island and ordered three small business owners to leave or get arrested, and to top it all, he rescued one terrified Shih Tzu puppy from the rising waters. The dog's collar identified the brown-and-white puppy as "Pumpkin," who had become Deputy Kennedy's partner for the remainder of his shift.

Deputy Kennedy was tired, overworked, and irritated.

By the time he backed his green-and-white cruiser under Todd's beach house on Ariola Drive, he was all too ready to fall into a deep sleep. He placed the cruiser in Park, locked the doors, and grabbed Pumpkin from the passenger seat. He made his way into the dark beach house, sat on the couch, lay back, and closed his eyes, with Pumpkin resting comfortably on his lap. The beach house belonged to Todd Warren, who was an old high school friend of Brian's, and Todd had given the deputy permission to use his beach house if he needed to during the storm. The wind blew the rain against the side of the beach house as Deputy Kennedy quickly sank deeper into unconsciousness. It was about twenty minutes past midnight when Tina, one of the county dispatchers, called for Deputy Kennedy over the radio.

"Four Adam Thirty-Eight," Tina announced and then waited a moment for Deputy Kennedy to answer.

"Four Adam Thirty-Eight," Tina announced a little louder once more over the radio.

"Four Adam Thirty-Eight, go ahead," Kennedy answered, half asleep. He sat up, startling the puppy.

"Four Adam Thirty-Eight, I know it's been a long shift, but we need you to respond to sixteen sixteen Ariola Drive in reference to a possible DB," Tina advised.

"Roger. Did I copy that correctly? It's a possible DB?" Deputy Kennedy asked. He knew DB was the acronym for a dead body. Kennedy wanted to make sure he had heard his dispatcher correctly.

"That's correct," she answered.

"Is there a reporting party?"

"Negative, the call came in anonymously."

"Anonymously. Really?" Kennedy responded surprisingly.

"Roger, Four Adam Thirty-Eight. I don't have another unit clear right now, but as soon as I do, I'll roll one your way for cover."

"Don't send a cover unit. I'll advise when I get there. I've been on Ariola all night, and there's no one out here but me. It's probably just some prank caller. I can't see anyone finding a DB this late at night, especially since there isn't anyone out here but me and my partner."

"Partner? Four Adam Thirty-Eight, I was told you were a lone unit tonight," Tina replied.

"I am. I'll explain later. Go ahead and show me en route."

"Roger, Four Adam Thirty-Eight. By the way, the DB is supposed to be under the house near the back."

"Roger."

"Roger, Four Adam Thirty-Eight. Twenty-four, twenty-five hours."

Deputy Kennedy stood up, stretched, held Pumpkin under his arm, and walked back out to his cruiser. The night air was cool. The strong, seventy-five mile-per-hour winds from Jerry were blowing the rain in from the Gulf of Mexico as a brilliant flash of white light streaked across the dark sky, followed by loud claps of thunder. Deputy Kennedy took a deep breath and held Pumpkin tightly as another flash lit the night, followed by another clap of thunder just above them. He quickly unlocked the passenger door and placed Pumpkin in the seat. He then walked out to the end of the driveway where it met the road and looked down the street through the darkness toward 1616 Ariola Drive. All the residents had been evacuated, and the power was out along the island. There should not have been any visible lights for miles in any direction, but there on the south side of the road, Kennedy noticed a small light moving about from the road toward the beach house. He squinted his eyes and tried to see through the darkness when another flash of light suddenly streaked through the night sky, revealing the silhouette of someone holding the light. "Hmmm, who is that?" Deputy Kennedy said quietly.

Kennedy went back to his cruiser and climbed inside, then

petted the frightened pup and used the radio to call dispatch once more.

"Four Adam Thirty-Eight."

"Four Adam Thirty-Eight, go ahead."

"Four Adam Thirty-Eight. Dispatch, why don't you go ahead and start another unit this way. It looks like there could be someone out here."

"Four Adam Thirty-Eight, are you on scene?"

"Negative. I'm just down the road from the beach house, and I can see someone moving around, carrying a light."

"Roger, Four Adam Thirty-Eight, I'll get a unit headed that way, but it may be a little while."

"Roger. I'll continue to the house. It's probably just a homeowner who refused to evacuate. I'll keep you advised."

"Roger, Four Adam Thirty-Eight. Twenty-four thirty hours."

Deputy Kennedy placed the car in drive and pulled out of Todd's driveway and onto Ariola Drive. He kept the cruiser lights off and allowed the car to move slowly toward 1616 in the Drive position without the use of the accelerator. As he got closer, he could see the light again, but now it was moving around under the beach house. When he was about three properties away from 1616, he placed the car in Park and called the dispatcher once more.

"Four Adam Thirty-Eight."

"Four Adam Thirty-Eight, go ahead," Tina replied.

"Four Adam Thirty-Eight. Show me on scene."

"Roger, Four Adam Thirty-Eight. Your cover unit is a few minutes out."

"Roger," Kennedy said.

"All units be advised, this channel is Code One for Four Adam Thirty-Eight at twenty-four thirty-five hours," Tina announced to all other deputies on the same channel. The Code One gave Deputy Kennedy priority use of the channel until he felt he was safe, by announcing he was Code Four and that dispatch could clear the Code One.

Deputy Kennedy reached down to plug his earpiece line into the radio on his belt and then looped the earpiece around his ear. He wanted to maintain noise and light discipline when he approached the unknown person or persons. Deputy Kennedy opened his cruiser door and once again stepped out into the hurricane environment. Before he could close the door, Pumpkin jumped out and ran toward 1616 Ariola Drive.

"No! Kennedy whispered, but it was too late. Pumpkin quickly disappeared into the darkness as she ran toward the light in the distance.

Deputy Kennedy ducked and quietly moved closer to the houses on his right. He decided to go around toward the back of the homes that lined the Gulf of Mexico. As he approached 1616 Ariola Drive, he used the sound of the waves breaking against the shore to cover his approach while keeping his flashlight off. When he got closer, he could see that some of the bottom blow-out panels of the beach house were missing. It appeared a surge of water had passed under the beach house, removing the bottom panels during the peak of Hurricane Jerry.

The light Kennedy had observed earlier continued to move back and forth, shining over the ground below it. It appeared as if a person was holding a flashlight, and he or she was moving it clumsily across the ground. Kennedy cautiously moved closer with his pistol drawn and aimed in the direction of the unknown figure holding the light. When he felt he had the element of surprise, Deputy Kennedy flipped his flashlight on and pointed it toward the figure.

"Sheriff's Office! Slowly turn around and face me," Deputy Kennedy ordered from behind one of the beach house support piers. He waited for a moment, but the person did not comply with his command.

"Turn and face me with your hands in the air! Kennedy yelled just as a bright white light streaked across the sky, revealing the unknown figure. Thunder clapped, and the deputy's eyes widened.

"What the…"

Lightning flashed overhead, exposing a female mannequin hanging from the trusses of the beach house with the flashlight tied to one of its hands. The deputy moved closer and saw Pumpkin standing under the mannequin, where she was tied securely to one of the support piers.

Deputy Kennedy quickly dropped to his knee, pulled the flashlight down, and used his light to survey the area around him.

"Who's out there?" he yelled as he passed the beam of light from one side of the house to the other, looking for a suspect.

"Four Adam Thirty-Eight, are you Code Four?" Tina asked after not hearing from the deputy for a few minutes.

Kennedy was about to answer when off in the distance, toward the water, he heard the unmistakable sound of a boat engine starting. He reached to his side for his more powerful flashlight, turned it on, and pointed it in the direction of the Gulf of Mexico. A few hundred yards offshore, he saw a large, fifty- to sixty-foot fishing vessel motoring its way out to deeper waters.

"Four Adam Thirty-Eight, Deputy Kennedy, are you Code Four?" Tina asked once more.

"Four Adam Thirty-Eight. I'm Code Four, and you can drop the Code One. Do we have any watercraft on the water near my location?"

"Negative, Four Adam Thirty-Eight."

Deputy Kennedy watched as the vessel's operator turned off its outside lights and went dark after reaching cruising speed. In its wake, Kennedy could see what appeared to be a small inflatable raft drifting in the surf back toward shore. He turned, put his light on the excited, barking Pumpkin, and walked toward her.

"I know, somebody's playing a very dangerous game with us," Kennedy said as he placed his pistol back into his holster. When Kennedy was almost to the excited pup, he tripped over something and fell to the wet sandy beach.

"Damn it!" Kennedy said out loud as he rubbed his knee in the dark.

"What did I trip over?" he asked himself and used his flashlight to survey the ground behind him.

"Holy…" Deputy Kennedy yelled as the light from his flashlight revealed the head and hand of a woman protruding upward out of the sand.

"Four Adam Thirty-Eight!" Kennedy shouted into the radio. "Four Adam Thirty-Eight, DISPATCH!" "Four Adam Thirty-Eight, go ahead," Tina answered quickly after hearing the excitement in the deputy's voice.

"I need additional units to my location, as well as major crimes. I need a perimeter set up as far as Panama City to the east and Fort Pickens to the west. I need units looking for a fifty- to sixty-foot fishing vessel, making its way to shore from the Gulf side of the island."

"Four Adam Thirty-Eight, roger. What do you have out there?"

"I got a DB at 1616 Ariola Drive!"

Chapter 2
Pensacola

Jaxson found his luggage quickly after his flight landed in Pensacola, Florida. Few flights were arriving and taking off from the Pensacola airport after Hurricane Jerry had moved through the area. After securing his luggage, Jaxson waited there for his prearranged contact, Detective Martinez, from the Escambia County's Sheriff's Office, but after forty-five minutes and three unanswered text messages to Detective Martinez, Jaxson decided to get a rental and drive to the scene himself. At the car rental company, he discovered he had a vast array of vehicles to choose from. He was greeted by a very tall, thin, and young teenager who spoke with a deep Southern accent. The young man, Jimmy, wore khaki pants and white shoes, with a brown polo that had his name pinned to it.

"We've got most of our cars to choose from. I guess folks thought the hurricane was going to be a lot worse than it was, and they left town or canceled their travel plans when Pensacola Beach got its evacuation order. Do you have a specific car in mind?" Jimmy asked the visiting FBI agent.

"How about I just get the least expensive, most gas efficient, and least noticeable car you have," Jaxson answered.

"Really? Because I have a convertible sports car available," the young man replied.

"I don't think Uncle Sam would approve of the additional expense for a sports car."

"Okay, no offense, but your uncle sounds like a dick, if you know what I mean."

"My uncle?" Jaxson said with a perplexed expression.

"Yeah, your uncle. Uncle Sam! I mean, if he paid for you to come to Florida, you'd think he'd want you to enjoy yourself. What better way to do that than from a convertible?"

"I don't think you understand…"

"No, I do. I got family like that. We all do, if you know what I mean," Jimmy explained while lowering his voice.

"Yes, we do, but still I'll just take the—"

"I know. The least expensive, most gas efficient, and least noticeable car," Jimmy said.

"Yes," Jaxson replied. He figured it was better to just end the conversation rather than try to explain who Uncle Sam was to the clueless young clerk. It took Jimmy about ten minutes to complete the paperwork and to give Jaxson the keys to a car. Before long, Jaxson found himself walking out of the terminal and into the hot and very humid Pensacola air. He made his way into the rental car parking lot and found the least expensive, most gas efficient, and least noticeable car sitting in space D3, right next to a red convertible sports car, where Jimmy told him he could find it.

Jaxson put his luggage in the trunk, got inside, and immediately turned the car on and started the air conditioner. He had already begun to sweat and could feel the wetness along his back. As Jaxson sat there inputting the address of 1616 Ariola Drive into the GPS, he thought about how he had made the right decision to have worn a white polo golf shirt and beige pants. *Pensacola may not be the tropics, but it certainly feels like it,* he thought.

Jaxson was on the road for about twenty minutes when his phone vibrated in his pocket. He thought it was Detective Martinez finally returning his previous messages or that maybe it was his boss, Steve Overton, contacting him to let him know he had given him the wrong contact information before he had left Virginia. *Why else would Detective Martinez not answer my text messages, and why wasn't he at the airport?* Jaxson asked himself.

When he stopped at a stoplight, Jaxson looked at the screen of his phone and noticed he had a message from an unknown number. He was about to open the text message when the person behind him honked his horn, indicating the light had changed and he needed to move on. Jaxson dropped his phone onto the passenger seat and continued on the route displayed on the screen. A few minutes later, he found himself crossing over a very long bridge that spanned straight over a large body of water. He then entered the city of Gulf Breeze and followed the route toward Pensacola Beach.

It wasn't long before he was crossing another bridge that took him to a toll booth. Jaxson pulled up to the toll booth where a uniformed deputy was checking people entering the area. The deputy was a short, thin man wearing a white polo, green shorts, and black tennis shoes.

"Can I see your identification and something that has your local mailing address on it if you reside outside of the area? Only residents, business owners, and people who own rentals are being allowed back on the beach for another couple of days," the deputy explained after Jaxson rolled down his window.

"I'm Agent Jaxson Locke with the FBI, and I'm here to assist with the investigation at sixteen sixteen Ariola Drive," Jaxson explained as he held up his credentials.

"Yep, they said you'd be coming through. Go on down the road here, and you'll turn right onto Avenue Twenty-Three. Don't make the mistake of going right at this light up there.

That road takes you to Ft. Pickens, and there's nothing out there except an old fort," the deputy explained with a slight Southern drawl.

"Thank you, Deputy," Jaxson replied and proceeded down Via De Luna Drive toward Avenue 23. As he drove, he saw people moving about the area, picking up debris from Hurricane Jerry. Some people were repairing windows and siding on their beach houses, while others seemed to be going about their day as if nothing had occurred. The hurricane may have come through the previous day, but today, the sun was out, and as he drove toward the crime scene, he thought about how, under other circumstances, he would maybe like to vacation at a place like Pensacola Beach one day.

After almost two miles, Jaxson found Avenue 23 and made a right turn onto it. He then turned left onto Ariola Drive and saw numerous police cars, a coroner's van, and of course the many national news vans and their eager reporters scouring about the area. Jaxson maneuvered the rental car past the news vans and pulled up to a barricade that was being overseen by a female uniformed deputy.

"Can I help you, sir?" she asked after Jaxson pulled up, stopped, and rolled down his window once more.

"I'm Agent Jaxson Locke with—"

"Yes, I know. Deputy Smith radioed that you'd be coming through in a few minutes. I'll open the barricade, and you can park anywhere up there along the road," she explained as she pointed toward the crime scene. She then walked over and moved the barricade aside for Jaxson to pass through. Jaxson did as he was told and found a spot on the right side of the road past everyone else. He parked the car, grabbed his phone, and stepped out onto Pensacola Beach.

The area had people running around, carrying evidence bags, shovels, and other equipment being used to recover the bodies of the victims. As Jaxson proceeded up the driveway of 1616 Ariola Drive, he stopped and looked at the beautiful Italian villa sitting before him. He then turned around and looked at the other beach houses lining the street, and he saw a woman.

Directly across the street was another beach house. It was almost as magnificent as the one he was about to enter. It was also built with an Italian-themed architectural design but not to the scale of 1616. On the second floor, there was a large balcony that extended over the driveway. Standing on the balcony was a woman. She was standing there in shorts and a T-shirt with her arms crossed. What really drew Jaxson's attention to her was the fact that she had locked her eyes directly on Jaxson Locke. *She's got something to say,* he thought.

Jaxson turned away and started for the front door when he saw a crime scene technician walking out from under the garage portion under the beach house. Jaxson walked that direction and made his way under the house, where he found different people working in some capacity in processing the scene. The crime scene technicians collected evidence, sifted through sand with large screens, or took photos of items recovered from the graves. Around the perimeter of the scene were uniformed officers. They ensured no one who was not part of the investigation entered the crime scene. In the center, watching over the collection of evidence, were two men in civilian clothing.

Jaxson carefully walked up to one of the men who had a bureau badge displayed on his waist. He was a large man who appeared to be uncomfortable in the hot, humid environment. He was sweating through all his clothes. Looking closer, Jaxson observed that even more sweat was dripping down his forehead and into his eyes.

"Hello, I'm Agent Jaxson Locke," Jaxson announced as he walked up to his fellow agent.

"Great! I'm Agent Travis Baker. I'm sure glad you're here,"

Baker said as he reached out to shake Jaxson's hand while wiping the sweat from his forehead.

"Who's in charge?" Jaxson asked as he looked at the man next to Agent Baker.

Baker replied, "Agent Locke, this is Detective Martinez with ESCO. He has been assigned to the case. And—"

"And did you sign in at the front? I need everyone who enters the scene to be accounted for. There's a deputy over there who will check your ID and put your name into the log. Don't touch anything and watch where you step," Detective Martinez ordered as he shook Jaxson's hand. He was a thin man with a short haircut. He was Hispanic but spoke without an accent.

"I was expecting you at the airport," Jaxson said in response.

"I thought that was tonight. The email I received didn't mention a.m. or p.m. I assumed it was this evening," Martinez replied.

"Well, I also texted you when I arrived."

"I'm sorry, but as you can see, I've been swamped, trying to solve a few homicides," Martinez said loudly. He put his arms to his side, pointed at the graves, and circularly moved his body. His body language, his performance, and general attitude toward Jaxson indicated he was not happy to have the FBI there and he wanted everyone watching to know it. Jaxson believed Detective Martinez enjoyed having an audience.

"I get it. Again, I'm Agent Locke with the FBI, and we were asked by Sheriff Thomas to assist with the investigation and—"

"I know, if—"

"If you require anything from me," Jaxson said, cutting off Martinez in response. "Then you can reach me on the number I texted you from earlier. Until then, I'll just look around and maybe ask the neighbors some questions."

"Fine. Make sure—"

"I know. I'll sign in the log with your deputy."

"Right," Martinez replied before going back to work.

Jaxson and Agent Baker walked to the deputy, where Jaxson provided his credentials and signed the entry log. The two agents then walked back out to the front of the beach house and stood in the driveway. Jaxson looked around and saw a few hundred people standing in driveways, on the dunes, and along the shoulder of the road. *Apparently, the deputies are only stopping vehicular traffic from entering the area*, he thought to himself.

"Detective Martinez is a bit of an ass. I would have warned you if he wasn't standing right there," Baker remarked.

"Yes, he is. But he's not much different than some of the other local authorities who think our job is to take over. I'll work on him a little bit, and eventually—hopefully—get him to understand that we're here just for support and assistance," Jaxson explained as he looked up and watched a drone fly overhead.

"I'm your liaison from the bureau's Pensacola office. If you need me for anything, just call my cell phone, day or night."

"Great," Jaxson said as he watched the drone fly over the beach house toward the water.

"Where do you want to start?" Baker asked.

"With whoever owns that drone," Jaxson answered. He followed the drone to the backside of the house as it continued toward the water.

From the side of the beach house, Jaxson and Baker could see that the back of the beach house was just as busy with people trying to see what was going on. It seemed everyone in Pensacola with access to a boat had made their way to the island. They then anchored nearby and made their way to shore in hopes of getting a glimpse at what was going on under the beach house. News crews were filming the area while reporters interviewed beachgoers and residents. Jaxson surveyed the crowd until he spotted the drone operator. He was a young man in his twenties wearing a white tank top and board shorts with a flowered pattern. He carried a backpack over his right shoulder while looking up in the air toward his drone.

"You see him over there?" Jaxson asked Baker.

"Yes."

"I want to speak to him, but I don't want to call any attention to him when we contact him."

"Okay, how do you suppose that we do that?" Baker asked.

"You stay here, and I'll go over and talk to him."

Jaxson untucked his shirt, removed his shoes and socks, rolled up his pants, and walked back to the front of the house. He made his way to the neighboring beach house. From the adjacent beach house, he casually walked out onto the beach where he carefully made his way through the crowd, pretending to look at the beach house that was crowded with law enforcement officials, just as everyone else was doing, until he reached the drone operator.

"That's a nice drone," Jaxson said to the young man.

"Yeah. It cost me a lot of money, but it takes great photos. I hope to get some good ones to sell to online media outlets," the young man explained.

"How much do you think you can get for the photos?"

"A couple hundred bucks maybe. Why?" he asked the oddly dressed man standing next to him.

"What if I gave you two hundred dollars just to fly your drone over the crowd and take as many photos as you can of everyone?"

"I could do that, but I don't know if the cops would allow it."

"I'm Agent Locke with the FBI. I guarantee you no one is going to say anything to you," Jaxson explained as he discreetly pulled up his shirt to show the young man his badge.

"Okay. I just got to take photos of the people in the crowd?" he asked.

"Yes. You see the man next to the beach house over there?" Jaxson asked as he looked toward Agent Baker. He was still standing next to the beach house where Jaxson had left him.

"Yeah."

"When you're done, just go over to him and give him the SD card with the images. He'll give you the other half of your money," Jaxson explained as he took five twenties from his wallet and handed them to the young man.

"How do you know you can trust me? I mean, you don't even know my name," the young photographer asked as Jaxson started to walk away.

Jaxson turned and answered. "Sure I do. You're Ronald Retting."

"How did you know that?" Ronald asked suspiciously.

"It's on your backpack. You're Ronald Retting of Ronald Retting Photography, correct?"

"Yes. I guess I forgot that was there," Ronald whispered as the agent continued to walk away.

Jaxson made his way back to Agent Baker using the same route he had taken to get to Ronald. Agent Baker was still standing there, uncomfortably waiting for Jaxson to return.

"Travis, I have the young man with the drone taking photos of the people in the crowd. I told him to come over here when he was done, and you'd give him the other hundred dollars I owe him for taking the photos," Jaxson said as he handed Agent Baker a hundred-dollar bill.

"Okay. How long do you think it will take?" Agent Baker asked.

"I don't know. Do you have an appointment or something?" Jaxson asked.

"No. I just don't feel well. I think I'm running a fever or something."

"That would explain the sweating."

"Yeah. I usually don't sweat this much."

"Are you okay to stay here for a little longer?" Jaxson asked.

"Yeah."

"Good. I'm going back into the crime scene to see if I can find anything useful."

Chapter 3
An Old Friend and a Garrote

Jaxson walked back under the beach house after signing in once more with the deputy controlling the access point for people entering and leaving the crime scene. He didn't speak to anyone. Jaxson had decided it was best to just walk around and observe. He watched as the crime scene technicians sifted through shovelful after shovelful of beach sand taken from inside and outside the areas surrounding the graves. Jaxson also watched as Detective Martinez moved from one grave to another, inspecting and overseeing different aspects of the collection of evidence. Martinez made comments to the technicians and made notes in his notepad.

In the corners under the beach house, large floodlights illuminated every square foot of the crime scene. There were more than three crime scene photographers taking pictures. After seeing the different photographers, Jaxson determined Detective Martinez was working the crime scene in a team approach. One team was charged with excavating bodies, another removed dirt and sifted through sand for evidence, and the third team photographed and documented the evidence collected. Each victim and their grave were assigned a detective from the sheriff's office. Every team worked under the direction of Detective Martinez, who moved from one team to the other when he wasn't checking his cell phone. *Sure, you were too busy to check your phone when I arrived,* Jaxson thought as he watched Martinez look at his cell phone more than ten times in ten minutes.

"I didn't know you were going to be here," Jaxson heard from behind him.

Jaxson turned around and saw his longtime friend Dr. Stefanie Mack standing behind him. "Hello. It's good to see you, Stefanie."

Stefanie was more than the eye could see, to say the least. She was an attractive woman with a PhD in Forensic Anthropology. She wore almost no makeup, kept her hair in a ponytail, wore glasses, and spoke scientifically, but she had the looks of a runway model.

"You got a profile yet?" Stefanie asked.

"I'm working on it. Why are you here? From what I can see, there's a little more meat on the bone than you usually like," Jaxson said jokingly.

"Ha, ha, I get it. Bone doctor! Meat on the bone!" Stefanie always enjoyed working with Jaxson, and it didn't hurt that she found him to be very attractive.

"I'm just kidding you," Jaxson said.

"I was asked to come and help with exhuming the bodies from their graves. Once an anthropologist, always an anthropologist."

"Dr. Mack, can you help us over here?" one of the crime scene technicians asked.

"I gotta get to work. Call me and we'll do dinner or something and catch up," Stefanie said as she rushed to the tech.

"I will."

Jaxson continued to walk the scene and watched from a few feet away as the last remaining victim was excavated. The victim appeared to be a woman. She had on some type of red dress that didn't completely cover her body. She looked to be buried shallower than the others, and her body wasn't as decomposed as Jaxson thought it should have been.

"You don't get squeamish, do you? I can't have you throwing up in my crime scene," Martinez stated from behind Jaxson.

Jaxson turned around and faced the detective. "No. I think I'll be all right."

"She was the one who was found first. When we got here, we set up the crime scene, and one of our guys noticed the ground under the piers supporting the beach house appeared to be sunken in more than the ground around it," Martinez explained.

"Interesting," Jaxson replied. Jaxson had decided not to say anything else, as he wanted Martinez to continue talking. Jaxson understood that people who displayed an extroverted personality, like Detective Martinez, needed to feel they controlled the conversation, and that was precisely what Jaxson was going to allow Martinez to do.

"Yeah. We brought out a ground-penetrating radar unit and discovered the other six graves. I made the decision to excavate the victims according to when or what order that I thought they were buried in."

"How did you make the determination?" Jaxson asked.

"I believed she looked pretty fresh. I think she was maybe in the sand for a couple of weeks, at the most. Then I worked backward. From her to the one next to her and so on after that, until I got to the first grave—or the one I think is the first victim's grave."

"So you believe the first victim was buried closest to the back of the beach house?" Jaxson asked.

"Yes," Martinez answered after he checked his cell phone once more and then sent a text message to someone.

"How did you determine she had been buried for only a couple of weeks?"

"She's not my first body buried at the beach. The moist and damp ground below keeps a body pretty fresh. I was surprised to find no scavengers had started feasting on her yet."

"I agree."

"The deeper the body is buried, the less likely scavengers would get to it. Sand crabs don't burrow down too deep, and they're usually found closer to the water." Martinez let out a deep breath as he read over another text message.

"That's good to know," Jaxson replied. He already knew the body would remain in better condition in the moist and damp environment but allowed Martinez to explain it to him.

"I gotta make a phone call," Martinez announced and walked a few feet away.

Jaxson continued to observe the excavation of the body. After the victim was lifted from her resting spot, Jaxson noticed something lying at the bottom of the grave. The victim's body had concealed the item until she was removed.

Jaxson heard parts of Martinez's conversation but acted as though he had not. "Yes. I don't know... I don't care... No, that won't happen... I'll talk to you later."

"We got anything?" Martinez asked after hanging up the phone.

"Yes. There's something down in the sand. It looks like she was lying on top of it," Jaxson said as he pointed at the object.

Martinez walked back to stand next to Jaxson. "Is it another flower?"

"No, it appears to be a garrote," Dr. Mack announced from beside the open grave.

"May be the murder weapon. Photograph it, bag it, and keep track of it," Martinez ordered.

"Yes, sir," the detective next to the grave replied.

"You mentioned a flower," Jaxson said to Martinez.

"Yeah, it looks like each girl was buried with a flower of some type, maybe a rose. Some were in pretty bad shape, but that's what we think they were," Martinez explained.

"Really…"

"Does that mean something to you?" Martinez asked sarcastically.

"Not yet."

"I didn't think so. We're almost done here. If you want to stay longer, I'll tell my deputies."

"I would like to look around a little more."

"What's your plan for tonight and tomorrow?" Martinez asked.

"I wanted to speak to the lady I saw across the street. Then I'm going to find a place to stay. As for tomorrow, I was hoping to meet up with you and discuss the case."

"We're meeting at the coroner's office tomorrow at one o'clock. There are plenty of hotels in Pensacola. Just stay off of Cervantes Street. I don't need another homicide! I'll text you the coroner's office address."

"Thank you, Detective Martinez."

Detective Martinez began to walk away but stopped and turned back toward Jaxson. "Be careful across the street with that lady. I think she's still upset with the entire sheriff's office. Probably me more than anyone else," Martinez warned and started to walk away again.

"Why?" Jaxson asked.

Detective Martinez stopped once more and turned toward the FBI agent after looking at his phone again. "Her friend owned this beach house. Her friend also came up missing a year ago. Her friend may be one of the victims we dug up today."

"Why would she be upset with you specifically?" Jaxson asked, continuing his line of inquiry.

"I got the missing person's case on her friend and did what I could. There were no leads. The case went cold. She came up to the sheriff's office and demanded to see me. We met, and things didn't go well. She didn't like the answers I provided, and she lost control. I had her escorted out of the building," Martinez reluctantly admitted and then started to leave again.

"What's her name?" Jaxson yelled. He wasn't finished with his questions and needed more information from Martinez, who appeared to be getting irritated with all the questions he was being asked.

"Taylor Long. Good luck! She's beautiful but a handful."

Jaxson wrote her name down in his notepad and looked over the scene once more. He drew a diagram of the beach house and where each grave was located. He then made notes to what he had already observed.

Four graves are lined up next to each other along the easterly side of the beach house directly in front of one of the beach house support piers.

Three graves are lined up next to each other along the southern side of the beach house directly in front of one of the support piers, just like the other four.

Jaxson looked at the piers along the easterly side of the beach house and noticed there was a total of ten piers supporting the structure on that side.

The graves start at the seventh and go to the tenth. Why not start at the first pier? It's more orderly. There's concealment from the road and the beach at those first six piers. You didn't start at the first one, nor did you stay in one row along the easterly side of the beach house, Jaxson thought to himself as he stood in the middle of the crime scene.

"Sir, I need to take some panoramic shots of the crime scene. Are you about done?" one of the crime scene photographers asked.

"Yes," Jaxson answered and walked to the deputy holding the entry log.

"Leaving?" The deputy asked.

"Yes, but I'll probably be back tomorrow."

Jaxson signed out of the crime scene and made his way to the driveway. He then wrote down some more notes.

Flowers/roses?

Garrote?

Odd placement of each grave. Maybe!

Chapter 4
Summer Rental

Jaxson found Agent Travis Baker waiting for him in the driveway. Jaxson looked up at the beach house across the street and once again saw the woman standing on the deck, the woman he now knew as Taylor Long. She had her hands and arms crossed across her body, and she was watching Detective Martinez walk out to his car.

"Here's the SD card with the photos Ronald took. He also gave me his business card in case you need it," Travis explained as he handed it all to Jaxson.

"Thank you."

"Here's my business card. If you need anything else, please don't hesitate to call me." Travis reached out and shook Jaxson's hand.

"I will. Thank you again."

Jaxson waited for Agent Baker to drive down the road and out through the barricade. Then he walked across the street toward the other house. Jaxson knew Taylor Long was undoubtedly waiting for someone to come over and ask her questions. *Everyone wants to say I told you so, and Detective Martinez was not about to listen to her say it. So I guess I'll take the hit,* Jaxson thought.

Jaxson knew he would catch all of Ms. Long's past years' frustrations with the people in law enforcement concerning her missing friend once he knocked on her door. It wouldn't matter that Jaxson was an FBI agent and not a member of the sheriff's office. *No, we would all be the same in her eyes. Here goes nothing,* Jaxson said to himself.

Jaxson walked across the street and made a direct path to the front door. He walked up the steps, stood in front of the door, and reached for the doorbell. The door quickly opened.

"I guess someone is *now* ready to listen to what I have to say!" Taylor Long said aggressively.

"If you're Taylor Long, I would very much like to hear what you have to say. I know that others working on your friend's missing person's case have fallen short of your expectations and—"

"Yes, I'm Taylor," she said sarcastically, cutting him off. "Fallen short! Is that what you call it? Your department did *nothing* to find Natalie, and then you had me forcibly removed from the building. I—"

"Please, I'm not with the sheriff's office. I'm Agent Jaxson Locke with the FBI. If you give me a chance, I promise I will do everything I can to help solve your friend's case."

"You're not a detective with the sheriff's office?" she asked in a more relaxed tone.

"No, I'm not. Can I come in and speak to you, or would you rather come out here on this very hot porch?" Jaxson asked and smiled slightly.

"Come in," she said as she turned around and walked back inside.

Jaxson followed her into her beach house and shut the door.

"We can talk in here," Taylor said as she walked through the living room and into the adjoining dining room, where she took a seat in one of the chairs along the side of the wooden dining table that filled the room. Inside the beach house, Jaxson had a better look at Taylor Long. She was beautiful, just as Martinez had said. She wore cutoff jean shorts, a sleeveless T-shirt, and what he thought was a red bathing suit underneath. "Please have a seat."

"Thank you," Jaxson said and immediately sat across from her. The table had two chairs on each side and one chair at each end. Her simple seat selection, not at the head of the table, expressed to Jaxson that she was approachable and willing to cooperate. He believed she had left the chair at the head of the table for him. The head of the table was, psychologically speaking, reserved for the leader, the person in command, and the person who, at times, may intimidate others in the room. Jaxson's seat selection reciprocated her unspoken intentions. He wanted her to know he was there as an equal, a team player, and he wanted to work together.

"Your home feels very welcoming and comfortable," Jaxson said.

"Thank you, but it's not my home. Well, it's mine, but I rent it out to vacationers. I have about fifteen vacation rentals up and down the Florida Panhandle. My actual home is down the road a bit," Taylor explained as she pointed toward the south.

"Is that what you do for a living? Vacation rentals?" Jaxson asked.

"Yes, but I also buy and sell real estate. It's how I met Natalie. She bought the house across the street," Taylor said as she teared up.

"When was that?" Jaxson quickly asked, attempting to move Taylor through the sorrowful memory of her friend.

"Um… four years ago. We became close friends after she bought the beach house and moved in. She was in commercial real estate. I was in residential real estate and vacation rentals. It was like we were meant to meet and to become best of friends."

"Did you two do a lot of things together?"

"Oh, yes. We took trips together and ogled handsome men on the beach from our decks while we drank large amounts of wine," Taylor answered. She smiled as she recalled her happier memories.

"When did you see Natalie last?"

"Right before I left to take care of my mother last year. You see, my mother hurt her back, and I went to take care of her during our 'Never Winter' vacation we had planned. That's when she met the man who did something to her," Taylor explained.

"Who did she meet, and how do you know this man harmed her?" Jaxson asked curiously.

"Well, she met Will while I was taking care of my mother. When I got back, she was gone. She never came back. She never called. Friends like we were don't do that to each other. Therefore, he had to have done something to her."

"Do you know Will's last name?"

"No. I think Natalie may have said it, but I forgot it. To tell you the truth, I thought Will was just a distraction for the summer. I never really gave him a second thought."

"What did you do when Natalie didn't call or come back?"

"I reported her missing. I kept calling Detective Martinez, the fucking asshole, but he didn't do anything except have me kicked out of the sheriff's office when I went up there to get answers," Taylor explained as a tear fell from her eye.

"I think I have enough for now. I would like to talk to you again, if that's okay," Jaxson said, realizing Taylor needed a break. Jaxson knew when to stop an interview. Taylor lived close by, and he could always reach out to her for more information. *Besides, it's a good possibility that Natalie was one of the victims who were buried under the house,* Jaxson thought as he wrote some notes down.

"That'll be fine. Where are you staying?" Taylor asked.

"I don't know yet. I flew in today, got a rental car, and drove over here. I'd like to find a hotel close to the scene, but Hurricane Jerry has many of them still closed."

"Then it's settled. You can stay here," Taylor declared as she stood.

"I don't think the bureau would approve of the expense of a place like this," Jaxson admitted.

"Hurricane Jerry forced a lot of people to cancel their vacation plans. This beach house is available for the next month. I'll rent it to you at the same rate you would pay at any hotel you can find. Besides, don't you want to be close to the crime scene?" Taylor asked as she took a key from her key ring and handed it to the FBI agent.

"I don't know what to say."

"Say you'll let me know if Natalie was one of those people I saw being carried out from under her beach house today in a black bag."

"I will," Jaxson said as he handed Taylor his business card.

"Thank you. Here's my cell phone number. Call me if you need anything or if you hear anything you can share with me," Taylor said as she handed him her card.

The beach house was crowded with people working the crime scene within the confines of the yellow police tape. Billy, along with the other civilians, stood on the other side of the tape. They watched and waited for anything interesting to happen. He had arrived before most of the crowd, but he had waited until there were plenty of people gathered around the area before he approached the front of the beach house to watch the "show," as he referred to it. Billy was surprised and slightly annoyed by the events that were unfolding. *How did this even happen?* he asked himself.

He mostly kept to himself and watched as different people came and went from the crime scene. He wasn't worried about any of them until he saw the man with the gold badge attached to his belt pull up in his car and cross the yellow tape. Billy had watched enough crime television shows, documentaries, and movies that involved serial killers, and he knew the man wearing the FBI badge was most likely an FBI profiler. "Shit," he mumbled when he saw him.

Billy was worried about the FBI agent. *I didn't leave any evidence that would trace anything back to me, but did* he *leave anything?* Billy questioned in his mind as people passed by him.

Billy was nervous about being just outside the perimeter in the open, but he was also confident he wouldn't be noticed as out of place in the crowd. He looked like a local, dressed like a local, and spoke like a local. He waited for about fifteen minutes more and was about to leave when he saw the FBI agent walk outside to the driveway. The agent stood there in the driveway and spoke to another man. Billy believed the other man was another FBI agent. Billy then watched as the FBI agent untucked his shirt, removed his shoes and socks, and made his way over toward the neighboring beach house, and then onto the beach.

Billy tried to keep an eye on the agent. He lost sight of him when the agent walked behind some sand dunes. A few minutes later, he watched the agent come back to the front of the house, where he spoke to the other agent again before going back into the crime scene. *What are you doing?*

He was concerned but wouldn't admit it to himself. Billy simply shook off his thoughts of the FBI agent being a profiler to his own paranoia. He was about to turn around and walk back to his truck when he heard a buzzing sound overhead. Billy looked up and saw a remote controlled drone flying over him with a camera attached to it. Out of panic, he quickly looked away and rushed toward his truck. *Way to go. Now you look guilty. FUCK!*

Billy sat in his truck for about thirty minutes and rationalized that he needed to get the photos from the drone. *More fucking photos!* Billy exited his truck and walked back toward the crime scene once more. When he got close, he saw the second FBI agent speaking to a young man, who was holding the drone. The agent gave him some money, and the drone operator handed him what appeared to be an SD card in return. A few minutes later, the SD card was given to the profiler. *Now what?*

Taylor left the FBI agent and headed back to her own beach house. As she walked home, she looked at Agent Jaxson Locke's business card. She thought that during their brief conversation, he seemed sincere and genuinely wanted to help. *He was also easy on the eyes.* She placed his card into her pocket.

As Taylor walked past Natalie's beach house, she thought about her friend and the times they had shared. Natalie was very much like Taylor. They both were very successful businesswomen in a career mostly dominated by men. They both worked hard but enjoyed the fruits of their labor. Deep down, Taylor knew in her heart that one of the bodies she saw carried out from under the beach house was her friend Natalie.

Before long, Taylor was walking inside her baby-blue stucco, traditional beach house on piers. Taylor's house, like Natalie's, was on the Gulf side of the island. She had decorated the inside with a country, beach-style decor. Her furniture was practical yet expensive. The walls in the living room and dining room had paintings of various lighthouses from different coastal shores found in the Southern states.

Taylor walked through the living room into the kitchen and poured herself a glass of sweet tea from the pitcher she had in the refrigerator. She then walked down the hallway past the numerous photos of her that hung on the walls. The images displayed were from her days of modeling. From thirteen to thirty-two, Taylor had modeled everything from bathing suits to wedding gowns, and once, she had modeled nothing except her birthday suit. Ultimately, that was her last photoshoot. She moved to Pensacola from California and used the money she had saved to start Oceanview Realty.

When she reached the end of the hallway, she took her keys out and unlocked the door on her right. She entered the room and stood there for a moment, looking at the timeline and the investigation she had been conducting into Natalie's disappearance, then sat down to write something onto a new sticky note tab. She placed the note on Natalie's timeline. She backed away from the board and looked at what she had written. A tear rolled down her cheek as she read it out loud.

Found!?

It was getting late, and the sun had already gone down. The moon shined brightly above. Billy had spent most of the day moving around from one beach house to the other, following the FBI agent and Taylor Long. Billy recognized Taylor from the news reports from the previous year. More than once, she criticized the sheriff's office in their lack of attention when it came to investigating the disappearance of her missing friend. Now, in the darkness under the late summer moon, he sat outside Taylor's place in the back near the water's edge, watching her from the back windows as she moved from room to room, preparing for bed. She wore a pink see-through chemise pajama set. Billy thought she was beautiful, but she wasn't his type. *You think you're something special, don't you? You rich bitch.*

He was moving closer to Taylor's beach house, hoping to get a better look, when his cell phone rang.

"Hello," Billy said to the caller.

"I don't know what you're thinking, but how did you fuck this up?" the man on the other end of the phone asked.

"Me? I didn't do anything! I heard it on the news."

"Bullshit! You're stupid, and you're playing one of your stupid games."

"I'm not stupid. You better watch how you speak to me."

"Where are you now?" the man asked.

"I'm outside of Taylor Long's place," Billy answered.

"Why?"

"She's been talking to the FBI. Somebody has got to keep an eye on what's going on. Are you going to do it?"

"I can't. What did Taylor Long have to say to the FBI?"

"How am I supposed to know? It's not like I can just walk up to them and ask."

"Fine. Just keep watching them but stay out of sight. Don't be seen, and don't let anyone get another picture of you. Have you fixed that fuckup yet?

"I'm working on it!"

"Work faster! I got to go for now. I need to make another phone call."

"Fuck off," Billy said in disgust and hung up the phone. He looked at Taylor's house just as she turned the lights off to go to bed.

Jaxson found the beach house to be very elegant. The accommodations weren't something the agent was accustomed to, but after about an hour, he warmed up to the beach house and its more exceptional amenities. After bringing his luggage inside, he made himself at home and sat in front of his computer. He checked emails and then began converting his notes from the scene onto a thumb drive for official use. He listed the people he'd contacted, what he observed, and things he knew to be factual.

When Jaxson was finished with his official file, he created his unofficial file. His unofficial files contained assumptions he had made based on his direct observations of the behavior of the people he contacted during the investigation. He then would move on to starting his profile of the killer.

Jaxson determined that Detective Martinez was ego-driven, self-conscious, overbearing, and displayed an extraverted personality that revealed itself when Martinez had drawn attention to himself earlier at the crime scene. He was also preoccupied with something other than the investigation. His two positive personality traits were active and dramatic, and his two negative personality traits were arrogance and conceitedness.

Jaxson then began his behavior analysis on Taylor Long. She was open, self-driven, outgoing, and cooperative. She appeared to genuinely want to find out what happened to her friend. Taylor's two positive personality traits were balance and compassion. Jaxson sat there for a few minutes but couldn't determine any negative personality traits.

When he was finished, he walked out to the back deck, down the stairs, and sat back in a lawn chair next to the pool. He was thinking about Taylor when his cell phone vibrated. Jaxson reached down to pick it up off the concrete patio and saw it was a call from a private number.

"Hello," Jaxson said after pushing the green button on the screen.

"Hello, Agent Locke. I hope I'm not catching you at a bad time," a man said in a deep voice from the other end of the call.

"No, who's calling?" Jaxson asked.

"This is SKO."

"SKO. I'm sorry, but I still don't understand who this is," Jaxson admitted.

"I'm the reason you're there in Pensacola."

"What?" Jaxson asked quickly as he stood and walked back inside the beach house out of the wind.

"I'm the reason you're there in Pensacola," SKO said once more but slower this time.

Jaxson didn't know what to say. He just stood there without saying a word for a moment and then reached for a pad of paper and a pen and started taking notes.

"Are you at a loss for words? I thought you would be happy that I had you assigned to the investigation. It's not going to be an easy one, and from what I've seen of you in the past, you like a challenge."

"Who is this?" Jaxson asked excitedly.

"Agent Locke, let's move on from me. I know you're probably running all kinds of thoughts through your mind right now. I was just calling to let you know that I'll be checking in on you periodically, to ensure you're up to the challenge," SKO assured and then hung up.

"Don't go—" Jaxson heard the line go dead.

Who was that?

Chapter 5
"Late?"

Jaxson awoke at seven o'clock, with the morning sun coming in through the bedroom window. He made some coffee, walked into the exercise room, turned on the big-screen television, and began his morning workout. About three years ago, Jaxson had made it a point to workout lifting weights three times a week, do some type of cardio exercise when he could, and practice his mixed martial arts skills regularly. After PPK stabbed Jaxson in Colorado Springs a few years back, he had decided he needed to learn hand-to-hand self-defense. He needed and wanted to be physically ready for anything that could ever happen.

Jaxson had stayed in the workout room for about an hour and was just about to go clean up when the national news came on. The news topic of the day stopped him from turning the television off.

"Jacob Mean, the former police officer, was taken into custody last night, and he is being held in the El Paso County Jail in Colorado Springs," the female news anchor announced.

Jaxson shook his head and turned the television off. He headed back to the master bedroom. He made a note in his cell phone to remind himself to call his old friend Detective Axel

Frost, to see how he was doing since Jacob Mean, Axel's friend, was arrested.

After a shower, Jaxson headed for breakfast. He found a small diner on the side of the road that was open. It was located on the south side of the island and had a view of the water. He ate a cheese omelet with bacon and washed it down with a glass of orange juice while he watched boats and ships of all sizes pass under the bridge. He then took out his laptop, inserted the SD card, and looked through the photos Ronald had taken with his drone. Jaxson quickly passed through the images of people without really inspecting each one. His mind was preoccupied with the man who called him last night. *Who is SKO?* he asked himself.

Jaxson left the diner to go shopping for groceries and then took them back to the beach house. He called his boss, Steve Overton.

"Hello?" Steve answered after one ring.

"Steve, Jaxson here."

"Hey, Jaxson, how are things going in Pensacola?"

"As expected, but I got a call from someone calling himself SKO."

"Yeah?"

"He said he sent me down here to Pensacola. I don't know what to think about it. I don't know if he's someone involved in the case or someone who's just messing with me. Either way, I thought you should know about it."

"I wouldn't worry. Hey, I gotta go. I'll call you later to discuss it," Steve said quickly and hung up.

"Wait," Jaxson said into the phone after Steve hung up.

What was that about? He just cut me off.

Jaxson put his phone away, made a sandwich, and at a little after twelve o'clock, he walked out to the rental car and headed for the coroner's office. The drive to the coroner's office wasn't a long trip. Traffic leaving Pensacola Beach was light. Traffic going to Pensacola Beach was, however, bumper to bumper, as residents were returning to their homes after their brief departure prior to Hurricane Jerry's arrival.

Jaxson pulled into the parking lot of the coroner's office a little before one o'clock. He walked inside the front entrance, made his way to the front desk receptionist, and displayed his credentials.

"Good afternoon, I'm Agent Jaxson Locke with the FBI," Jaxson said to the young man sitting at the counter.

"Hello. Everyone's inside waiting for you," the man said in a tone that indicated to Jaxson he was late. "Follow me."

Jaxson said nothing. He just followed the man through a solid wood door, down a long hallway, and through a set of double doors. Inside, he found Detective Martinez sitting in chair, along with many other people who were assisting with the investigation.

"Finally. We didn't think you were going to make it," Martinez said.

"I thought you said we were meeting here at one o'clock," Jaxson replied.

"Did I? I could have sworn I told you twelve," Martinez replied sarcastically as he looked around the room at his audience.

"My apologies to everyone," Jaxson said in response and looked at Martinez, who stood there with a smirk on his face.

"No problem. I'm Dr. Kendrick, the pathologist."

Jaxson walked over and shook hands with Dr. Kendrick. He was a middle-aged man with brown hair that had started to gray on the sides. He was tall, thin, and dressed in green medical scrubs.

"You can make the formal introductions with everyone else later. I would like to get started," Dr. Kendrick explained.

"That's fine. I understand," Jaxson said in response and took a seat next to Stefanie Mack. The seating for everyone involved in the investigation was directly across from Dr. Kendrick. The victim was laid out on a steel gurney. The body was white, naked, and had minimal decomposition.

"The body is of a thirty- to forty-year-old female, found partially buried in beach sand. The body is currently identified with toe tags and coroner's band on the left ankle as a Jane Doe PB Number Seven. The body is an unembalmed, refrigerated, adult Caucasian female. The body weighs one hundred twenty-five pounds and measures sixty-six inches and is well built, muscular, and fully nourished. The body appears to have extensive dental work completed, which may help in the identification of the body. The body also has breast implants, which may also be used in the identification process. The lot and serial number located on the breast implant will be collected after the initial autopsy and after the classification as to the cause of death has been determined."

The people in attendance listened to Dr. Kendrick proceed through his initial examination. Jaxson looked over and saw a table that held the victim's personal belongings. On the table, Jaxson saw a small evening purse, a red dress, red shoes, the possible murder weapon, and a few small items he couldn't make out. He then surveyed the other people in attendance. There was Stefanie, Dr. Kendrick, his assistant, a crime scene photographer from the sheriff's office, and a man whom Jaxson believed was the detective assigned to the victim. In the corner of the room, not seated, was Detective Martinez, who was preoccupied with his phone. *That's a surprise,* Jaxson thought to himself.

"The body appears to have an approximate six-millimeter neck abrasion that circles the neck in its entirety. This abrasion is a possible ligature mark. There also appears to be petechial facial hemorrhages, which is an indication of cerebral hypoxemia or strangulation."

The group listened, took notes, and exchanged looks while

they observed Dr. Kendrick complete the autopsy of the victim. It was about four o'clock when the autopsy was completed.

"My determination is the victim died from compression of anatomical neck structures leading to asphyxia and then death. It is also my determination that the cause of death is a homicide. Are there any questions?" Dr. Kendrick asked.

"No. I'll call you if there are," Martinez answered quickly.

"Actually, I have a question," Jaxson said as he walked to the table that held the victim's personal belongings.

"What is it, Agent Locke?" Dr. Kendrick asked.

"On the table over here in this evidence bag is a possible strangulation weapon. A 'garrote' as it's commonly known. Can you take a look and let us know if it's possibly the same size as the ligature mark on the neck?" Jaxson asked.

"Certainly."

Martinez watched as Dr. Kendrick walked to the table, picked up the evidence bag, and measured the garrote through the plastic bag protecting it. Dr. Kendrick took his time and carefully held it in his hand as he examined it.

"It is approximately six millimeters, the same diameter as the ligature marks on the body," Dr. Kendrick declared.

"Thank you, Doctor," Jaxson replied.

"I think that just about does it, unless Agent Locke has another question," Martinez sarcastically commented as he looked at Jaxson.

"Nothing right now, but if I do, I'll be sure to speak up," Jaxson replied directly.

"We'll meet in the coroner's conference room in thirty minutes to discuss the case," Martinez announced to the group while keeping his eyes on Jaxson.

Some of the investigation team members moved toward the conference room, while others found their way to the bathroom or breakroom. Jaxson made his way toward the direction of the conference room while checking his phone.

"What was all that about?" Stefanie asked.

"All what?" Jaxson asked, as if he were unaware as to what Stefanie was inquiring about.

"You and Detective Martinez. You walking in late. The look Martinez gave you when you asked Dr. Kendrick to measure the garrote. All of that!"

"I don't know. Yesterday, Martinez told me everyone was meeting here at one o'clock, not twelve. I think he's got an inferiority complex. He's in charge, he makes the decisions, no one is telling him anything different, and he feels he needs to let people know he's in charge."

"Well, he's in charge for a reason," Stefanie said with a tone that led Jaxson to believe she knew something more about Martinez and the case.

"What do you mean?"

"I heard through the rumor mill that Detective Martinez had received the missing person's reports on some of the victims, and apparently he just sat on them. He didn't contact the family, didn't interview possible witnesses, and didn't go out to the victim's last known locations. In other words, he did nothing. Now, the sheriff assigned the entire case to him. The sheriff has given him as much support as Martinez has asked for, and when this case blows up in the media, the sheriff is going to point the finger at the one person who did nothing from the beginning," Stefanie explained.

"That explains why there are so many people here," Jaxson replied.

"Absolutely. Detective Martinez will be done if he doesn't solve this case and bring the killer in," Stefanie said as she and Jaxson made their way into the conference room.

"You'd think he would be more open to my help," Jaxson remarked.

"You'd think."

CHAPTER 6
JANE DOE PB #7
(PENSACOLA BEACH BODY NUMBER 7)

The conference room was large. There was a circular table in the center with room for fourteen people to sit around it. On the far wall, away from Jaxson and Stefanie, was a projection screen. A projector hung from the ceiling above the table, and a computer sat on a small table at the other end of the room. Everyone who had viewed the autopsy came in and took a seat. Detective Martinez walked in and stood at the other end, in front of the screen, and after everyone was seated, he addressed the group.

"I think we'll start with the photo images of the scene. I'll explain each image as we move from one to the other. When I'm done, we'll have another person come up and brief everyone on what they've learned."

Jaxson sat there quietly. He listened, he viewed each image, and he took notes. The one thing that stood out to him in the photos was the placement of the graves. To Jaxson, they appeared to be misplaced. He couldn't reason as to why the killer had buried four girls on one side of the beach house and the other three on another end of it.

It makes more sense to bury them all in one row. Why did you do that? Jaxson thought as he watched Martinez flip quickly from one image to the next.

Detective Martinez was quick and to the point. When he finished, he asked Dr. Stefanie Mack to come up and explain what she had found while she led the teams in exhuming the victims' remains. Stefanie was confident as usual, and after she loaded her thumb drive into the computer, she stood in front of the group to share her findings.

"Jane Doe PB Number Seven was partially buried in the sand under the beach house. Her head and left hand were exposed. She was not positioned like the other victims. The other victims were laid flat and then buried. PB Number Seven was buried with her torso and head higher up than her waist and legs," Stefanie explained as she pointed at the screen with a laser pointer.

"So she was in a reclining position?" Jaxson asked.

"Yes, the other victims were not. PB Number Seven was also buried shallower than the other victims. The four victims buried along the easterly side of the beach house were buried anywhere from three feet to three and a half feet deep. The other two victims along the southerly side of the beach house were buried lying flat as well but only at two and a half feet down."

"How deep was PB Number Seven buried at her deepest point?" Jaxson asked.

"Two and a half feet, just like the first two," Stefanie answered.

Jaxson wrote the findings down in his notepad and listened as Stefanie continued.

"Each victim was fully clothed, each victim had a purse with her that contained some type of identification, and each victim was buried with a single rose. The only additional item discovered was the possible murder weapon found underneath PB Number Seven."

"After reviewing all the crime scene photos, it appears each victim is in relatively good shape in regard to the rate of decomposition. Does anyone know how long these girls were buried under the beach house?" Jaxson asked.

"I do," said the man whom Jaxson believed to be the detective in charge of the victimology for PB #7 while raising his arm in the air. He was young, dressed professionally, spoke with a Southern drawl, and appeared to be nervous.

"Who are you?" Jaxson asked.

"I'm Detective Waterman," the detective replied.

"What do you have?" Jaxson asked and then looked at Detective Martinez, who, in Jaxson's opinion, should have been asking the same questions.

"If we believe that PB Number Seven is Abigail Johnson, based on the identification we found in the purse near her body, then she has been missing for about two weeks. I have the missing person's report that was completed by her supervisor at the bar where she worked," Waterman explained nervously.

"Do we have any information on the other victims?"

"Yes," Waterman said and looked over toward Detective Martinez, who did not appear to be very happy.

"Please share," Jaxson said, encouraging the young detective to continue.

"I completed some of the victimology on all the bodies that were found. If, in fact, they are the people in the identifications that were found with their bodies," Waterman said and paused after looking at Martinez again.

"And…" Stefanie said, trying to move the young detective along.

"PB Number One is presumably Bethany Porter. She was reported missing by her family two years ago this month," Waterman explained as everyone in the group took notes. "PB Number Two is presumably Brook Evans, but there is no missing person's report for her. PB Number Three is presumably Samantha Farmer, and she too was reported missing two years ago this month. PB Number Four is presumably Jodie Lawrence, and she was reported missing by her son one year ago this month. PB Number Five is presumably Natalie Adams, and she was reported missing by her friend, Taylor Long, one year ago this month. PB Number Six is presumably Trina Tyler, and she was reported missing by her friend one year ago this month."

"Does that tell you anything, Dr. Mack?" Detective Martinez asked somewhat sarcastically.

"Yes, it does. Let me explain. The rate of decomposition is slower in the beach sand. I know that sounds odd because of how hot it is here. I also know the Pensacola winter has very few cold days, but the temperature two feet down and lower varies. The variation comes from being outside under the sun to being under the beach house in the shade. The water table is closer to the surface as well and changes with the weather throughout the year. Any water that comes in under the beach house seeps down into the ground, where the sand acts as a filter, cleaning it. Taking all of these factors into consideration, you can understand why the rate of decomposition is slower, which results in the bodies being in fairly good condition."

"So the victims were preserved in an environment where the temperature stayed below a temperature of…" Martinez looked over at Stefanie.

"Maybe forty-five to fifty-five degrees," Stefanie replied.

"Anything else, Doctor?"

"Yes, PB Number Seven had the seawater directed in such

a way that additional sand would not be redirected toward the burial site."

"Which means?" Martinez asked.

"Which means someone didn't want her upper body covered or hidden by the sand that was being shifted from the floodwaters of Hurricane Jerry," Jaxson offered.

"Exactly!" Stefanie responded.

"Okay, so what else do we know about PB Number Seven, or Abigail Johnson?" Martinez asked.

"She was a bartender and had come here to work for the summer," Detective Waterman answered.

Abigail Johnson (PB #7)

All over social media, the party at Casino Beach was already being called "epic," and it hadn't even started yet. Three live bands were scheduled to play, seven bars were going to be open, hundreds of people would be there, and it was going to last all night. Abby took one last selfie, laid her phone down, quickly slid the red, keyhole open-back dress over her head, and pulled it down past her hips. She turned sideways and checked how the tight polyester made her backside look. *Perfect, girl! But damn those panty lines. Oh well, I don't need them anyway. Besides, it'll be a pleasant little surprise for Will later,* she thought to herself as she reached under the dress and slid her panties off. She then looked at herself once more in the mirror and adjusted her breasts until she felt they were even. *All eyes will be on you girls tonight. Damn the bands, and damn little boys and their fantasies.* The man she had dated when she was twenty-eight had paid for her implants, but he was long gone now. *His loss,* she thought.

Abby hurried into the bedroom and sat on the edge of a

chair. She slid her feet into her red four-inch-high heels Will had bought for her after her mani-pedi earlier in the day. She loved dressing to impress him, but she loved how free he was with his money even more. She had met Will at Snappers on the Gulf, where she was bartending for the summer.

Each year, for the past fifteen years, she chose a sunny destination, found a beach rental, flew out from Denver, Colorado, and scoured the local bars until she found a job, which she usually had her choice of anywhere along the boardwalk. In Denver, Abby worked at various bars in the LoDo, Lower Downtown Denver, area until the end of April, but when the weather changed, she headed south every year. She had no kids, no man, and no real friends to speak of, but that didn't bother her. She saw herself as a free spirit who could up and move at any moment if an exciting opportunity presented itself.

Abby never ever thought much about her future nor her progressing age. She was thirty-nine and felt she looked better than most other women who came into the bars, and they were in their twenties. She had been in the bar scene for nineteen years now, and she enjoyed every minute of it. Her life was an endless party until February fourteenth of this year. It had been a Thursday night when a well-dressed and handsome young man came into the bar and ordered a Screwdriver. He was polite, charming, and was able to carry on a conversation intelligently throughout the evening. By the end of the night, she thought he was just as attracted to her as she was to him. When the last call was announced by the DJ, she approached the young man and asked if he wanted to go back to her place for more drinks.

Now, as Abby tightened the strap of her heel around her ankle, she heard his words again: *"No thanks, ma'am. I'm not into cougars."* She sat there quietly. *Cougars. Am I a cougar?* she asked herself.

His words hurt, and they were followed by her having

trouble finding a job this summer in Pensacola. She felt dirty for having to flirt and then have sex with the owner of Snappers to get her current job, which was something she had never done before and never wanted to do again. She had decided this summer she needed to make a change. She was going to find a wealthy husband and finally settle down, no matter what she had to do. *The party has to end,* she thought to herself.

Abby was still sitting on the chair when Will walked into the room wearing his baby-blue board shorts and a white short-sleeve camp shirt that was tight around his biceps. He stood there with a smile, holding a single red rose. She thought he was handsome, sexy, fit, wealthy, and best of all, he was single and, like her, he was looking for a change.

Abby was happy to see Will when he swaggered into the bedroom. She allowed *her man,* as she liked to call him, the freedom to come and go as he pleased. It was six weeks into their fling when Abby decided to make an attempt at a long-term relationship with him. It was also then when she gave him the combination to the lockbox that contained the key to her beach house. He had accepted it willingly, but at the same time, he did not offer a key or the combination to his place for her. At first, Abby was a little upset but never said anything to Will about it. Instead, she simply wrote it off as one of those things that men didn't think about.

After the summer was over, the key, the beach house, and everything else wouldn't matter anymore. If things went as Abby planned, she'd be leaving at the end of her vacation and not back to Colorado as usual. Abby was going anywhere Will wanted to take her. She was determined to make Will *her man* forever.

"Is that for me?" Abby asked as she walked toward Will.

"Yes. A beautiful rose for a beautiful woman," Will answered as Abby took the rose from his hand, wrapped her arms around his neck, pressed her breasts against his body, and kissed him passionately. Will reached around Abby, pulled her dress up, and caressed her naked buttocks. *Wow, just amazing,* he thought to himself.

"You like that, baby?" she asked as she backed away slightly and pulled the top of her dress down, revealing her breasts.

"I like it all very much," Will answered and lowered his head to kiss her breasts.

"You want it now, baby?" she asked as she pulled his head back up and kissed his cheek.

"I do, but we should wait until after we have dinner. Tonight, is going to be special. I have big plans for us later this evening."

Abby backed away from Will, who just stood there, staring at her alluring body.

"Are you sure?" she asked as she slowly pulled her dress farther down.

"No… But we have plenty of time for that later," he answered as Abby slowly caressed her own breast before pulling her dress top back up.

The drive to Joe's House of Seafood was not a short commute, but the two lovers didn't complain. Will maneuvered the convertible sports car down the road while Abby fondled and teased him from the passenger seat. More than once, Will had to swerve back into his lane and lift Abby's head back toward the passenger seat. She insisted on pleasuring him while he drove. At one point, Abby had pulled her skirt up and her top down until she was completely exposed. She then stood on her knees in the passenger seat as the wind blew past her naked body, while the car sped along the coastline. If there was anything about her that Will really enjoyed, it was Abby's casual lifestyle and her openness about sex. She was the most sexual woman he had ever had the pleasure of meeting, loving, and later killing.

In the restaurant parking lot, Abby fixed her makeup

before going inside with Will. She always enjoyed the different places he took her to for dinner. He never seemed to pick the same place twice. He continuously ordered her whatever her heart desired. Never once did he ask her to pay for anything. In return, she felt she gave him new experiences in the world of cocktails, expensive whiskey, and old drinks that had long since been forgotten by most. She also believed she gave him the most mind-blowing sexual experiences he had ever had. In her mind, she pulled all the stops to influence *her man* to make him see her as *his woman.*

Abby enjoyed the lobster, mixed vegetables, and a small salad followed by two Mai Tais she ordered each night. She was eager to get back to his beach house on Pensacola Beach. Abby enjoyed staying at Will's place. She admired the Italian-style villa he had rented for the summer. Abby had only spent the night there a few times and spent most of her time either inside or lounging in a chair she carried out from under the house to the white sandy beach that overlooked the Gulf of Mexico. She always wore tiny bikinis on the beach for Will. She made it a point to never speak to other men who approached her when she was alone. Abby never wanted to give Will the impression that she was interested in any other man but him. In her mind, Abby was for Will and Will only.

The air conditioner was on when the couple arrived back at Will's beach house. Abby felt a bit chilled, but she was in the mood to please him. She did not let the coolness of the room distract her. She also did not hesitate to demonstrate her intentions. After Will walked in behind Abby, he turned around and locked the door. Abby, while Will had his back toward her, slipped out of her dress. She allowed it to fall to the floor. She then stood there with the rose he had given her earlier situated pleasantly between her breasts. Will turned around and saw her beautiful naked body glowing in the light of the full moon shining through the front window.

"What's on your mind?" she asked sensually.

"A lot." *Maybe I should kill you some other night,* he thought to himself.

"Well then, follow me," she said as she turned and walked up the stairs toward the bedroom. Abby knew how to tease a man, and she loved every minute of it.

Will watched as she took each step very slowly in her red heels.

"Are you coming?" Abby asked over her shoulder after stopping halfway.

"Yes," he replied after checking to make sure the garrote was still in his front pocket.

By the time Will entered the bedroom, Abby was already on the bed, bent over on her hands and knees. She had situated herself so that Will would have a pleasurable view from the door.

"You see something you like?" she asked, looking over her shoulder while she slowly wiggled her hips back and forth.

"I do," Will softly whispered while he removed his shirt. He reached into his pocket to remove the garrote and slid his shorts off.

"Come get it, baby!" Abby whispered as she continued to wiggle and moan seductively.

"Okay," he answered as he walked toward her. He caressed her buttocks and entered her from behind. Abby moaned louder as he started slowly moving in and out of her.

"I like that. Keep going!" she said excitedly.

Will did as he was instructed until Abby reached orgasm.

"That feels wonderful," she said as she sat up. She reached her hands back, pulled his head toward hers, and kissed him. Will laid the garrote next to him on the edge of the bed. He then placed his hands around her body. He rubbed her breast and slowly moved down the front of her stomach, where he played with her until she couldn't take any more. Abby moaned louder and pushed her hips back toward him.

"Fuck me," she ordered.

Will pushed her back down toward the bed to move in and out of her faster. He then reached next to him and secured the garrote. When he was close to finishing, he quickly looped the garrote over her head and pulled it tightly around her neck.

Abby was able to get her fingers in between her throat and the strangulation device, but it was no use. It was too tight. She soon fell forward onto the bed with Will still on her back. Abby felt him moving in and out of her quickly. She tried to speak, but only wheezing sounds came out of her mouth. Then, when she thought Will was almost finished, she noticed darkness closing in around the outsides of her eyes, and Abby realized without a doubt that she was *his woman*, and for her, the party was over.

"You, by far, were the most sexual woman I had ever had the pleasure of being with," Will said as he removed the garrote from her neck. He rolled her over and ran his hand along her perfectly round breast. "You would have done anything for me," he said and then kissed her lips.

CHAPTER 7
SNAPPERS AND HOW TO MAKE MONEY!

J axson and the rest of the investigators left the coroner's office a little after five o'clock. Instead of going back to the beach house, Jaxson drove to Snappers, the bar Abigail worked at before she went missing, to speak to her boss. The autopsy, the meeting afterward, and Detective Martinez's short conversation hadn't been helpful. Jaxson wanted to talk to Martinez about the missing person's reports, but Martinez told him he didn't have time to speak with him. The only real help the sheriff's office had provided was that of the young Detective Waterman. Detective Waterman had given everyone a thumb drive on Abigail Johnson. The thumb drive consisted of all of Abigail's personal information, her place of employment, the missing person's report, and a copy of her lease for the beach house she had rented when she had arrived at Pensacola Beach. It also had her social media and every text message she had sent in the past six months.

Detective Waterman was thorough, to say the least, Jaxson thought as he pulled into the parking lot of Snappers on the Gulf.

Jaxson walked in and was surprised to find the bar to be as busy as it was. The twenty-something customers, of the male persuasion, walked around in board shorts, no shirts, and no shoes, and the women dressed accordingly in their tiny bikinis. Some of the more modest women wore see-through cover-ups too. Jaxson determined that the bar drew in young single adults. He casually made his way to the bar and took a seat. He felt out of place in his dress slacks, pull-over polo, and wingtips. The woman tending the bar walked over after placing a large glass of beer in front of another patron. She had her hair pulled back in a ponytail. She was tall, thin, and her tiny bright-blue bikini left nothing to the imagination.

"I'm Brittany. What can I get you, honey?" she asked with a friendly smile.

"Nothing. I'm looking for Stewart Barnes," Jaxson said as he presented his credentials.

"Oh, are you here about Abby?" she asked quickly.

"Yes, did you know Abigail?" Jaxson asked. He was surprised by Brittany's question.

"Did I know her? Was she one of the bodies that was taken out from under the beach house I saw on the news last night?" Brittany asked sorrowfully.

Damn! Jaxson thought to himself. He had been clumsy with his choice of words, especially since the coroner hadn't positively identified Abigail Johnson as Jane Doe PB #7.

"I really should talk to Stewart and…"

"Wait, come over here," Brittany said as she walked from behind the bar over to a corner.

Jaxson didn't say anything. He just got up and followed her.

"Stew doesn't know anything. I'm Brittany Cole, and Stew only reported Abby missing after me and some of the other girls insisted that he call the police when she missed so many shifts."

"Really?" Jaxson replied as he began to take notes.

"Yeah, Stew is a sleazy scumbag. He takes twenty percent of our tips, makes us work longer shifts than scheduled, and takes other privileges, if you know what I mean," Brittany explained and looked away, embarrassed.

"He sounds horrible," Jaxson replied.

"He is, but there's not much we can do about it. This is the busiest bar on the boardwalk. Guys come in here to look at the girls working in these skimpy bikinis, and girls come in here looking for guys. For some of the girls, the money they make over the summer pays for a lot of things, things they need to get through during the slower winter months. Personally, I use it to pay for tuition and books."

"That's smart."

"Yeah, if I learned anything from Abby, it's that I'm not working here for the rest of my life," Brittany declared frankly.

"It sounds like you have a plan."

"I do."

"Well, what can you tell me about Abby?" Jaxson asked.

"Abby wasn't like the rest of us. She was a little older, and she took care of us. She was all business when it came to doing what needed to be done to make money. Abby taught us how to make more money than we were already making."

"Make more?"

"Yeah, she taught us how to work the male customers, like flirt a little more than usual."

"Flirt how?" Jaxson asked. The forensic psychologist in Jaxson wanted to know more about Abby's behavior. He knew that learning more about the victim's behavior could help him understand the killer's behavior, which would help with the profile Jaxson was putting together.

"Okay, a pretty face, a curvy figure, a nice smile, and a great attitude goes a long way in getting a good tip. Abby taught us how to get a great tip. A slight body rub with your breasts or your bottom in these tiny bikinis, followed by a little flirty comment, goes much further with the men," Brittany explained.

"I see. What else can you tell me?"

"Abby increased the sales in the bar. She taught the other bartenders how to pour drinks correctly. She introduced a menu of specialty drinks that only Snappers made. She convinced Stew to charge more for those drinks and to give the girls a commission on selling them. Those two things increased sales substantially. I heard Stew on the phone one day tell someone that his sales were up by thirty percent this summer," Brittany explained and then looked over at the bar at her customers.

"Do you know of anyone who would want to hurt her?" Jaxson asked.

"No one here. We all liked Abby. Even Stew."

"Do you know if she was seeing anyone?"

"Yeah, she was dating some guy she met here a few months ago."

"Did you ever meet him?" Jaxson asked excitedly, hoping she could provide a description.

"No, she met him on a slow night, probably a Tuesday. It's really slow on Tuesdays. The only reason I knew she was dating someone is she told me one night."

"Did you and Abby talk a lot?"

"Yeah, here at work. I mean, we worked really well with each other. Occasionally we told each other some stuff about our personal lives, but we didn't do things together or go out. The only reason I knew Abby was seeing someone is because one night, this handsome guy came in and was laying it down hard for her. This guy was tipping her big time, telling her how beautiful she was and how he was in town for the summer *alone*. I mean, he was trying hard to get with her, but when he asked her out, Abby turned him down flat. When I mentioned it to her later that night, she told me she had met someone and wasn't going to ruin it."

"Okay, is Stew around?" Jaxson asked.

"No. Stew's on a three-week fishing trip. He won't be back here for another two weeks," Brittany answered as she walked back behind the bar to get a customer another drink.

"If you can think of anything else, please call me. This is my cell phone number," Jaxson said as he handed her his business card.

"I will. How can I find out about Abby's funeral arrangements?" Brittany asked as her voice cracked slightly.

"You can call the coroner's office, and they can let you know when she'll be ready for that. They'll need to positively identify her first, but it shouldn't take too long. I'll see what I can do as well. I'm sorry about having to bring you bad news," Jaxson explained. He then took down Brittany's contact information while she continued to attend to her customers. "You've been a lot of help. I'll see what I can do for Abby."

"Thank you," Brittany responded in return.

Billy waited around the back of 1616 Ariola Drive, near the water with other beachgoers, pretending to fish while he waited for FBI Agent Jaxson Locke to return. He positioned himself so he had a view of Agent Jaxson Locke's beach house across the street. Billy had called the FBI, from his burner phone, and informed them he had information about the women found under the beach house in Pensacola and needed to speak to the agent in charge. A short time later, he was connected to Agent Locke's voicemail, and he, of course, hung up before leaving a message.

Billy cast his fishing line far past the breaking waves. He wasn't worried about catching anything because he had left his line without bait. He occasionally surfed his phone for information about the agent and texted his friend.

"Where are you?" Billy asked in the text.

His friend texted back: "Working on finding out more about the FBI agent. Where are you?"

"Sitting outside his beach house."

"Fuck, don't get caught!"

"I know what I'm doing." Billy didn't like being told what to do by anyone, especially him.

"I don't think you do. You've been photographed twice now!"

"I'm working on that! STOP FUCKING WITH ME. I'M DOING EVERYTHING! YOU'RE NOT EVEN HERE!" Billy was growing impatient with his friend. Billy always felt his friend believed he was better than him, and that bothered him.

"Okay, do you need more money?"

"Yes. Do you want another girl?" Billy replied.

"No, I have my eye on one already. I just have to decide if she's worth the risk."

"REALLY, NOW WHO'S BEING CARELESS?" Billy texted back.

"FUCK YOU. The money will be in your account this evening. I got to go."

Billy put his phone away and looked back toward the beach house just as Agent Locke pulled into the driveway. He tried to look inconspicuous as he watched the water and his empty fishing line while occasionally looking back at the house as the sun dropped closer to the Gulf of Mexico in the distance. Eventually, the beachgoers packed their belongings and walked back toward their cars they had left parked on the street, but Billy needed the photos taken by the drone, and he needed to know where Agent Locke kept them in the beach house. Billy had decided he wasn't leaving until he had the photos.

Jaxson entered the beach house and sat in the dining room, where he removed his shoes. He then went into the kitchen, took a diet soda and a premade deli sandwich from the refrigerator, and went back into the dining room. He took out his computer, inserted the thumb drive, and began reviewing Abigail Johnson's social media while he ate his dinner. It was about ten minutes and a half-eaten sandwich later when his cell phone vibrated on the table. Jaxson reached over and picked it up. The number was, once again, private.

"This is Agent Locke."

"Agent Locke, how are you this evening?" SKO asked.

"I'm fine," Jaxson answered but consciously added nothing more.

"That's it? Nothing else?" SKO inquired suspiciously.

"Yes. I don't know who you are. I won't be sharing any information with you or speaking to you until you agree to answer my questions."

"Fine, but you can only ask the question once, and my answer is the only answer. I will not add any other information or clarify my answer. If you ask me to do so, then our conversation will end. I also get one question and one answer from you for every question you ask that I answer. Do we understand one another?"

"Yes," Jaxson said in agreement. He was going to take anything he could get.

"Then ask your first question, Agent Locke."

"Who are you?" Jaxson asked.

"SKO, but you knew that."

Jaxson was disappointed in himself. He had to start formulating his questions better.

"Now, did you learn anything useful today?" SKO asked.

"Yes," Jaxson answered but added nothing more.

"Did you kill the victims who were discovered buried under sixteen sixteen Ariola Drive in Pensacola, Florida?"

"That's something you should be figuring out. It's not for me to solve. I've given you plenty already," SKO answered.

Jaxson took notes quickly as he prepared for his next question.

"My turn. Agent Locke, can you tell me what happened to Lisa?" SKO asked point blank and waited for an answer.

"No. Now, can you tell me how you selected your victims?"

"No, why won't you tell me anything about Lisa?" SKO asked.

"You've broken your own rule. You're asking for clarification on your previous question. Now, I can either end the conversation, or we can agree that you have forfeited a question," Jaxson reaffirmed.

"Very well," SKO replied to Jaxson's suggestion.

"How do you know so much about the investigation?" Jaxson asked.

"It's what I enjoy doing."

"Did you know that you are being watched?"

"No, by whom?" Jaxson asked before thinking.

"That would be a clarifying question, Agent Locke, and I choose to end the game. Good night."

"Damn," Jaxson whispered to himself.

Jaxson placed the phone down and wrote in his notebook.

Billy waited for it to get darker before making his way to the beach house. It wasn't quite dark enough to do what he wanted, but Billy was anxious and getting nervous about the entire investigation. He slowly made his way through the shadows. He passed the pool and then quietly climbed up the back stairs of the deck. From the rear-facing living room window, he could see Agent Locke sitting in the dining room, talking on his cell phone.

"Agent Locke, are you out here?"

Billy quickly turned when he heard the woman's voice. She was walking toward the back of the beach house from the front. Billy looked to his left and then his right. He quickly moved across the deck, stepped over the rail, jumped down to the soft beach sand, and ran toward the street.

Jaxson was standing there thinking about the phone call when he heard something or someone on the back deck. He reached for his gun, turned off the dining room light, and walked toward the living room very cautiously. When he got to the sliding glass door, he paused. Then he quickly flipped on the deck light and looked outside with his pistol at the ready.

Taylor was startled when the light came on and was frightened when she saw Agent Locke standing there with his gun pointing at her. Jaxson immediately dropped the gun to his side, slid the door open, and looked at Taylor, not knowing what to say.

Jaxson tried to explain. "I'm sorry. I just got off the phone and—"

"And was about to shoot me," Taylor interjected, holding her hand to her chest.

"Again, I'm sorry. Please come in," Jaxson said as he moved to the side while gesturing with his other hand for her to come in.

"Okay," Taylor said. She walked inside while Jaxson put the pistol back in the holster on his hip.

"I came to get my sunglasses I left on the deck yesterday. I thought I heard you out on the deck. I yelled for you, but I didn't hear anything back. I came up the stairs and grabbed my glasses and then I saw the light go off inside. Then there you were with your gun." Taylor explained as she stared at the agent's deli sandwich.

"I don't know what to say. I had a strange phone call and thought maybe... Never mind. Are you okay?" Jaxson asked.

"I am now," she answered and then picked up the sandwich.

Is this what you had for dinner?" She asked with a disgusted expression on her face.

"Yeah, I got pretty busy today and didn't have time to stop anywhere." Jaxson didn't know why he felt embarrassed, but he did.

Taylor nodded. "Then tomorrow night I'll take you to dinner, somewhere where the food doesn't come wrapped in plastic," she decided while holding the sticky plastic Jaxson's food had been wrapped in.

The agent shook his head from side to side. "I couldn't ask you to do that."

Taylor walked toward the front door. "You're not asking. I'm telling."

"I don't know what to say." Jaxson knew he shouldn't go to dinner with her, but something inside him told him he should. "Okay, I can maybe pick you up at six."

Taylor opened the front door and looked at Jaxson's rental car. "No, I'll pick you up at six."

"All right. I'll see you tomorrow then."

"Yes, you will. Good night, Agent Locke."

Jaxson watched Taylor until she got into her car and drove away. He then went back inside and sat at the table to review Abigail's social media. There were numerous selfies of her, at different vacation destinations she had ventured to in the last few years. She posted often, and most of her posts were of her at work. Jaxson determined Abigail knew how to promote herself.

If Abigail flirted like Brittany had said, then she shared her social media with customers, who would come in and see her at the bar. The more men who came to the bar to see her, the more money she made. She also knew that tight shirts with lots of cleavage got more happy faces, thumbs-up, and general comments from her customers on her social media accounts.

There was also something else about Abigail that caught Jaxson's attention. After her arrival in Pensacola, she had copied a poem and posted it to her timeline. The poem was Shakespeare's "Sonnet 29."

When, in disgrace with fortune and men's eyes, I all alone beweep my outcast state, And trouble deaf heaven with my bootless cries, And look upon myself and curse my fate, Wishing me like to one more rich in hope ,Featured like him, like him with friends possessed, Desiring this man's art and that man's scope, With what I most enjoy contented least; Yet in these thoughts myself almost despising, Haply I think on thee, and then my state,(Like to the lark at break of day arising From sullen earth) sings hymns at heaven's gate; For thy sweet love remembered such wealth brings That then I scorn to change my state with kings.

Jaxson searched the internet for "Sonnet 29" and learned one analysis of the sonnet described it as a poem about being alone and jealous of others, and from what Jaxson concluded, it explained Abigail's life at the time she'd been killed. She was an aging female bartender who felt out of place among the younger people she worked with, and at that moment, she must have fallen out of favor with the world she had come to know.

"Abigail was not in the best state of mind when she arrived here. She longed for something more out of life," Jaxson said out loud.

After a few weeks, she met someone named Will. Jaxson saw the two had texted each other often and called just as much. Apparently, Detective Waterman had already discovered Will's cell phone had been a burner, which had been purchased at a convenience store two years ago by someone named Hector Gonzalez. There were no pictures of Will anywhere to be found. Abigail stopped posting pictures of herself as much as she had when she first arrived, and when she did, the photos weren't as revealing.

Jaxon reviewed the text messages between Abigail and Will and didn't find anything unusual about them. The messages were like any text messages that people who were dating sent to each other. The only thing Jaxson knew for sure was that Abigail was finally happy with her life and she had appeared to have found her true love. She posted numerous poems and comments about love, happiness, and having a partner.

Will must have shown up and made everything right. Abigail posted everything she desired in the perfect man, her likes and her wants. Jaxson wanted to read more, but it was getting late, and he had to get up early to be at the coroner's office by eight. He removed the thumb drive, placed his computer back into his bag, locked the beach house, and went to bed.

Chapter 8
On Time

Jaxson got up early and made it to the coroner's office fifteen minutes before eight. When he walked in this time, he was greeted by Detective Waterman. Detective Waterman had gotten there early and had brought a box of donuts with him.

"Have a donut. They're fresh from one of the most iconic donut places in the South. Everyone loves them," Waterman said as he walked toward Jaxson and opened the box. Jaxson smiled as reached in and took a crème-filled glazed donut.

"Thanks," Jaxson said right before taking a bite.

"This is an interesting case. Wouldn't you say?" Waterman asked.

"I would," Jaxson answered. He felt Detective Waterman wanted to say something but didn't really know how to approach the topic. "How did you get assigned to this case?"

"I asked for it."

"You asked for it. Really?"

"Yeah. Once there was the discovery of multiple bodies, I asked for it, and now I'm here in charge of the victimology," Detective Waterman said.

"How did Detective Martinez get assigned as the lead

detective?" Jaxson asked, hoping he would get the answer to the question he was most curious about.

"I think you've already heard the rumors, Agent Locke."

"Jaxson. Please call me Jaxson."

"Okay, then call me Newt."

"All right, Newt, what's the story?" Jaxson asked.

"Well—"

"Are you guys ready for the autopsy?" Martinez asked as he entered the lobby.

"Yes, I even brought donuts," Newt responded and offered them to Martinez.

Detective Martinez walked past Newt, reached in the box, and removed one donut. Jaxson noticed Martinez had on the same pants and shirt from the previous day. His face was unshaven, and his hair was unkempt.

"Glad to have you here on time Agent Locke," Martinez said as he moved through the doorway leading into the autopsy room.

"Yes, and it's nice of you to dress for the occasion," Jaxson responded without thinking.

Martinez stopped, turned, and looked Agent Locke over. "I was in the office all night, looking over the crime scene photos. I didn't get a chance to go home and change clothes or shower. So please excuse my appearance," Martinez said in defense and then turned back around to walk to the same spot he had occupied the previous day.

Jaxson stood there, unsure of what to say or do. Suddenly the front door opened, and Stefanie walked in.

"Good morning, men!" Stefanie said out loud to the two of them.

"Why the long face, Jaxson—ooh donuts!" she said as she hurried toward Newt. She took two from the box and walked into the autopsy room.

"Don't feel bad," Newt said to Jaxson.

"Why shouldn't I? He was working on the case all night. I assumed otherwise," Jaxson replied somberly.

"Because he's lying. I was in the office until two this morning, putting victim files together. Detective Martinez wasn't there," Newt explained as he walked toward the door.

"Is that right?" Jaxson asked as he followed the young detective.

"Yeah, we should talk later," Newt suggested.

Jaxson and the rest of the group made their way to the same seats they had sat in the previous day. They sat there quietly as Dr. Kendrick began his autopsy of the next victim. This time, he started off slightly differently.

"The body is a thirty-six-year-old female found buried in beach sand. The body is currently identified with toe tags and coroner's band on the left ankle as Bethany Porter. The body is an unembalmed, refrigerated, adult Caucasian female. The body weighs one hundred twenty-one pounds, and measures sixty-five inches, and is well built and fully nourished. The body was originally identified as PB Number One but was then identified through dental records overnighted to the Escambia County Coroner's Office. DDS Leon Melton, a recognized Forensic Odontologist, compared the dental records of Bethany Porter to PB Number One and confirmed they were the same."

Dr. Kendrick followed the routine autopsy procedures just as he had done with the first autopsy. Jaxson sat there listening and taking notes along with everyone else in attendance, except Detective Martinez, who, on more than one occasion, left the room during the autopsy after receiving a text on his cell phone. Martinez's behavior was becoming more intriguing the more Jaxson observed him.

"There is substantial damage to the soft tissue around the front of the neck. The soft tissue damage is consistent with manual strangulation. The neck injuries suggest someone was over the victim, choking her from the front with both hands. There are also extensive facial injuries. The nasal bone is fractured, the mandible on the left side is fractured, and the supraorbital bone above the left eye is fractured as well. My determination is the victim died from compression of anatomical neck structures leading to asphyxia and then death. The victim also suffered severe facial fractures consistent with being struck in the face with a fist or other fist-like object. It is also my determination that the cause of death is a homicide. Are there any questions?" Dr. Kendrick asked.

"Dr. Kendrick, did any person in your office have an opportunity to recover evidence from the body that could be used to identify a suspect?" Jaxson asked.

"I take your question to refer to any possible DNA?"

"Yes, that's what I'm referring to, Doctor."

"Fingernail scrapings from underneath the victim's nails were taken. Swabs from around the neck for possible DNA belonging to someone other than the victim were also collected. If there is any DNA from those locations, then we will know it in a few weeks when the results come in. We have also taken DNA swabs from other locations on the victim, and they too will take time to get back," Dr. Kendrick explained.

"I don't suppose you know who the killer is yet, do you, Agent Locke?" Detective Martinez asked sarcastically.

"No, I do not, do you?" Jaxson fired back.

"No. I just thought that since the FBI and one of their top profilers were involved, then we would have some answers by now." Detective Martinez looked around the room at his audience for their approval.

Jaxson's patience with Detective Martinez and his poor attitude was wearing thin, and Jaxson decided he wasn't going to allow it to continue. "Maybe when we review the victim's victimology and the missing person's report, we'll have more information to help identify the killer. That is, if someone actually followed up on the missing person's report when it was completed. Any information collected at that time could provide a lead or even point to a possible suspect."

"Maybe," Detective Martinez replied.

The other people in the room could feel the tension between the two law enforcement professionals. Stefanie Mack looked at Jaxson and thought he was about to say something back to Martinez. She took the awkward moment of silence between the two men to interject.

"What about the rose that was found with the body? Other than the victim's clothes, her purse, and her identification, there wasn't much evidence left behind by the killer. I can have a friend of mine, Dr. Lori Parker, a botanist, examine the roses found with all of the victims," Stefanie suggested.

"Do you think we need a botanist to tell us the dead roses are dead roses?" Martinez asked sarcastically.

"I—"

"I think that would be a great idea, Dr. Mack," Detective Waterman said, interrupting Stefanie as he stood. "I think we should take a quick break and then meet back in the conference room. Once we're all back together, I'll brief everyone on what we've learned about Bethany Porter, unless you have anything else to add, Dr. Kendrick."

"No. A break sounds like a good idea," Dr. Kendrick said as he removed his gloves and walked away from the table.

Jaxson and the rest of the group got up from their seats and moved about the area. Jaxson was standing up along the wall when Stefanie walked toward him. She had a look on her face that told Jaxson she was disappointed in him.

"I know," Jaxson said and looked away.

"You know what?" she asked.

"I know I shouldn't allow myself to be drawn into a confrontation with him."

"That's right. You're one of the smartest people I've ever met. You're also one of the most professional people I've had the pleasure of working with in the field. What was all that about in there?"

"It's about him not doing anything to help solve this case when he's the one who dropped the ball from the beginning," Jaxson said in frustration.

"Well, it's not going to help if you end up throwing punches at each other," Stefanie said, gesturing toward the conference room with her hand.

"You're right," Jaxson replied as he walked toward the room.

"I know, and I didn't need someone with a PhD in Forensic Psychology to tell me that either."

Once the group was back together in the conference room, Detective Waterman began his presentation.

BETHANY PORTER (PB #1)

Bethany was excited about her date with William. William was perfect. He was the type of man she had wanted her entire life. He was smart, good looking, educated, and rich. But most importantly, her parents would approve. William was precisely the type of man her parents wanted her to marry. William didn't listen to grunge bands, did not wear clothes that looked to be from a thrift store, wasn't a beach bum, and was not superficial. He had come by his money the hard way; he had earned it by creating online computer games, apps for phones, and anything else found on the internet to take people away from the strains of everyday life.

Panama City was the picture-perfect setting for her dream vacation. *You only turn thirty once. Well maybe three or four times if I need to,* she thought to herself as she got ready for her evening with William. She had found the form-fitting red spandex dress online and ordered it immediately. She even paid more to have it shipped by Next Day Air so she could wear it for him this evening. William was a perfectionist. He required Beth, as he liked to call her, to wear the outfits he liked. On many occasions during the summer, William took her shopping and bought her countless outfits, bathing suits, lingerie, and shoes. *Man, does he like shoes,* she thought as she slipped the red high heels on that accented her freshly pedicured toes. Bethany thought the bright-red toenail polish was perfect, and William had matched it perfectly with the shoes he purchased earlier in the day.

Bethany had met William at the Sunken Treasures Nightclub two months ago in June when she first arrived in Panama City. William had been there alone, and she had spotted him from across the bar when she was trying to avoid an aggressive man who kept following her around. The man was attractive enough, but he used immature college pick-up lines to impress her, and it was a huge turnoff. Besides, he wore clothes that appeared, to her anyway, to be purchased secondhand. Bethany had gone to the nightclub to meet her friend Sara, but Sara had texted her, an hour after Bethany had arrived, to inform her she had decided she would be staying in for the evening. Bethany, not wanting to be alone, made her way toward William, who was conversing with some woman. Bethany thought the woman could use a self-help video that focused on fashion selection, makeup application, and how to flirt with single men in a nightclub.

Bethany had gone to Panama City to have one glorious summer with her friend Sara, who was supposed to be staying with her at Bethany's summer rental. But Sara had met Matt two months before their vacation, and Matt had convinced Sara he should go with her to Panama City and that she should stay with him in the beach house he was renting. Matt had promised Sara she could go out and party with Bethany, but that didn't happen either. Eventually, the topic of Matt led to an argument. Bethany hadn't seen Sara in two months, and she hadn't even met William. *Matt's probably the reason Sara didn't show up that night at the nightclub. Insecure men! Who needs them?* Bethany thought.

Bethany smiled at the thought of how she had first met William and how quickly she had run the other woman away that night. *If a slut is afraid of the truth, then she shouldn't venture out in public dressed that way,* Bethany thought. *Besides, a man like William would never be interested in a woman like her. Real men prefer a woman like me.* Bethany fastened the last strap around her ankle, stood in front of the mirror, and admired her slim, tight, and curvy figure. *This is what a man like William wants in a woman.*

Then it was one last look in the mirror, one more smell of the beautiful roses sitting on the nightstand, and off she hurried downstairs to her William.

William was sitting in the leather lounger with his feet propped on the matching ottoman that sat directly in front of it. He watched Beth make her way to the stairs above him. He smiled when he saw her stop at the top, where she leaned over and slightly pulled her dress over her hips, baring herself to him.

"Nice!" he said from below.

Beth stood back upright and walked down the stairs with her dress still pulled up around her waist. William stood and walked to the bottom of the stairs and waited for her to come to him.

"It's a bit cold in here. Don't you think?" Beth asked as she got closer.

"Maybe it's because you forgot to wear underwear."

"Maybe, but if it bothers you, I can go back upstairs and put some on," Beth said playfully and then pretended to turn around and go back up the stairs.

"No, you don't!" William said out loud as he grabbed her by the waist. He pulled her to him and kissed her passionately.

Beth enjoyed the way William kissed, and she liked how he reached behind her and cupped her bare bottom with his strong hands. If there was one specific thing she looked for in a man, it was strong hands, strong arms, and vascularity running up and down his arms. Beth was a small woman at five four and one hundred ten pounds. All her life, from the time she had started dating anyway, she found herself attracted to men who were over six feet tall and very fit. She often told close friends she enjoyed the feeling of security that a strong man provided.

"Where are you taking me?" she asked.

"Dinner!" he answered sarcastically.

"I know that, but where?" she asked again as she backed away and pulled her dress back down.

"The Red Fish Restaurant and Oyster Bar," William answered proudly.

"I don't think we've been there before."

"We haven't. I thought it would be a nice place. I read the reviews online, and they're pretty good. Besides, this is a big night for the two of us," William explained as he opened the front door.

"Okay, then let's go," Beth ordered.

"Did you pack some clothes to stay at my place tonight?"

"Oh, yes, it's right here," Beth said as she reached down to pick up the expensive travel bag next to the door.

"I'll carry that. Now let's go," William said as he took the bag from her hand and slapped her bottom to get her moving out the door.

"Ouch!" Beth screamed and grabbed William's hand.

"You're so bad!" She stretched up and kissed him once more before stepping out into the hot summer night air.

Beth enjoyed riding in William's expensive convertible. She always insisted the top was down, if it wasn't raining, so she could be looked at by the people they passed.

William knew Beth was a beautiful woman but believed she always needed the attention of others, no matter the circumstances. William thought that Beth, if allowed, would take the focus away from a bride on her wedding day or from a dead man at his own funeral. *The center of attention, that's Beth,* he thought as he shut the car door and dropped her bag in the back seat.

William drove the convertible from Panama City to Destin in just over an hour. During the drive, he played with his passenger sexually, and she, in turn, played and teased him back. William had resolved he had fallen for Beth, but he knew the two of them couldn't be. For William, the mere thought of being outdone by his opponent wasn't something he could swallow. Therefore, by the time the evening came to an end, so would Beth. *I must keep up with him. There's no doubt about that! The score is the only thing that matters,* William thought to himself as he drove along the shoreline while looking at his beautiful passenger. Beth smiled when she caught him staring at her.

Once they arrived at the restaurant, William ordered dinner for the two of them, and after a few minutes, the food came. The couple enjoyed the blackened snapper and white wine while they discussed the future. Beth tried in earnest to get William to hint about what else he had planned for the evening, but he wouldn't tell her anything. Beth believed William was planning on asking her if she would like to move their relationship beyond their summer romance. Their dinner was followed by a slice of mud cake covered in milk chocolate and chocolate ice cream that the two shared in the corner booth away from the other guests.

William paid for dinner and bought Beth a rose from a girl with a cart selling outside the restaurant. On the way to William's beach house, Beth smelled the rose, rubbed William's thigh, leaned over, and kissed his neck while he drove. William was excited about his plans, and he desperately wanted to get there quickly. Before long, the couple made it back to the beach house on Pensacola Beach, and they hurried inside. William closed and locked the door while Beth stripped her dress off, rushed up the stairs, and stood at the top.

"Come and get me," she called and ran into the bedroom.

William placed his hand on the railing and slowly walked up the stairs. A smile crossed his face as he began to think about what he was about to do to Beth. Halfway up the stairs, William heard the unmistakable sound of *Beethoven's 5th Symphony in C Minor* coming from the bedroom. He stopped and listened for a moment. *She really does know me,* he thought as he walked up the stairs again. *Beethoven's 5th Symphony in C Minor* was a favorite of William's. *How appropriate it is for this evening.*

William entered the bedroom and found Beth lying in the middle of the bed completely naked, with the red rose he had bought for her lying on the nightstand next. He stood there for a moment, creating a memory he could relive at another time. Beethoven continued to play from the speakers around the room.

"Come to me, lover," she said as she sat up onto her knees, caressing her breasts.

William slowly undressed and moved across the floor to the edge of the bed. *She's beautiful,* he thought as he reached out for her and pulled her close. He kissed her passionately while caressing her back.

"Do you love me, William?" she asked.

"Yes."

"Then take me," she whispered in his ear.

William reached down and pulled her legs out from under

her, forcing her onto her back. He then lifted her legs and climbed on top of her.

"Yes, just like that," she said encouragingly.

William moved slowly at first but sped up as Beth's breathing and pleasurable moans increased. She ran her hands down his back and gripped his buttocks to pull him into her.

"Faster. Harder, baby!"

William did as he was instructed, and when he thought Beth was close to orgasm, he raised himself and placed his hands around the front of her neck. He slowly applied pressure. At first, Beth went along with it, but soon the pressure became too much, and when she reached up to stop him, he used one hand to punch her in the face.

"No, William! Stop!" she shouted over the music.

William continued to squeeze her throat. When she pulled his hand away once more, he hit her repeatedly in the face until she finally stopped fighting back. He continued to choke her while increasing his thrusts in and out of her until it was too much for him and he couldn't take it any longer.

"Yes, oh, yes!" he yelled as he squeezed her neck until he felt the soft tissue collapsing. William stayed on top of Beth for a moment. He ran his hands across her bloody face, through her hair, and down her neck. He then rolled off Beth's lifeless body and lay there next to her, listening to the last of *Beethoven's 5th Symphony in C Minor*.

CHAPTER 9
FOR SALE

Jaxson and the rest of the group left the coroner's office a little after two o'clock in the afternoon. As Jaxson was leaving, he noticed Detective Martinez walking to his car. Jaxson thought about walking over and saying something to the detective but decided it was probably better not to contact him. *Better to let sleeping dogs lie,* Jaxson thought to himself as he walked to his own car.

"Do you know how many missing person's reports we get every year?"

"No," Jaxson replied after turning around to face Detective Martinez, who had pulled up next to him.

"More than I care to count. You see, single lonely women come out here on vacation, they meet some man, and they leave town with him without telling anyone. Their family and friends get worried and fill out a missing person's report. A few months later, after the romance wears off, these missing women turn up in another town," Martinez explained as he looked out the windshield of his car.

"I get it," Jaxson said.

"Good, so before you go pointing fingers at people for

not following up on a missing person's report, make sure you know your facts," Martinez said and looked at the agent disapprovingly.

"If it were just one report, then I would agree with you, but it wasn't just one, was it? These women haven't been missing for months. They've been missing for over a year, and some of them for over two years," Jaxson retorted in a disgruntled tone.

"So?" Martinez remarked harshly.

"So, someone failed to do their job."

"Well, why don't you start doing your job and give us something we can use to catch this guy?" Martinez asked and then sped out of the parking lot without allowing Jaxson to respond.

Jaxson shook his head slightly and climbed into his car. He headed back to the beach house. While he drove, he thought about his conversation with Martinez and how he wished he could stop allowing the detective to get under his skin. He then began to review and question Martinez's behavior.

Why is Martinez against me?

Is it me or the entire bureau that he dislikes?

Why does he feel a need to put me down or place me in a bad light in front of others?

Why didn't he follow up on the missing person's reports when he was assigned to them?

Why did he lie about being in the office last night?

Where was he last night?

Jaxson then recalled the items he had observed in Detective Martinez's car when he was standing next to it.

"I think I know more about you than you realize, Detective Martinez," Jaxson said under his breath as he drove onto the long bridge leading back to the beach house.

Jaxson parked in the driveway. When he got out of the car, he heard the ocean waves splashing against the shore off in the distance. He also heard and then looked up and saw the seagulls flying overhead. Jaxson went inside and placed Bethany Porter's file folder and thumb drive on the dining room table. Back outside, he made his way across the street to the crime scene. In the driveway, there was a green-and-white police cruiser with a deputy sitting inside. The deputy appeared to only leave the comfort of the air-conditioned cruiser to check the identification of the people coming into the crime scene, which was what Jaxson was about to do.

"Can I help ya?" the deputy asked in a strong Southern accent once Jaxson walked up to the scene.

"Yes, I'm agent Jaxson Locke with the FBI, and I need to go back into the crime scene to have another look around," Jaxson replied as he looked the deputy over. He noticed the deputy was older. He was slightly overweight but had a pressed uniform and shined shoes.

"You're that profiler, ain't ya?"

"Yes, I am," Jaxson answered as he displayed his credentials to the deputy.

"They say you profilers are pretty good at reading people."

"I guess a little, maybe," Jaxson said.

"What can you tell about me?" the deputy asked as he stood up straight and placed his hands on his duty belt.

"Well, I can tell you're very passionate about your career, that you probably don't get a lot of complaints from citizens, and that you enjoy helping others," Jaxson said to the deputy. Jaxson really thought the man enjoyed the job and that he took pride in wearing the uniform, but he also felt he should boost the deputy's ego and to be polite. *It never hurts to make friends,* Jaxson thought to himself.

"I do!" the deputy exclaimed and smiled proudly. "If you need something, just come on out and get me, Agent Locke.

There's another deputy around back in a four by four, watching the back of the beach house. By the way, I'm Deputy Turner, but everyone calls me Bo, and you can too."

"Great, Bo, I'll do that. My friends call me Jaxson," Jaxson said in return and then walked under the beach house as the deputy made his way out of the heat and back to the cooling comfort his car provided.

Once he was back under the beach house, Jaxson stood in the center and looked around at the seven grave sites. He walked over to the foot of the first grave, knelt down, and looked over the site where Bethany Porter's body had once lay. The hole was still there. Dirt had been piled up around it, and the support pier at the top acted as a grave marker of sorts. The pier support was nothing more than a round pole of wood similar to a telephone pole. People had used the pole to express their love and affection for another with the shape of a heart with their initials inside. Some people carved their initials, and others carved designs. Jaxson stayed there for a moment, trying to figure out why the killer had chosen this spot to leave his victims.

After a few minutes, he moved on to the next grave, where he surveyed the burial site before moving onto the next one. Before long, Jaxson was standing at the last grave, where Abigail Johnson had once been buried. She, like the others, had been laid to rest directly in front of a support pier. Jaxson looked up at the pole for a moment. He tried to put himself in the mind of the killer, and that was when he saw it. Carved in the wood support pier was a "Ø" at the very top. He looked over at the other two graves next to Abigail Johnson's and observed the same "Ø" above them. Jaxson hurried to the other four graves and looked for the markings but could not find them. "Damn!" Jaxson said out loud as he inspected each pole individually. He was about to give up when he saw "S" engraved into the wood piers above two of the graves. Jaxson then became excited and inspected the other two graves but couldn't locate the "Ø" or the "S" on either of them. He did, however, notice that in the same location on the other two piers was what appeared to be a "K" instead.

"What does Ø, S, and K mean?" Jaxson stood there and pondered his question for a few minutes until he heard people talking in front of the beach house.

Jaxson walked out to the driveway and found Taylor and an unknown man standing in front of Deputy Turner's cruiser, speaking to the deputy. Deputy Turner was shaking his head at Taylor and the man standing with her. The man was tall with dark hair and had an athletic build. He wore pressed slacks, a blue silk polo, and expensive wingtip shoes.

"I'm sorry, but I can't allow you to enter the home without authorization," Deputy Turner said politely.

Taylor appeared disappointed. "Well—"

"Hello," Jaxson said, interrupting Taylor.

"Hello," Taylor said in return.

"What's going on?" Jaxson asked.

"Agent Locke, this is Jeff Carlisle. He owns Largo Coastal Realty, and he'd liked to look inside at Natalie's home. He'd possibly like to buy it for an investment property," Taylor explained.

"Hello, Agent Locke," Jeff Carlisle said as he extended his hand toward the FBI agent.

Jaxson shook Jeff's hand and smiled. The forensic psychologist inside of Jaxson looked the man over and couldn't help but to notice that Jeff Carlisle, the real estate investor, was wearing a thirty-thousand-dollar watch and designer sunglasses. Jaxson determined that Jeff was flashy, successful in his business dealings, and wanted others to notice it. Especially Taylor.

Jaxson turned toward Taylor. "I didn't know the beach house was for sale."

"It's been for sale for about six months now. Natalie's trust has it set up that way. I didn't want to sell it, but her family contacted Natalie's attorney and had him put things in motion to liquidate her assets after she had been missing for six months," Taylor explained.

"My family and I tried to buy it a few years ago, but Natalie beat our offer. It's a great property, and we would like to add it to our Prestige Destination Series," Jeff explained.

"They want to go inside and look around, but I can't authorize that," Deputy Turner said once more.

"Yes, I know. The sheriff's office hasn't released the crime scene yet. I think it'll be tied up for another two weeks, at least," Jaxson said to the two visitors.

"That's okay. We can wait as long as Taylor here doesn't sell it out from under me," Jeff said as he looked at Taylor and smiled.

"I won't. Largo Coastal Realty will be first in line. I have your offer, and I'll send it over to the trust attorney, and he'll get things ready if the family accepts your offer. If another offer comes in, I'll call you and let you know you need to come back with your highest and best offer," Taylor said and smiled back. Jaxson watched the two of them and found himself slightly jealous.

"Thank you for your time. I'll be in touch," Jeff said as he shook everyone's hand and walked to his expensive car to leave.

"Thanks, Jaxson," Deputy Turner said gratefully before walking back to the confines of his cruiser.

"Yes, thank you, Jaxson," Taylor said not so gratefully.

"I'm sorry, but we can't let the scene go yet."

"I know. It's not you. It's everything with Natalie. I just…"

"I know. If we're still on for dinner tonight, I'd like to hear more about her."

"We are, and I think I'd like that. I'll see you tonight."

Taylor walked toward the street. Jaxson watched the beautiful woman walk away. He didn't realize he was staring at her until Taylor turned around and caught him. She smiled and waved good-bye once more.

Don't even think about it, Jaxson thought to himself as he walked back to his beach house.

Was he staring at my ass? Taylor asked herself. *It does look good in these pants! Hmm.*

Inside the beach house, Jaxson sat to look over the thumb drive and file folder concerning Bethany Porter. He found the missing person's report and saw it had been taken by the Panama City Police Department. Beth, as she apparently liked to be called, had rented a beach house there for the summer. "How did you end up under a beach house two hours away from your own beach rental?" Jaxson asked himself out loud. The file folder contained nothing more than the missing person's report, her rental agreement, and various copies of photos that Beth's parents had provided to the police department when they reported their daughter missing.

Jaxson made his way into Beth's social media accounts and discovered a beautiful thirty-year-old woman who seemed to have everything going for her. She took photos with her parents, friends, and her fellow animal rights activists at the different places she visited over the years. There were numerous photos with her parents at her college graduation, her sister's wedding, and other family gatherings. It didn't appear Beth had had a job at any time in her life. She did, however, make sure everyone who followed her on her social media platforms knew she volunteered at animal shelters, rescued puppies from dog mills, and donated, what Jaxson believed to be her trust money, to organizations that protected animals.

Beth had also made comments about finding the right man. She believed a man took care of and protected his woman. She often referenced fairy tale stories of a prince rescuing a damsel in distress. Sometimes Beth posted memes of men saving women, to which she captioned with popular songs that emphasized men being heroes and women needing rescuing.

Jaxson determined Beth was the type of person who needed the attention of others and the approval of her parents. She made many posts that centered on family and friends and the need for both in a girl's life. The only thing that bothered Jaxson about Bethany Porter was she seemed to be a phony. He noticed in the animal rescue photos, she was dressed nice and remained clean, while other people in the pictures appeared to be dressed down and slightly dirty from crawling around the puppy mills. She also stood in the power position, on the right side of everyone in almost all of her selfies. She tried to focus the attention on her and what she was doing. In one photo, Beth wore the same pink dress as the other bridesmaids at a wedding, but Beth's dress was cut lower in the front and displayed more cleavage than the other girls. Once again, the attention was on her.

All of Bethany's social media photos were centered on her and what she was doing, until June of the year two months before she went missing. In June, Bethany seemed to almost disappear from social media altogether. There were no more stories of puppy mills or animal rescues, and her selfies seemed to dwindle as well. One of her last posts, on all of her platforms, was one sentence.

Prince Charming does exist!

When Jaxson finished reviewing Bethany Porter's files, he determined the man who had entered her life in June of that year had made sure Beth felt as though she was the center of the world, in a manner of speaking.

"Where are you, Prince Charming?" Jaxson asked himself out loud before he turned his computer off and walked toward the master bedroom to change clothes before his dinner with Taylor Long.

Chapter 10
Car Salesmen and Married Women

Jaxson was worried about having dinner with Taylor. It was while he was getting ready when he started to get concerned about the plans for the evening, and he questioned whether he should go out with her or not. After all, Taylor Long was very close to the case. She might ask questions about the investigation or her friend Natalie, which he knew he would not be able to answer. After putting on a fresh set of clothes, Jaxson determined he would still go to dinner with Taylor, but he would keep it professional.

Jaxson was walking out of the bedroom when he heard someone knocking on the door. He looked at himself once more in the hallway mirror and then walked over and opened the front door.

"Hello," Taylor said when the door opened.

Jaxson was speechless for a moment. Taylor wasn't wearing cutoff jean shorts with a T-shirt this time. She wore a short one-piece royal-blue sleeveless dress that needed three to four inches more at the bottom to reach her knees. She stood about three inches taller in her high heels. Her blonde hair was down and circled her face.

"Umm, hello," Jaxson managed to say as he tried not to appear surprised.

"I hope this is okay. I didn't know what to wear. We really didn't talk about it, and I haven't dressed up since I don't know when." Taylor ran her hands across the sides of her thighs as she stood there looking slightly nervous.

"You look great. I hope I look okay," Jaxson replied.

"You're perfect. Are you ready to go?" she asked.

"I am," Jaxson answered as he followed her to her car. Taylor's car was a white convertible with a cream-colored leather interior. *Expensive,* Jaxson thought to himself as he politely opened the driver's side door for Taylor. He then walked to the passenger side and got inside himself. Taylor started the car, backed out of the driveway, and headed down Ariola Drive. Jaxson didn't know the destination, but he enjoyed the view both outside and inside the car. The top was down, and as Taylor accelerated to merge into traffic, the wind carried the sweet smell of her perfume.

The drive was short, and before long, the two of them were pulling into the parking lot of the Amberjack and Lobster House restaurant. Jaxson got out first and made his way to the driver's side and opened the door for Taylor.

"Old-fashioned. No one's opened the door for me in a long time," Taylor said as she stepped out of the car.

"I guess a bit," Jaxson said in return. Taylor walked beside him as they made their way to the entrance.

Billy had been watching Taylor's house, and when she left in her car, he followed her to the other beach house where Agent Locke was staying. At the beach house, Billy was surprised to see the FBI agent leaving with her in her car. Billy thought about breaking into the agent's place after they left, but then he saw the two deputies sitting across the street at the crime scene at 1616 Ariola Drive. For the moment, Billy decided to wait until it was darker before breaking in. In the meantime, he decided to follow the two of them to see what they were up to.

"Is this a date? Has Taylor fallen for Agent Locke?" Billy asked himself. He then waited a few minutes before walking into the restaurant after the two of them had gone inside. Billy walked by the young hostess and into the bar, where he found a seat that provided him a view into the dining area so he could see the two of them sitting next to each other at a table for two. Billy ordered a longneck and a shot from the bartender and sat there spying on them from afar.

Taylor had sat in her chair and moved it closer to Jaxson. Jaxson was confused. He didn't know what to expect from his attractive dinner guest. Being confused wasn't something the experienced profiler was accustomed to. The two made small talk and ordered drinks and dinner.

"So, how does one become an FBI profiler?" Taylor placed her elbows on the table, interlocked her finders, and placed her chin on top of her hands while smiling at Jaxson.

Jaxson recognized her body language. To most people, her behavior didn't mean anything, but Jaxson knew her subconscious behavior revealed to others that she enjoyed the company she was in and she was inviting him to look at her face. The presentation of one's face in this manner was usually reserved for attracting other people. It was then Jaxson realized this was a date, and that changed things. He decided he was going to enjoy it.

"I never told you I was a profiler," Jaxson replied.

"No, no, you didn't. I spoke to the deputy across the street earlier today. He was eager to tell me about his new friend, who was an FBI profiler," Taylor replied and smiled at her date.

"Bo. Yeah, he seems to be a nice guy who enjoys his work."

"I agree. So how did you end up becoming a profiler?" Taylor asked again.

"Well, I've always been interested in human behavior. Our behavior explains a lot about who we are, what we're thinking, and what we may do next."

"Really?"

"Sure. Ralph Waldo Emerson once said, 'Your actions speak so loudly, I cannot hear what you are saying.' It merely means you can say one thing but your actions or behavior says something else," Jaxson explained.

"What do my actions say about me?" she asked.

"No, I learned a long time ago not to profile people I'm friends with."

"Okay, then profile that couple over there," Taylor said as she nodded her head toward a man and woman sitting in the corner of the restaurant.

"I usually have more time with the people and have an opportunity to study them a little more, and I…"

"Well, if you can't do it, just say so," Taylor said humorously and took a drink of her red wine.

"Okay, I like a good challenge," Jaxson said and turned his attention to the couple.

"They're not married. Well, she's married, but he's not. She looks to be in her mid-forties, wears a wedding ring, and likes the attention from the younger man. The way she's dressed tells me she wants to be noticed and that she wants the man sitting with her to be the one to notice her. She uses her arms to push her large breasts closer together, hoping it draws his focus to them. For her, she believes her breasts are her best asset. She wants to be more intimate with him, and she's letting him know it. She's trying to let him know without coming out and saying it directly. Instead, she occasionally reaches over and touches his hand and laughs at his jokes," Jaxson explained and took a sip of water.

"Wow! Okay, what about him?" she asked.

"He's not married. He has no wedding ring, no sign of a white band where he would normally wear it, and in this area of the country, there would probably be one, especially on someone with dark skin like he has. He's younger, and he's dressed like a single man trying to impress women."

"What else?" Taylor asked excitedly.

"They probably met when he sold her a new car."

"How do you know that?" she asked surprisingly as she turned toward the couple and looked for something Jaxson saw that she did not.

"His tight shirt and pants tell me one thing, but his shoes tell me he's on his feet and walks around a lot. They're scuffed on top around the toes from getting in and out of cars, and they seem pretty worn on the bottom as well."

"You can tell all of that just by looking at them?" Taylor asked, shocked.

"That and the fact I saw them in the parking lot getting out of a new car with temporary plates on it. Then while we were waiting to be seated, I saw him take his name tag off his shirt in the waiting area."

"Oh, so you're messing with me!"

"No, not really. Everything I suggested about them was true. Everything mentioned was observable. I mean, I expect a car salesman to have worn shoes and to dress nice. I expect men who are looking for companionship will dress accordingly to attract a woman. A married woman who's not happy in her marriage may look for the attention of a handsome young man."

"Now I understand, but how do you know she's really interested in him?" Taylor asked.

"Body language. She's flirting. I'll bet you the check tonight that they'll end up holding hands across the table at some point. Will that prove it?"

"Yes, I think it will," Taylor admitted.

"Good. Then you, like her, will be buying dinner tonight," Jaxson professed confidently.

"Oh, she's buying dinner and not him?"

"Yep. She wants to thank him for giving her such a good deal on her car."

"We'll see about that," Taylor replied as their dinner arrived.

Billy ended up ordering something to eat and watched as the two of them ate their dinner. He so wished to be a fly on the wall so he could listen to what they were saying. When he saw the waitress walk over with a dessert menu, Billy decided he needed to get back to the agent's beach house before they left so he could locate the drone pictures. Billy quickly dropped fifty dollars on the bar, nodded at the bartender, and left the restaurant.

"There it is," Jaxson said as he drew Taylor's attention back to the couple in the corner, where she now saw the couple holding hands across the table.

"You were right!" she admitted as she turned back toward Jaxson.

"Wait for it," Jaxson said as the waiter approached the couple with the dinner bill in hand.

Taylor's mouth dropped open. "Are you kidding me?" she said out loud, as she and Jaxson watched the woman reach into her purse, remove her credit card, and hand it to the waiter.

"She's got something for you too," Jaxson said as he nodded toward their own waitress who had just walked to their table with their check.

"I know, but I was going to buy dinner anyway." Taylor retrieved her own credit card from her purse.

"Yeah, but this made it more interesting."

Jaxson and Taylor left the restaurant after paying the bill. They got into her car and started back toward Jaxson's beach house. The sun had fallen from the sky, only to be replaced by a full moon. The two of them exchanged glances at one another as they drove along the coastline.

"Why give up the modeling career you told me about over dinner?" Jaxson asked.

"I guess it was a moment of self-reflection. One day I looked in the mirror, and I just didn't want to be that person anymore," Taylor said without giving any more insight into the question.

"It appears real estate was a good transition for you."

"It was, and I'm glad I did it. It gives me the choice of traveling when I want to and not because I have to. It also allows me to choose the people I work with day to day." Taylor explained in a tone that insinuated, to Jaxson anyway, that Taylor's career in modeling was one where she didn't get much say so in what was planned or being planned. He also believed Taylor had met some people she disliked or who may have taken advantage of her.

Billy made it back to the FBI agent's beach house and forced his way in through the sliding glass door was off the back deck. Once inside, he looked through every room but couldn't locate the agent's shoulder bag or anything related to the case. Billy knew the agent didn't leave with it, and he was sure the agent would not leave it in his car. He was frustrated but looked around once more. In the master bedroom, he stood at the door and surveyed the room. At the foot of the bed was an armoire that held a flat-screen television. At the bottom was a large cabinet door. Billy opened the door and found a metal safe wedged snugly inside. He rushed to the end table and turned on the light so he could see the safe more clearly.

"Damn it!" Billy said after he reached down and tried unsuccessfully to pull the safe out.

Jaxson and Taylor pulled up and parked in the driveway. Jaxson wanted to invite her inside but was too nervous.

Taylor, seeing Jaxson hesitate, took the lead.

"Do you mind if I come in and look at the kitchen stove? The last person who stayed here said one of the burners wasn't working," she said as she shut the car off.

"Sure, come on in," Jaxson answered and then hurriedly opened his door, walked to the driver's side, and opened the door for her.

Taylor smiled and stepped out. She looked up at Jaxson, who was now looking at the beach house. He had a look of concern on his face.

"On second thought, maybe you should wait here for a minute," Jaxson suggested.

"Why? Is something wrong?"

"Yeah, I'm pretty sure I turned off all the lights before I left," Jaxson answered as he looked toward the bedroom window where light shone onto the driveway.

"Should we call the police?" Taylor asked quickly.

"What?" Jaxson asked, surprised.

"Well, I mean, I know you're like the police, but should we—"

"I'll go up and look around. You stay here, and if you hear anything crazy, go across the street and get the deputy. I probably just forgot to turn it off," Jaxson said and cautiously walked to the front door while Taylor moved back toward the street. When Jaxson reached the front steps, he reached down and drew his compact 9mm from his ankle holster and then slowly made his way up the steps to the door.

Billy was still trying to figure out how to get the contents out of the safe when he heard something at the front door. He reached into the center of his back and removed the .45 from his waist. Billy then moved across the room, flipped the light off, and hid behind the wall next to the bedroom door, with his pistol at the ready.

Taylor was standing at the end of the driveway when she saw the light go off in the bedroom just as Jaxson walked inside the house. "Jaxson wait, don't! There's…" It was too late. Jaxson was gone.

Jaxson moved through the door very quietly, and once he was inside, he saw down the hallway that the bedroom light was now off. The trained agent took up a position of concealment behind the corner wall leading into the dining room. The position afforded him to be out of the light from the front door while keeping cover on the hallway.

"FBI. Come out of the bedroom with your hands up," Jaxson ordered to the intruder.

Billy heard the agent's voice. He looked at the bedroom window and thought about jumping out of it onto the driveway below.

"Jaxson, someone's in the bedroom!" Taylor said as she burst into the door.

"Taylor, NO!" Jaxson yelled as he turned toward Taylor, who was standing in the light from the street.

Billy heard the FBI agent and Taylor. He took the opportunity to make a break for it. He readied his pistol and ran down the hallway, firing blindly.

Jaxson moved toward Taylor and grabbed her around the waist just as Billy entered the living room, still firing his gun. Taylor was frozen in fear. Jaxson carried himself and Taylor outside. The two of them fell hard onto the porch. Jaxson quickly stood, just as one bullet struck a large bronze statue of a dolphin sitting next to the door. The bullet ricocheted and grazed Jaxson on the side of his head.

Billy ran through the living room and fired two shots at the large sliding glass door that led to the back deck. He leaped up and into the damaged glass and fell onto the deck as it shattered around him. Quickly, he stood and heard gunfire coming from inside, just as bullets whizzed by his head. Billy ducked and jumped off the deck as he had done before. He ran madly into the darkness, back to where he had parked his truck.

Jaxson didn't chase after the intruder. He rushed back to the front door and found Taylor picking herself up off the porch.

"Are you all right?" he asked quickly.

"Yes, but what about you?" Taylor asked as she walked toward the agent.

"I think…" The light around Jaxson's eyes started to darken until it engulfed the light entirely. He fell backward onto the floor. Taylor rushed to his side and applied pressure to the cut on his head.

The deputy from across the street ran in with his gun drawn.

"Call an ambulance!" Taylor screamed.

Chapter 11
Houseguest

When he opened his eyes, Jaxson saw a man standing over him. The man was older. He wore glasses, he had on green surgical scrubs, and he was singing "Good Morning" from the 1950's hit movie *Singin' in the Rain.* Jaxson blinked his eyes and began to move his arms. He could smell the odors of alcohol and the rubber from the gloves the man was wearing.

"What are you doing?" Jaxson managed to ask as he tried to push the man's hands away.

"Jaxson, it's okay. You're in the hospital emergency room," Taylor said as she pulled his hand back down on to the bed.

"What?" he asked.

"You've got a nasty cut across the left side of your head from where the bullet grazed you. I'm Dr. Reynolds. I'm putting in a few stitches, and I'm just about done," Dr. Reynolds explained as he looked over the rim of his glasses at the sutures.

"What happened?" Jaxson asked.

Taylor looked from Dr. Reynolds to Jaxson. "Well—"

"Looks like you made a friend or enemy, depending on your point of view," Martinez said as he walked in and looked at Jaxson and then Taylor.

"Aren't you a sight for sore eyes?" Taylor said sarcastically as she looked back at the detective.

"I imagine I am, to you anyway," he replied just as sarcastically.

"What do you want?" Jaxson asked in a low, groggily voice.

"I got a few questions about this evening that I need you to answer," Martinez answered.

"He's not answering any questions tonight," Agent Baker ordered as he entered the room.

"Well, your agent here was involved in a shooting this evening, and the shooter could have been the suspect I'm looking for." Martinez turned back toward Jaxson, who still appeared to be slightly disoriented from his head wound.

"Detective Martinez, you expressed your jurisdiction and authority at the crime scene at 1616 Ariola Drive earlier in the week to Agent Locke and me. Now, I'll do the same. Agent Jaxson Locke of the Federal Bureau of Investigation was performing his duties under the jurisdiction of the Department of Justice when he was involved in a shooting. Agent Locke was working in his official capacity as an agent of the federal government when the shooting occurred. In doing so, the FBI, under the authority of the DOJ, will be taking over this shooting investigation. We will be happy to share our findings after our investigation is complete," Agent Baker explained. It was apparent Agent Baker had recovered from the fever he'd had earlier in the week, and like Jaxson, he had grown tired of Detective Martinez and his poor attitude.

"Fine, but I'll make sure Sheriff Thomas is aware of your decision," Martinez said as he began to walk out of the room.

"That won't be necessary. I've already called the sheriff and explained it to him, but please go ahead and call him again if you feel the need. I'm sure he won't mind being awoken again at two o'clock in the morning," Agent Baker said as he watched as Detective Martinez walked out without saying anything back.

"Are you okay?" Travis asked Jaxson as he moved closer to the bed and examined the cut on the agent's head.

"Yeah. I think so. Thanks for that with Martinez," Jaxson replied.

"Ms. Long told me what happened at the beach house. I'm sorry I wasn't in here when that asshole came in. I had to call your boss and let him know what happened."

"That's okay. I'm getting used to him. I guess the shooter got away, but did anyone see him or anything else?" Jaxson asked.

"No, we got crime scene technicians from the Pensacola Police Department collecting evidence. They'll collect the evidence instead of the county, and the bureau will investigate the shooting."

"Are they taking me off the case?" Jaxson asked.

"Oddly enough, no," Travis answered.

"Really?"

"Personally, I thought you'd be on the next plane back home, but they insisted you stay on the case unless you're physically incapable of doing so."

"That's interesting," Jaxson said and then looked at Taylor. He noticed her makeup was slightly smeared around her eyes.

"Are you okay?" Jaxson asked softly.

"Yes. Earlier I was scared. I didn't know how bad you were hurt. When we arrived at the hospital, I guess I broke down in the waiting room, but I'm fine now," Taylor answered unconvincingly.

"Well, we're going to admit you to the hospital for the next twenty-four hours," Dr. Reynolds advised after covering the wound with a bandage.

"I'd rather not," Jaxson replied.

"Do you have someone who can look after you for the next twenty-four hours?" Dr. Reynolds asked.

"He can stay at my place. I have three extra rooms, and besides, his place needs some repairs," Taylor quickly said.

Jaxson lightly shook his head. "I couldn't do that, I—"

"Sounds good. My wife would kill me if I brought you back to our house," Travis said.

"It's settled then," Dr. Reynolds said as he turned and walked out of the room.

"Good," Taylor replied.

Before Jaxson could say anything else, he found himself being wheeled out to Agent Baker's car. Agent Baker took Jaxson and Taylor back to Taylor's beach house after they picked up Jaxson's personal belongings and his car from his place.

Jaxson made several attempts at refusing Taylor's request to stay at her place, but his words fell upon deaf ears. Taylor Long had already made up her mind, and no one was going to change it. When Jaxson found himself in her beach house standing in her junior master suite with his belongings in the closet, he decided to give up and accept the invitation, for now anyway. Besides, Jaxson was in no condition to argue. His head hurt, and he had many unanswered questions running through his mind. He wanted nothing more than to put his head on a pillow and sleep it all off.

"I'll be in to check on you from time to time," Taylor said as she walked Jaxson toward the bed.

"Taylor, I'm all right. I can walk."

"I know that. I'm just trying to be helpful. Maybe you should be a little more open to it," Taylor suggested.

"I'm sorry if I sound ungrateful. It's just that I—"

"Need some rest. I'll wake you up after I know you've rested enough," Taylor said and walked toward the door.

"Okay." Jaxson smiled back as Taylor walked out of the room.

Jaxson changed his clothes, washed his hands and face, and made himself comfortable in the California king. He lay there on his back, looking up at the ceiling fan and listening to its motor hum as it spun around and around. Many questions flashed in and out of his mind.

Who was the shooter? What was he after? The case files! What's in the case files that he doesn't want discovered? Is he SKO? Why is Detective Martinez so difficult? Why did the killer leave his murder weapon? What's with the roses? Why did the bureau leave me on the case? The standard procedure is to have me removed pending an investigation into the shooting, isn't it?

Jaxson soon fell asleep with the hypnotizing hum of the ceiling fan's motor overhead, with his questions still unanswered.

Taylor stood in the shower, allowing the warmth of the water to comfort her. She replayed the events of the shooting in her mind. Suddenly Taylor realized how dangerous the entire situation had been and how she would have been killed if it had not been for the man now sleeping in her guest room. Once more, just as she had done at the hospital, she began to break down. Taylor sat in the center over the drain as the warm water continued to fall over her. She pulled her knees to her chest and allowed all of the frustrations surrounding Natalie, the shooting, and other deeply buried emotions come to the surface at once. She let out a breath of air, accompanied by an uncontrollable sob. Her somber tears ran down the drain along with the remnants of the day.

After the shower, Taylor dried off, put on a large T-shirt, and retrieved an item from the closet, something she had hidden away many years ago. She turned the air conditioner down, added a blanket to the bed, and climbed inside where she pulled the bedding up to her neck. She then rolled over on her side and looked at the item she had recovered from the closet. The metal of the gun shimmered in the light of the moon.

I was a victim once, many years ago, and I won't be one again, Taylor thought to herself before falling asleep.

Jaxson woke to the warmth of the sun that had found its

way through the window shades. He slowly rolled over to look at the clock and realized it was after eleven. "Damn," he said as he sat up, grabbed his cell phone, and saw he had a text from Stefanie Mack.

"Jax, I hope you're okay. I had Detective Waterman postpone the autopsy for today until tomorrow. Detective Martinez was pissed, but he'll get over it. I'll try to come by later to check on you. Take care."

Jaxson put his cell phone back on the nightstand, grabbed the remote next to the bed, and turned on the news.

"In national news, Jacob Mean was released from the El Paso County Jail in Colorado Springs earlier this morning. The county prosecutor, John Steadman, cited lack of evidence as being the reason for the release of Mr. Mean after his arraignment. Mr. Mean was represented by Walter Braxton. Both Mr. Braxton and Mr. Mean left the county jail without providing a statement."

Jaxson watched and listened to the reporter as a video played, of Jacob Mean and a man he presumed to be Walter Braxton walking out of the county jail, followed by an army of reporters.

"He's going to be hunted down for the rest of his life," Jaxson said quietly.

"What?" Taylor asked as she walked into the room.

"Nothing. I was just watching the national news," Jaxson answered.

"Let me see that head of yours," Taylor ordered as she walked to the edge of the bed. She was wearing yoga pants and a loose-fitting T-shirt. Taylor reached over and gently placed her hand on the back of Jaxson's head and pulled it downward. She removed the bandage and leaned in to inspect the injury. Taylor's T-shirt opened up around the top, revealing her breasts. Jaxson looked for a moment but realized he was staring and immediately closed his eyes.

"What'd you think?" Taylor asked as she released Jaxson's head.

"About what?" Jaxson asked nervously. He backed away while consciously avoiding looking at her chest.

"Last night. Who do you think the shooter was?"

"I don't know yet. Someone interested in the case, I think."

"The killer?"

"Maybe, but I don't know," Jaxson admitted.

"You'll figure it out. Now, get cleaned up, and I'll make us some lunch," Taylor said before leaving the room and closing the door behind her.

Jaxson got up, showered, and checked his emails on his cell phone. He then allowed Taylor to change the bandage on his head. The two of them sat on the deck overlooking the ocean, eating the lunch Taylor had ordered from a local deli. Jaxson figured that ordering and making lunch meant the same to Taylor. The two enjoyed a conversation about Pensacola while they sat on the deck next to the pool under a large umbrella. Jaxson liked listening to Taylor speak about something other than the case that had been consuming his thoughts. The beautiful woman was a welcomed distraction. The sound of the doorbell interrupted them.

"I'll get it. Finish your sandwich."

"Okay," Jaxson replied as he took the last bite of his hot pastrami on wheat. He was leaning back in the chair, looking at the beach and the waves crashing against the shore, when he heard the unmistakable voice behind him.

"Glad to see you're up and around, Agent Locke," Detective Martinez commented.

"Thanks," Jaxson replied without looking at the man.

Martinez didn't like that the agent wasn't giving him his full attention. He moved around the chair and stood in front of Agent Locke, blocking his view while looking down at him.

"Do you think you can answer some of my questions about last night?" Martinez asked.

"No," Jaxson said in an irritated tone.

"You know, you think—"

"I think you were told the bureau is investigating the shooting. Not you," Jaxson interrupted.

Martinez looked at Taylor, who had followed him out on the deck. Usually, Detective Martinez enjoyed having an audience, but not this time. He didn't know what to expect from the agent, and he didn't want the agent to make him look bad in front of Taylor Long.

"Ms. Long, this is official business. Could you go back inside?" Martinez asked.

"I—"

"No. This is Ms. Long's home, and you and I are guests. You're not here on official business because I just reminded you the bureau is investigating the shooting. Now, did you ask to come inside her home, or did you walk by her when she opened the door?" Jaxson asked as he stood from the chair.

"He just walked in," Taylor said quickly and confidently as she crossed her arms.

"What are you looking for, Detective Martinez?" Jaxson asked.

"What do you mean?" Martinez asked suspiciously.

"You've had a chip on your shoulder since I arrived. You've spoken down to me and others who are trying to help you in this investigation. You've given me the runaround ever since the moment I arrived. Up until now, I haven't said anything to you about it, but now your unacceptable behavior is spilling over into other people's lives. So what are you looking for, Detective

Martinez?" Jaxson had finally had enough of Martinez, and he was going to get some answers from him.

"I want to know who the killer is, and I don't think your 'profiling' technique is worth anything. I don't think you can help with any aspect of this investigation. Some of my coworkers think you're something special, but you're not. You think you know me, but you don't."

"Really? Well, you're looking for a white male, between the ages of thirty-five and forty. He's intelligent, socially competent, sexually competent, lives alone, has money, and he's playing a game of sorts. He follows the case in the news and may even try to get close to it, just like the shooter did last night," Jaxson explained confidently.

"What else?" Martinez asked.

"What else? What else are you asking about? Are you asking me about you?" Jaxson asked.

"Sure, Agent Locke, what do you think you know about me?" Martinez asked angrily.

"You have the characteristics of a narcissist. You also display characteristics of someone who has an addiction. Your addiction is gambling. I saw the betting sheet on the seat of your car the other day, along with many other betting sheets discarded in the floorboard. You're sleeping at the Emerald Isle Inn, which is evident by the dirty clothes and the numerous Styrofoam coffee cups from the hotel piling up in the back seat. You're married, but your wife has probably kicked you out. You think the next bet you make will get you back to being even. You owe money, probably to people you should be investigating rather than consorting with, and you don't even realize that everyone else around you can see it. Lastly, your biggest fear is happening as we speak."

"Yeah, what's my biggest fear, Agent Locke?" Martinez asked in a low voice.

"Failure. You're failing. You know it, I know it, and everyone around you knows it," Jaxson answered.

"Go to hell!" Martinez shouted and then stormed out of the beach house.

Jaxson sat back down in the chair and looked up at Taylor. He was embarrassed by his actions. He hadn't wanted that to happen, but he was in no mood to be polite anymore.

"I'm sorry about all of that," he said after Taylor moved over and stood in front of him.

"Don't be. He needed that. I'm just glad you refused to profile me the other night." She smiled down at her houseguest.

Jaxson and Taylor spent the rest of the afternoon talking about anything and everything from their careers to relationships. They had a small dinner of fish and chips and then walked down the beach along the water's edge and watched as the sun dipped down out of sight and the moon took its place. At about eleven o'clock, the two of them retired to their separate bedrooms with thoughts of the other carrying them to a much-needed restful night's sleep.

Chapter 12
A New Day

Jaxson woke up to the smell of bacon and eggs. He had set the alarm for seven o'clock, with the hope of completing a workout in the exercise room Taylor had introduced him to after they returned from their walk on the beach last night. Unfortunately, when the alarm went off, he didn't feel like working out. Jaxson had experienced some bouts of dizziness all through the previous day and now apparently into the next. He finally got out of bed, removed his bandage, quickly got ready for the day, and made his way downstairs, where he found Taylor. She was sitting on the deck, looking at the ocean with a cup of coffee in one hand and a book in the other.

"Good morning," Jaxson said from the sliding glass door.

"Good morning, did you sleep well?" she asked as she stood and made her way back inside.

"I did. Did you?"

"Yes, I even got up early to make breakfast. I already ate, but I made a plate for you," Taylor said as she removed a dish filled with bacon and eggs from the oven.

"Wow! That's a breakfast," Jaxson replied, seeing a large

plate filled with what he believed to be six scrambled eggs and a large stack of bacon next to it.

"You don't have to eat it all. The eggs were about to expire, and I figured they would be really good warmed up if I decided to have an egg sandwich for lunch," Taylor explained.

Jaxson ate his breakfast while Taylor sat there drinking her coffee and sharing her experiences of visiting places when she had been a model. She described the beaches of Fiji in the summer and the mountains of Switzerland in the winter. Jaxson listened as she reminisced about her former career and the places she had visited. The two seemed to be enjoying the other's company.

After Jaxson finished, he stood but quickly sat down, as he became dizzy and unsteady on his feet. Taylor jumped from her seat and helped guide him back to his chair.

"Maybe you should stay in bed. I read your paperwork from the hospital, and it indicated you could have continuing symptoms from the concussion," Taylor explained from behind him, rubbing his shoulders. He felt better but didn't want her to stop. He could smell her perfume, and he enjoyed her soft voice and the touch of her hands.

"I really need to be there this morning," Jaxson said as he slowly stood again.

"Fine. Then I'm driving you." Taylor walked to the counter and picked up her purse and keys from the table near the front door, then stood by the door waiting. Jaxson thought about refusing the ride but remembered how persistent Taylor could be. Taylor Long wasn't the type of woman who was accustomed to taking no for an answer.

"All right, but I buy dinner tonight," Jaxson said as he walked out the door with his chauffer close behind him.

Jaxson made it to the coroner's office on time, thanks to Taylor's heavy foot, and once he entered the building, he was bombarded by Stefanie and Newt. They were full of questions and concerns for Jaxson's safety. Newt told Jaxson the sheriff's office was assigning a deputy outside Ms. Long's residence until the investigation was completed. It was then when Stefanie learned Jaxson was staying at the home of the former model she had heard about. *He's sleeping under the same roof as a former bathing suit model,* Stefanie thought to herself.

The three of them soon found themselves in front of Dr. Kendrick, as the doctor once again dived into another victim. He spoke his typical legal script concerning the body.

"The body is a thirty-five-year-old female, found buried in beach sand. The body was first identified with toe tags and coroner's band on the left ankle as a Jane Doe PB Number Two but has since been identified through dental records as Brook Evans. The dental identification was completed by DDS Leon Melton, a recognized Forensic Odontologist. The body is an unembalmed, refrigerated, adult Caucasian female. The body weighs one hundred twenty pounds, and measures sixty-seven inches, and is well built, muscular, and fully nourished. The body has apparent breast implants and a three-inch scar on the left knee."

Jaxson and everyone else listened and took notes as Dr. Kendrick conducted his autopsy, everyone except Detective Martinez, who had not shown up. Jaxson had already decided to apologize to the detective if he had the opportunity. The experienced agent didn't want what had occurred at Taylor's place to have happened between the two of them. Jaxson had written the confrontation off as a side effect of his concussion. Whether it was or not, he felt he needed to make amends and try to bury the proverbial hatchet with the troubled detective.

"There is substantial damage to the soft tissue around the front of the neck. The soft tissue damage is consistent with manual strangulation. The neck injuries suggest someone was over the victim, choking her from the front with both hands. My determination is the victim died from compression of anatomical neck structures, leading to asphyxia and then death. It is also my determination that the cause of death is a homicide. Are there any questions?" Dr. Kendrick asked.

"Yes, Dr. Kendrick, are there any injuries to the facial bones or soft tissue around the victim's face?" Jaxson asked.

"No," Dr. Kendrick answered quickly.

"Thank you, Doctor."

There were no further questions, and soon the group took a break and eventually made their way into the conference room. Before the meeting started, Jaxson walked toward Newt, who was preparing for his portion of the briefing.

"Have you heard from Detective Martinez?" Jaxson asked.

"Yeah, he texted me earlier and said he was taking a sick day."

"Really?" Jaxson asked in response.

"I know. Surprising, right? He's in charge of the biggest case in Pensacola history, and he takes a sick day."

"Yeah," Jaxson answered and took his seat as Newt began his briefing.

Brook Evans (PB #2)

Brook was excited as she got ready. She had big plans for the evening. Bill, her boyfriend, was taking her out for a romantic evening, a picnic dinner on the beach. Carl, the club manager and her boss, didn't want to give Brook the night off from the club, but Brook was persistent and threatened to quit and go work for another club if Carl didn't agree. Reluctantly, Carl agreed, if Brook agreed to pull a double shift next Friday and Saturday evening. Normally, she worked one shift on Friday and Saturday nights at Motions Gentlemen's Club. It was at Motions where she had met Bill one night three months ago. Bill had come into the club alone and appeared to be distracted by something. Brook approached him and introduced herself as Candi and asked if he wanted a lap dance in the back room.

At first, Brook thought Bill was just another one of the many men who came to the strip club for a distraction from their job, their wife, their girlfriend, or from some other life stressor. It was in the private rooms in the back where "Candi" made most of her money, when she danced and grinded herself on top of different men. On some occasions, Candi, not Brook, performed extras if the customer was willing to pay for it. Candi was not Brook at the club, and Brook was not Candi, most of the time, outside of it. The transition from one person to the other was a common activity she made when needed.

Brook could transition from Candi to Brook once she walked out of the club and back to Candi if the need suited her. She had grown up in a home where she had to transform into another person on a regular basis. Her mother had married, remarried, and dated multiple men through Brook's childhood. Many of the men moved into the trailer with her mother and Brook at the Shady Acres Mobile Home Trailer Park in Pensacola. Her mother, Candi, eventually grew tired of each man, and soon the guy would be on their way out of the trailer, but not before finding their way into Brook's room when she was sleeping. Brook thought her mother kicked the men out for what they did to her, but when Brook was sixteen, she learned her mother was selling her daughter to them for a nice profit and had been doing so since Brook was ten years old. It was during those many occasions when Brook learned how to make the transition into someone else.

Brook moved out of the trailer park at the age of seventeen

and never finished high school. She found out early on in her young life that she could make a lot of money with her looks and her flirtatious nature. On the weekends during the summer, Brook made anywhere from three to four thousand dollars at Motions, and during the winter months, she flew back and forth to Las Vegas for two weeks at a time. In Las Vegas, she made even more money escorting and dancing at various strip clubs. When Brook was twenty-eight, she started saving her money in the hopes of moving far away from the coastal community of Pensacola and retiring for good somewhere on the western coast. She worked multiple jobs and dated almost no one unless there was money to be made and for the most part, she followed a plan to do just that until Bill came into the club one night.

Bill agreed to a private dance in the back room, and when the two were alone, she asked how much money he had to spend on her. She discovered Bill only had enough money for one dance. She could see he was embarrassed, but she agreed to the dance with a smile. When the music started, Bill stopped Candi and asked her to simply sit on his lap naked and talk to him for a few minutes until the song was over. In those few minutes, she learned his mother had died a few weeks ago, while he had been out on an offshore oil rig, working. When he got back, he came home and found her in her bed, dead of an apparent aneurysm. Brook always held resentment for her mother for what she had done to her as a child. Still, Brook loved her mother up to the day she had died of an aneurysm herself.

Brook, after hearing of Bill's mother's death, felt sorry for him and believed they somehow had a connection. What was supposed to be a three-minute lap dance for an attractive, fit man turned into a two-hour date. After that night, Brook worked less at the club and spent more time with Bill. Eventually, she felt she was falling in love with him and he was falling in love with her. After a month of dating, Bill left for two weeks to work on the oil rig, but Brook found she missed him deeply, and when he returned, she insisted he quit the job and move in with her at her beach house.

Bill never got jealous of Brook working at the club, but he did ask her to stop dating other men and to refrain from performing extras in the back rooms of Motions. Brook figured with the money she had already saved over the years and the few bills she had, she could stop escorting services outside the club, but Candi could still perform extras in the back room, especially if there was good money to be made. *Besides, everyone likes Candi, and that's Candi in the back room giving blow jobs and hand jobs, not Brook,* she told herself.

Brook had rushed home and gotten ready for their date. She found his favorite red dress and high heels in the closet. Brook had her fingernails and toenails painted red to match. As she got dressed, she moved around the bedroom, dancing sexually to the sounds of rock and roll coming from the radio. She thought about how sweet Bill was when she walked past the single red rose sitting in the glass vase next to the bed. The rose was Bill's signature. No matter how little money he had, he always found a way to get her a single rose three to four times a week. Since Bill moved in, Brook had taken on the expenses for both. Bill, with Brook's help, had begun working on starting his own business, with Brook's financial backing.

It's okay. Bill doesn't cheat on me, he doesn't hit me, and he cares about me. He really cares, she thought as she got ready.

Brook walked down the stairs looking for Bill, who had gone down to the kitchen earlier to prepare their picnic basket. The living room was dark, and as she stepped off the last step, she noticed the window shades were closed. Brook enjoyed the view of the bay from the living room, and it was the main reason she had bought the beach house two years ago. The asking price was more than she could afford, but she met the owner—by chance, of course—when she was out jogging by one day and asked about the home he was selling. Brook had done her homework. She knew the man was married and that his wife had left for work earlier than her husband, and that was when Brook made her move.

Brook had asked to see the house, and the owner, George, the lawyer, escorted her inside. Before long, Candi had George in the master bedroom. George undressed her and had his way with her. Brook filmed the quick affair from her cell phone that she had propped up on the dresser next to her clothes. Three days later, Brook drove to George's law firm and presented him with the video. When Brook was finished with George, she had gotten the beach house for two hundred fifty thousand dollars less, since Candi was quiet about the affair and agreed to give him the only copy of the recorded sexual encounter.

Brook smiled as she walked over and pulled the shades back slightly to see the evening sky over the bay.

Extortion. That's what he called it, she thought to herself as the sound of classical music began to echo from the kitchen. "Schubert Fantasie in F minor, *no doubt. How could a kid from the poor side of town come to enjoy that shit?*" Brook whispered to herself as she quietly made her way into the kitchen. She found Bill standing next to the center island with his eyes closed. He slowly moved to the tempo of the music. His arms and hands were in the air as if he were the conductor controlling the pace of his own imaginary symphony.

"Maybe that's the career for you," Brook said over the sound of *Fantasie.*

"What?" Bill asked as he picked up the remote control and turned the music off.

"I said, maybe that's the career for you. A band conductor," Brook replied.

"Hey, don't tease. You have your air guitar, and I have my air baton."

"I'm not teasing you. I love the way you get into your classical music," Brook said as she placed her arms around his waist and kissed him. She then reached behind him and squeezed his butt cheeks. "Besides, I love how you move this cute little ass of yours to the music." Brook giggled as she squeezed it again and gave him another kiss.

"Well, I love how this ass looks in this dress," Bill said in return. He placed his hand under the backside of her dress and slid it up until he was cupping her naked left cheek.

"Mmm. Are we about ready?" she asked and kissed him once more.

"Yes, are you ready?" he asked.

"Yes."

"Then let's go," Bill said as he smacked Brook's backside and headed for the door with the picnic basket in hand. The two quickly walked out into the humid, warm evening air and made their way to Brook's two-door sports coupe. The expensive car had been a gift from an old client, who didn't want his wife to find out he was spending her inheritance on a costly escort in Las Vegas. Brook had been able to make sure the man's wife would never learn of her husband's infidelity if Brook got something in return—a little white sporty something with four tires.

The couple laughed and enjoyed the ride together as they passed more expensive beachfront property down Via De Luna Drive toward the public beach access. Before long, they pulled into Parking Lot H, where they could access the beach. Soon they were walking down the shoreline, away from the parking lot and out of sight of other beachgoers. The sun was setting over the Gulf of Mexico to the west. The waves were crashing onto the shore.

How beautiful is this? Brook thought to herself as she held Bill's hand and kissed his strong shoulder. *I'm happy, really happy, for the first time in my life.* After a short walk, they found the perfect spot behind a large sand dune that provided protection from the brisk winds blowing off the water. Bill handed the basket of food to Brook, then took a large blanket and spread it out over the sand.

"I think this will do," he said and fell forward onto the blanket.

"I think it's perfect. Just perfect."

The two removed their dinner from the picnic basket and enjoyed it with a bottle of wine. The sun continued dipping further and further into the ocean in front of them.

"What do you want more than anything in the world?" Bill asked.

"You," she replied as she leaned close to him and kissed his lips.

"Me too." He slowly reached into the picnic basket and removed a single rose. "This is for you," he said as he handed the rose to her. He then pulled her dress down, unveiling her beautiful breasts to only him and the moon hovering above. Brook reached down the front of Bill's shorts and caressed him. After a moment of fondling each other, Bill removed his shorts and shirt, and Brook pushed him back onto the blanket and mounted him after lifting her dress above her waist.

"I love you," she whispered in his ear as she moved her hips faster and faster on top of him.

Bill could hear her breathing getting heavy, and he reached under her and grasped her bare buttocks. Brook placed her hands on his chest and continued to move faster until she screamed out in pleasure. Bill immediately rolled her over and began moving in and out of her quickly.

"Oh, yes!" she moaned just as Bill moved his hands to her throat and squeezed.

"That hurts," she managed to say as she tried to pull Bill's hands away.

Bill was too strong, and he kept squeezing her neck as she

desperately fought to stop him. Bill was relentless, and he kept moving in and out of her while choking her harder and harder until she stopped breathing. Bill continued his assault until he was finished, and he lay on top of her until he caught his breath.

"Everyone likes Candi," Bill said out loud as he rolled away from Brook's lifeless body.

Chapter 13
Dinner For Five?

Everyone at the meeting had insight into the life of Brook Evans. When Newt was finished, the attendees either asked follow-up questions or provided feedback. Stefanie followed Newt in briefing the group. She explained the body's rate of decomposition and how she had exhumed the victim. She then updated everyone on the status of her friend, Dr. Lori Parker, the botanist who had arrived that morning to Pensacola on other business but had taken the time to examine a sample of each rose. Stefanie explained she had hoped to hear from Lori later this evening.

It was after four o'clock when it was time for Jaxson to brief everyone, but first, it was decided by everyone that they should take a break and allow everyone to get something to drink, check emails and phone messages, or to simply use the bathroom. Jaxson was standing in the hall next to Newt when Stefanie walked toward the two of them.

"I just heard from Lori. She can meet with us tonight. She says she has something very interesting to tell us," Stefanie said excitedly.

"When can she meet?" Newt asked.

"Seven o'clock. Will that work?"

"Yeah, we can make it a dinner meeting," Newt suggested.

"All right, but Taylor was picking me up, and I had promised to buy her dinner," Jaxson said.

"Bring her, and you can buy everyone dinner. We can discuss what Lori found at seven o'clock, and you can have Taylor show up at seven-thirty," Newt replied. He knew that Jaxson's involvement with Taylor would not be tolerated by the sheriff's office. Still, he also knew that Agent Jaxson Locke was their best shot at solving the case. He wasn't going to jeopardize that because the agent was crossing the line regarding his relationship with a woman who was close to the case. For Newt, solving the case and finding the killer was all that mattered.

"Yeah, bring her along," Stefanie said in a teasing tone.

"Where?" Jaxson asked.

"Captain John's Seafood Buffet on the Bay. My high school friend owns the place, and I think we can get a private room," Newt explained.

"Great, sounds like a plan then," Jaxson said in agreement.

Jaxson texted Taylor with the plan and then entered the briefing room and started his Q and A with the group. The group had lost most of its attendees, but that was fine with Jaxson. He always believed that the fewer the number involved in the investigation, the better it was. He explained to the group, which now only consisted of Newt, Stefanie, the county coroner, one representative from the police department, and the sheriff's personal advisor, about the profile he had told Detective Martinez about previously.

"The man we're looking for is a white male between the ages of thirty-five and forty. He's intelligent, socially competent, sexually competent, lives alone, and has money."

"Do you have anything else?" Newt asked.

"I have some other theories, but they're just theories and nothing solid," Jaxson answered.

"I'm open to theories," Newt replied.

"Well, he's playing a game of sorts. I don't know what his game is, but—"

"What leads you to believe he's playing a game?" Stefanie asked.

Jaxson didn't want to share, and hadn't thus far, that he had been in contact with SKO. Now, he figured it was as good a time as any to tell the group. Jaxson started with the first text message he had received before his arrival in Pensacola and then ended with the last phone call he'd had with SKO. The group sat there and listened without interruption until Jaxson was finished.

"Do you think he's the killer?" Newt asked.

"I don't know. He certainly seems to know a lot about the case."

"Could he have been the shooter?" Stefanie asked.

"Your guess is as good as mine," Jaxson answered.

"Yes, but I've come to rely more on your guess than my own when it comes to predicting human behavior," Stefanie admitted.

"Okay, no. I don't think he's the shooter."

"Why?" Newt asked.

"The shooter was sloppy. SKO doesn't come off as someone sloppy. I think SKO is intelligent, methodical, and that everything he does is part of his plan. He speaks very well, and he sounds educated. I don't think he would've done something like break into my rental without considerable thought and planning," Jaxson explained.

"Anything else?" Newt asked.

"Not really," Jaxson answered.

After the meeting, Jaxson and Newt decided they would go by and speak to the manager of Motions Gentlemen's Club. The manager, Carl Grant, had been the one to report Brook Evans missing. Stefanie told the two of them she would meet them at seven at the restaurant after she picked up her friend Lori.

Billy had spent the past day and a half recuperating from the injuries he had suffered from jumping out the window. He had gotten up late in the day and made his way back to Taylor Long's beach house, where he followed her to the agent's beach house. There, he observed a large panel van with a trailer parked in front of the house. A police officer from the Pensacola Police Department was next to the street. The officer was speaking to the deputy guarding the home across the street. On the side of the van was written Shore to Shore Window and Repair. Taylor had gone inside with the window man and came back outside after about an hour. The man handed Taylor a sheet of paper that Billy assumed was a bill or an estimate, and she, in turn, gave him her credit card.

"I caused a lot of damage. In more ways than one, I'm sure," Billy mumbled under his breath as he walked back toward his truck with his fishing equipment. Once inside, he turned the truck on and started to pull away when he heard his phone ringing.

"What?" Billy said after seeing the familiar number.

"Are you a complete idiot?" the man on the other end asked.

"Fuck off!" Billy said in response. He didn't have any other response to refute the accusation and had nothing else to say. He knew he had screwed up, and he had been dreading this call.

"Well, it sure seems like it. You're on the news once again. You're getting a lot of attention. It's only a matter of time before you get us both caught," the man explained with disappointment.

"I'll take care of it."

"No, I'll take care of it."

"Fine!" Billy shouted into the phone and then tossed it into the passenger seat.

Newt and Jaxson pulled into the parking lot of Motions Gentlemen's Club at about six o'clock. They walked inside and showed their identification to the doorman. The doorman took them inside and had them wait near the front. The two were immediately approached by two exotic dancers, who were dressed very provocatively. One girl, a blonde dressed in a see-through teddy, placed her arm around Jaxson's waist and asked if he'd like a private dance. The other, a redhead, ran her hand up Newt's pant leg. Newt quickly reached down and stopped her.

"Ladies, thank you for your attention, but we're here on business," Jaxson explained and displayed his badge.

"Oh, then we'll leave you to it," the redhead stated and quickly walked away, with the blonde close behind her.

"Man, this place is crazy. The city cops spend a lot of time here, you know," Newt said as he looked around the club at the naked and half-naked women dancing and enticing the all-male customers in various fashions.

"I imagine they do!" Jaxson replied.

A few minutes later, a large man walked over and identified himself as Carl Grant. He asked the two law enforcement professionals to follow him to his office. The office was cramped and cluttered with papers, boxes, and video screens that captured every inch of the club affixed to one wall.

"What can I do for you?" Carl asked.

"We're here because you reported Brook Evans missing," Newt answered.

"Did you find her under that beach house?" Carl asked excitedly.

"Yes," Jaxson said, answering before Newt.

"What can you tell us about Brook?" Newt asked.

"What do you want to know?"

"Why did you report her missing?" Jaxson asked.

"Brook was an attraction here. She had a lot of customers who missed her. Her customers started asking questions, and I felt as though I had an obligation to report her missing." Carl didn't sound convinced.

"Do you know if she was seeing anyone?" Newt questioned with his notepad and pen at the ready.

"She was, but it's none of my business. I don't ask the girls personal questions like that. I just want them here when they're supposed to be here."

"How do you know she was seeing someone if you don't ask?" Jaxson asked the man who seemed to have an unsympathetic attitude toward hearing about Brook's death.

"She wanted time off to go somewhere with him or to do something with him. I told her no at first, but she threatened to quit. I couldn't have that. So, we compromised. That's how I know." Carl stood there with his arms crossed across his large belly.

"Did this guy ever come into the club?" Newt asked.

"Maybe."

"Do you think we can review the video you have and try to see if we can see him, just in case he came in?"

"No," Carl answered quickly.

"Why not?" Newt asked with a surprised and disgusted look on his face.

"Because the cameras don't record anything," Jaxson stated.

"Exactly," Carl said in agreement.

"Are you one of the owners here?" Jaxson asked.

"No, felons can't have a liquor license," Carl answered.

"Okay, are you one of the investors who manage the day-to-day operations?" Jaxson asked, rewording his question.

"Maybe, but that's not illegal," Carl answered, visibly uncomfortable.

"I think that's about it, Carl. Do you have any questions for us?" Jaxson asked.

"Yeah, can I get a copy of Brook's death certificate?"

"Why do you need a copy of the death certificate?" Newt questioned.

"Because he and the other owner took out a life insurance policy on Brook," Jaxson said before Carl could say anything. "It's called 'dead peasant' insurance. The two of them are named as beneficiaries to the policy. Corporations do it, which opens the door for other companies that are corporations to do it as well."

"So? That's not illegal either. Brook made us a lot of money. We're owed something. She signed off on it!"

"How much was Brook Evans worth, Carl?" Newt asked with disgust in his voice.

"Three hundred fifty grand!"

"You're disgusting," Newt said, then reached up and grabbed Carl by his collar.

Jaxson pulled Newt back and stood between the two men.

"Yeah, you better stop him before he gets hurt!" Carl said confidently, with Jaxson in between him and the young detective.

"Actually, I'm saving you from him. By the way, I think the city and county will be looking at this place a little more in depth from now on. Wouldn't you agree, Detective Waterman?"

"He can count on it," Newt answered and walked out of the office with Jaxson close behind.

The two men got inside Detective Waterman's car and started for the restaurant to meet the others. Newt was quiet at first, but after he had cooled off a little, he looked at Jaxson.

"How did you know the cameras didn't record anything?" Newt asked.

"No strip club in their right mind would ever record the activities of their dancers in the back rooms. If they did, especially at clubs with a questionable reputation, then they would be setting themselves up for legal issues both criminally and civilly," Jaxson explained.

"Really?"

"Sure, no strip club owner wants illegal prostitution being caught on camera, or drug use, or the possible sexual assault of a dancer, or an over-served intoxicated customer being taken advantage of financially by the dancers."

"I never knew," Newt stated as he looked at the road and thought about what Jaxson told him.

"Hello," Taylor said after answering her cell phone on the second ring.

"Taylor, Jeff Carlisle here. How are you doing?" Jeff asked.

"I'm good, how are you, Jeff?"

"Good as well. The reason I called is I spoke with my family, and we would like to increase our cash offer for 1616 Ariola Drive by three hundred fifty thousand, but we want an answer within three days," Jeff explained.

"Wow! You guys really want to add this beach house to your Prestige Destination Series, don't you?"

"No, actually. We want it for our own family vacation home. My mother really likes it. I only said we wanted to add it to the series so it sounded more like a business deal and not a personal one. Now my mother is getting anxious, and she wants me to up the offer and let you know the beach house is for our family and not for our business."

"I get it. I'll call the attorney and let him know and then I'll let you know."

"Thank you, Taylor."

"You're welcome, Jeff. Bye for now," Taylor said and ended the call.

There's always a hook or something in real estate, Taylor thought to herself before calling Natalie's family attorney and leaving a message for him about the increased offer. Taylor was excited about another dinner with Jaxson. She was becoming accustomed to his company, and while she was making the arrangements to get the sliding glass door repaired, she thought about their evening walk on the beach together. Taylor enjoyed Jaxson's conversation, his laugh, his smile, and his rugged yet gentle demeanor. All of that and his good looks were enough for Taylor to delay the glass repair for two weeks, in the hope that Jaxson Locke would continue to stay at her place. After meeting with the window repairman, she spent the afternoon getting ready for the dinner with her handsome houseguest and some of his friends.

Jaxson and Newt were waiting for the others to arrive in the private room of Captain John's Seafood Buffet on the Bay. The two men were looking out of the large, hand-carved wooden-framed window that faced the bay, talking about the shrimping boats going out for another trip. Newt shared that he had worked on a shrimp boat during the summer months when he was in college.

"What did you study in college?" Jaxson asked.

"Sociology with an emphasis in criminology."

"Interesting. Are people born criminals, or are they made after they're born?" Jaxson asked.

"Well—"

"Both!" Stefanie answered from the door. "They can have a psychological impairment they're born with, and if raised in a negative or criminal environment, they could be created to be a criminal."

"I agree, to an extent," Jaxson replied as he turned around to see Stefanie standing at the door with another woman.

"Hello, I'm Detective Waterman, but you can call me Newt," Newt said as he hurried toward Stefanie's female companion.

"Hi, I'm Dr. Lori Parker, and you can call me Lori," Lori said and smiled flirtatiously at the good-looking detective.

Jaxson and Stefanie looked at each other and grinned. The two of them quickly surmised that the detective was infatuated with the botanist, and apparently, the botanist was infatuated with the detective.

The four of them sat at the large table and ordered drinks. Newt sat at the head of the table, next to Lori. Stefanie sat next to Lori while Jaxson sat on the other side of Newt, across the table from the two ladies.

"Lori, have you discovered anything about the roses?" Jaxson asked after the male server left the room with their drink orders.

"Yes, I've determined that you have two different types of roses."

"Two?" Newt asked. Newt focused his attention on the beautiful brunette with designer eyeglasses sitting next to him. She smelled lovely. She dressed modestly but with a hint of sexiness. Newt had concluded that Dr. Parker was the most beautiful woman he had ever laid eyes on.

"Yes," she answered and looked at the handsome man next

to her. She liked that he seemed to be interested in what she had to say. He also smelled nice, had dark-brown eyes, and seemed to be very confident.

"Well, what can you tell us about the roses, Lori?" Jaxson asked.

"The roses found with Jan Does one, two, four, and five are the types of roses you can purchase almost anywhere. It's known as the 'Mister Lincoln,' which is a hybrid tea rose, created in 1964. You can find them in any store that sells flowers," Lori explained.

"What about Jane Does three, six, and seven?" Jaxson asked.

"That's what's most interesting. The roses found with those bodies are an exceptional and rare rose that costs a lot of money to acquire or to grow. It's known as the 'blood rose' or the 'Osiria rose,' and it's a hybrid tea rose created by crossbreeding two different roses, giving it an appearance of being artificial. It's a beautiful white-and-red rose that's very difficult to crossbreed," Lori explained as she showed everyone a picture of the rare rose she had pulled up on her phone.

"It's beautiful!" Stefanie said and then passed the phone to Jaxson.

"It certainly is beautiful," Jaxson said in agreement.

"A girl likes to be given roses," Stefanie said as she locked eyes with Jaxson. She took the phone from him and handed it back to Lori.

The four of them sat there and exchanged thoughts and theories about the roses, the victims, and the killer. The three people at the table who were not profilers attempted to create a profile of what kind of person they thought could kill another without any regret. Jaxson didn't add anything or tell anyone they were wrong. He had grown accustomed to other people trying to be profilers, and he was often amused at their attempts. When the drinks arrived, Jaxson looked up and saw

Taylor standing at the door. She was wearing a pair of white shorts with a pink shirt that exposed her arms and shoulders. Her hair was down once again, and Jaxson couldn't help but notice how beautiful she looked.

"Taylor, come in and sit down," Jaxson said as he quickly got up and walked toward her. He thought about kissing her cheek but decided against it. Instead, he awkwardly placed his hand behind her back and escorted her to the empty chair next to him. Jaxson then introduced her to everyone at the table. Stefanie, who seemed to be very comfortable a few minutes ago, appeared slightly uncomfortable with Taylor's arrival. Still, she smiled and greeted the new dinner guest. Lori saw Stefanie's demeanor change and immediately knew what was wrong with her longtime friend.

"Oh my God!" Lori blurted.

"What?" Newt asked.

"No, really, I told you. Taylor is a model you've probably seen on the cover of a magazine, and you would possibly recognize her," Stefanie said and pointed toward Taylor before Lori could say anything else.

"Yes, you're right!" Lori replied as she reached across the table and shook Taylor's hand. Before long, they were all seated around the table. They exchanged war stories from cases they had worked in the past. Taylor ordered water and a glass of wine, and when the waiter returned with her drinks, he invited all of them to enjoy the seafood buffet.

Everyone got up as a group and moved toward the buffet to select their favorite dishes. Taylor invited Jaxson to go with her so she could help him in choose the best seafood. Newt excused himself to wash his hands, while Lori followed Stefanie to the salad bar.

"Are you kidding me?" Lori remarked as she grabbed a plate.

"What?" Stefanie asked, pretending as if she didn't know as to what Lori was referring to.

"You have a thing for the very handsome Agent Jaxson Locke. I should've known. All those conversations we've had about the cases the two of you have worked together… Then when I saw how jealous you got when he walked her in… It all made sense."

"I'm not jealous!" Stefanie replied as she piled spinach leaves onto her plate.

"You know you're just as beautiful as she is," Lori said before she joined Newt at the bread counter.

At the table, the dinner group continued to tell war stories and other topics that did not involve the case. Jaxson finished his plate of boiled shrimp and looked back toward the buffet, trying to decide what to try next.

"If you go back to the buffet, make sure you take your silverware off your plate. The waiter comes by and picks up the used plates, and if you leave your silverware on it, he'll think you're finished and take them away with the plate," Taylor explained.

"What?" Jaxson said as he looked at her with surprise.

"If you leave your silverware on the plate, it means you're done," Taylor said, trying to explain it again.

"That's it!" Jaxson said excitedly.

CHAPTER 14
WENDY COLLINS

Wendy was walking toward her home on 88th Street in the very sought-after Carnegie Hill area of New York City. She had planned on meeting her husband, Richard, at their home before going to their favorite restaurant for dinner. *My favorite, anyway,* Wendy thought to herself as she slowly walked down Madison Ave. toward 88th St. It was getting later in the evening, and her mind, for the moment, was on her plans for the evening with her husband. As she rounded the corner onto 88th St., she thought about the phone call she had received earlier and her close friend Trina Tyler.

She had been in a meeting when she received the message from Detective Waterman. It was, without a doubt, about her dear friend Trina, who had disappeared about a year ago. In the back of her mind, Wendy knew Trina was most likely one of the women who had been carried out from under the beach house a few days ago that she and Richard had watched on the national news. At the time, Richard had tried to convince her Trina had probably just run off with the man she had met in Pensacola and that she would eventually turn up one day, working for another publishing house.

Wendy knew that scenario was a fiction story only a mystery writer could weave into a best seller. If anything, Trina would have brought William back to New York with her, and Trina, William, Richard, and herself would be going to dinner this evening if she were still alive. Wendy was sure William had killed Trina, and probably the other women as well. When Wendy had gone to dinner with the two of them in Pensacola that night, over a year ago, Wendy knew there was something about William she did not like, and she told Trina, but Trina wanted someone in her life, and William filled the order.

The evening was cool, and as Wendy got closer to her home, she saw a police car, an ambulance, and bystanders gathered near the entrance to her townhouse. *Are they at my house?* Wendy asked herself. She walked faster toward the commotion when suddenly a man blocked her path.

"Excuse me!" she said and moved to the right to go around him.

"No, excuse me," he said in return.

A strange feeling came over Wendy. She stood motionless and looked up at the face of the man in front of her. She was speechless, and then the uneasy feeling of fear came over her. The man standing before her was a man she had met before. He was the man she had once had dinner with, and he was the man she suspected had harmed her friend Trina.

"William!" she managed to say in a shaken voice.

"Yes. It's nice to see you again, Wendy."

"I… Don't know what to say!" Wendy was afraid. She wanted to scream or run away, but she could not. Her fear kept her still.

"No need to hurry home. Richard won't be joining you for dinner this evening. He was killed a few minutes ago, just before you got here," William explained.

"But, no wait, I—" Wendy felt pain in her chest. She reached out with her right hand and grasped the light pole next to her to steady herself. Wendy tried to breathe but could not. Slowly, she dropped to her knees and watched as William walked away.

William didn't need to make sure Wendy was dead. He knew two bullets to her heart was all that was needed to end her life. He placed the gun with its silencer back into the newspaper he was carrying and made his way down 88th Street.

No one needs a witness, the killer thought to himself as he turned left and strolled down Madison Avenue.

Everyone was still looking at Jaxson, waiting for an explanation. For a moment, the profiler just sat there, looking down at his plate. It was Stefanie who broke the silence.

"What is it?" Stefanie asked as everyone anxiously waited for Jaxson to say something.

"He's done!"

"Who's done?" Taylor asked and looked at Newt.

"The killer. He's done." Jaxson picked up his fork and looked at it.

"How do you know?" Stefanie asked.

"He left his weapon. Don't you see it? He doesn't need it anymore. He left the garrote with the last victim because he's done," Jaxson explained.

"So, he won't kill again?" Taylor asked and looked around at everyone else at the table.

"I don't know for sure, but my gut says he will. He stopped for a reason, but I don't know what the reason is yet.

Stefanie didn't say anything as she drove herself and Lori back to their hotel. Her thoughts were on Jaxson and the woman he was spending the night with. Taylor Long was beautiful, and Stefanie knew Taylor had her eye on Jaxson.

"Are you going to stop, or should I prepare to jump out as we pass by our hotel?" Lori asked as she pointed at their hotel and its entrance.

"Oh shit!" Stefanie said as she quickly slowed the car and then turned the wheel sharply into the hotel parking lot. She pulled into a parking space, placed the car in park, and looked at Lori.

"What?" Lori asked.

"You know what. Jaxson is what!"

"Men are stupid. You know, for someone who studies human behavior, he couldn't be more in the dark on how you feel about him."

"Well, I haven't said anything or made a move myself, so I guess I can't blame him. Besides, he was more focused on the supermodel sitting next to him than anything else this evening. Did you see how great she looked? Her outfit was to die for! Look at me. I look as if I got my clothes off the rack at the homeless shelter after everyone else picked through it."

"Oh, yeah. Her outfit was easily four hundred bucks. She did look hot, and she wore it for him," Lori said without thinking about what she was saying.

"That doesn't help, you know," Stefanie replied.

"I know, and it's hard to hate her because she's so nice."

"Right?" Stefanie replied in agreement and laughed along with Lori.

Jaxson and Taylor made it back to her place just before eleven.

Taylor suggested a walk together along the beach with a glass of wine. Jaxson accepted the offer, and before he knew it, he was strolling alongside his hostess under a full moon, with the sound of the waves gently washing up along the shore.

"So, do you think you're close to solving the case?" Taylor asked and looked up flirtatiously into the FBI agent's alluring deep-blue eyes. She desperately wanted to kiss him but thought she should allow him to make the first move. *A girl should play hard to get,* she thought to herself.

"I don't know. I'm still trying to put things together." Jaxson looked back into her light-green eyes. He wanted to lean down and kiss her full lips. *Don't do it! She's involved in the case. Talk about a conflict of interest,* Jaxson thought to himself.

"What's your next move?" she asked as she moved in closer to Jaxson. *A girl who plays too hard to get sometimes doesn't get anything.*

"This," Jaxson answered as he reached behind her to pull her into him and kissed her passionately. *This is not a good idea,* Jaxson thought for a very, very brief moment.

Billy sat at the piano, drinking whiskey on the rocks while he played Johann Sebastian Bach's "Come, Sweet Death, Come, Blessed Rest." He had planned to get drunk with every strike of the keys. Billy knew he had to do something about the FBI agent before things got too far out of his control. He needed the photos, and he needed them soon. Billy stopped playing the piano, picked up the glass once more, and drank the remainder of its contents. He then picked up the pistol in front of him, pulled the slide back, and placed the barrel to his head and pretended to pull the trigger.

Come, sweet death, come, blessed rest, Billy thought to

himself.

Someone knocked on the door. Billy jumped up, hurried to the door, and looked out the peephole. Standing there was his attractive new neighbor.

The woman spoke from the other side of the closed door. "Hello, I heard you playing and figured you were up. I was too and I—"

"Thought you'd come over and meet your late-night piano-playing neighbor," Billy said charmingly as he opened the door. A beautiful blonde stood in front of him, holding a bottle of whiskey.

"I saw you the other day and figured you weren't a wine kind of guy," she said as she moved forward, holding up the unopened bottle.

"You were right, I'm not. I'm Billy, by the way." Billy moved to the side so his neighbor could walk inside.

"I'm Jessica, but everyone calls me Jess."

"Welcome, Jess. Billy said and closed the door, after looking up and down the street for anyone who could be watching.

Jaxson sat on the edge of the bed in the dimly lit room, with an array of thoughts running through his mind. He almost stood and walked out of Taylor's bedroom when suddenly the bathroom door opened. Taylor stood there, glowing in the light illuminating from behind her. She wore a pink silk baby doll that dropped to just below her buttocks. Jaxson didn't say anything. He watched as Taylor slowly and seductively walked toward him. Within seconds, she was standing in front of him. She ran her hands over his shoulders, leaned over, and kissed him, while she gently unbuttoned his shirt.

Jaxson reached up and placed his hands around her waist

and pulled her on top of him as he leaned back onto the bed. He knew it was a terrible idea, but he also knew it felt terrific. She smelled beautiful, and her touch was gentle.

Taylor loved the feel of his strong arms, and as he pulled her into him, she pulled his head into her breasts and held him there tightly. The two were wonting, and everything was perfect. The moment felt right to them both.

Billy and Jess moved quickly through small talk and a few drinks; they both knew what the night would bring. It wasn't long before Billy had his new neighbor naked in his bedroom and on his bed.

She was intoxicated, and she wasn't going to let anything stop her from having a good time. Jess had been admiring her handsome neighbor for a few days but hadn't dared to talk to him until this evening. Besides, up until yesterday, she had a boyfriend, but now he was gone and Billy was available.

Billy needed a distraction, and Jess was perfect. A girl like Jess was up for anything, and he didn't hold back his lustful desires. She allowed him to explore her without yield. He first took her from behind and then aggressively flipped her over and lifted her legs high in the air as he moved his hips faster and faster. When he couldn't hold off any longer, he reached down and placed his hands around her neck.

Jaxson and Taylor lay there, holding each other in the center of the bed. Jaxson enjoyed the feeling of being wanted by a stunning and desirable woman. Taylor embraced the intimacy and being held by a strong, confident man.

"Is this okay?" she asked.

"Yes," Jaxson answered and kissed her again and again.

Billy lay there naked, next to the equally naked Jess. She didn't move, and as she lay there in the dimly lit room, Billy heard her breathing heavily. Billy hadn't killed her, nor had he choked her into unconsciousness. Jess was his neighbor, which meant she was a high-risk victim he couldn't kill. Besides, he knew nothing about Jess, and that too was dangerous.

"Wow! That was fantastic! Are you ready to go again?" Jess asked as she rolled over onto Billy.

"Yeah."

The night soon turned into day, and Jaxson awoke next to a sleeping Taylor. He gently kissed her cheek, walked out of her bedroom, and returned to his bedroom to prepare for the day, feeling rejuvenated.

Chapter 15
Bumps And Bruises

Jaxson left Taylor's beach house after kissing her good-bye. It was the kiss that made Jaxson think about his behavior during his drive to the coroner's office. *What am I doing?* he asked himself as he drove the rental car along the coast. When he approached the bridge leading off the island, Jaxson, along with everyone else, was stopped to allow a tractor trailer with an oversized load to cross the bridge using both lanes. Jaxson took the opportunity to check out the surroundings at the island entrance near the bridge. He noticed people carrying their fishing poles and other fishing gear toward the water. Other visitors to the island moved in and then out of the many tourist shops with bags full of souvenirs.

Billboards on the side of the road enticed visitors to various local attractions. All the signs seemed to fit the beach atmosphere except for one billboard, which advertised a school for children. The Legacy Classical Academy of Pensacola advertised to local commuters that registration was now open for fall enrollment. The advertisement displayed the school's logo along with images of some of their students performing their chosen art. Jaxson dismissed his belief that it looked out of place as to being a profiler and how he always looked for things that stood out or didn't fit in everything he saw or heard. Soon he turned his attention to his inner thoughts, about the case and about Taylor.

What would the bureau do if they knew I was involved with someone from the case? Who is SKO? How does he know so much about the case? Is he the killer? How did he know I was coming here? Wait, did he really have something to do with bringing me here?

The impatient driver behind Jaxson honked their horn, alerting the distracted agent that it was time to continue over the bridge.

Before long, Jaxson was moving along in traffic with the other commuters, and a short time later, he was pulling into the parking lot of the county coroner's office. By the time he arrived, Jaxson had concluded that his relationship with Taylor would be viewed as unprofessional by the bureau, but it was their problem. He wasn't going to stop it from happening. For him, it felt right. Jaxson wanted to see where their relationship would go.

Stefanie was running late, and she found herself rushing out of the hotel door and into her car only a few minutes before she was supposed to be at the coroner's office. She was about to back out of the parking space when she looked across the parking lot and saw Detective Martinez talking with another man. Their conversation didn't appear to be friendly, in Stefanie's opinion. The man Martinez was speaking to seemed to be angry, and his body language confirmed it. Instead of just pulling away, she watched the two men. Suddenly and without warning, the mysterious man punched Martinez. The impact sent Martinez to the ground. He tried to stand, but the man kicked him hard in the ribs three or four times before he walked to a black sedan and left the hotel parking lot.

Stefanie didn't know what to do. She slid down slightly in her seat and waited until she saw Martinez pick himself up off the ground. She then watched as he walked back inside one of the hotel rooms. When she felt she wouldn't be seen, she sped out of the parking lot.

Jaxson was standing with Newt when Stefanie hurried into the coroner's office. She appeared to be excited about something as she frantically scanned the foyer area of the coroner's office. When she spotted Jaxson standing next to Newt, she rushed toward them.

"Is everything okay?" Jaxson asked as he placed his hand on her arm.

"No! I just saw Detective Martinez in the parking lot of my hotel."

"I guess he moved from the Emerald Isle," Jaxson said, in a manner that left everyone knowing he was not concerned about the happenings of Detective Martinez.

"No, you don't understand. He was there in the parking lot arguing with some man!"

"That doesn't surprise me. I think Dr. Kendrick is ready for us to come in," Newt said.

"Wait, the man punched him and kicked him in the ribs numerous times," Stefanie explained frantically.

"Did you call nine one one?" Newt asked, appearing to be more concerned.

"No, the man left, and Martinez got up and walked back

into a hotel room. He seemed okay. I drove over here as fast as I could to tell you two."

"I'll call dispatch and let them know to send a cruiser over to check on him," Newt said as he reached for his phone.

"No need," Jaxson said as he nodded toward the door. Detective Martinez walked in sporting a shiner around his left eye.

"Do we say something?" Stefanie asked.

"No. Let's just go inside as usual," Jaxson answered as he turned toward the door.

Everyone took their usual places and listened to Dr. Kendrick go over the autopsy of Jane Doe PB #3, who had been identified as Samantha Farmer. There was nothing unusual about Samantha, and she had been identified through dental records by the forensic dentist the previous day. Jaxson had determined that Dr. Kendrick had his standard routine, as most medical professionals did, which covered the basics of body identification, height, weight, and other points were both procedural and legal requirements for all autopsies. The only part of the autopsy that was not standard routine was both the cause and the manner of death for each victim.

Jaxson listened and took notes but occasionally looked over at Detective Martinez. Jaxson noticed Martinez was not looking at his phone this time. He simply stood in the corner, and every so often, he reached up and felt the red puffy skin around his very swollen eye. He was not paying attention to Dr. Kendrick, or anyone else. He seemed to be distracted by something other than his eye and the case. That something drew Martinez's attention away from the victim. He stood there staring at the autopsy room's unimpressive concrete floor, appearing to be consumed by his inner thoughts.

"The body appears to have an approximate six-millimeter neck abrasion circling the neck in its entirety. This abrasion is a possible ligature mark. There also appears to be petechial facial hemorrhages, which is an indication of cerebral hypoxemia or strangulation. Before anyone asks, I've also determined that the suspected strangulation device found with PB Number Seven is of the same diameter and matches the injuries around this victim's neck. The weapon was likely used on both PB Number Seven and PB Number Four, but a DNA test needs to be completed to confirm."

Dr. Kendrick paused for a moment and looked at his audience before continuing.

"My determination is the victim died from compression of anatomical neck structures leading to asphyxia and then death. It is also my determination the cause of death is a homicide. Are there any questions?"

Everyone in attendance kept quiet and waited for Detective Martinez to say something. Detective Waterman looked at Jaxson for help. Jaxson nodded at the detective as if to say he should adjourn the group.

Newt stood. "All right, everyone, if no one has a question for the doctor, then let's meet back in the conference room in about fifteen minutes."

Detective Martinez walked over and pulled Newt to the side. Jaxson and Stefanie watched but did not approach the two men as they spoke in private. After a few minutes, Newt walked to the two of them as Martinez walked out of the autopsy room.

"What was that about?" Jaxson asked.

"He says he's not feeling well and needs to leave."

"No shit, he's not feeling well. That guy beat the crap out of him," Stefanie stated out loud and without filter.

Jaxson looked at Stefanie and shook his head. If there was anything he loved about Stefanie, it was her unfiltered opinions. Newt looked at the two of them, smiled, turned toward the conference room, and motioned his arm as to invite them inside.

Samantha Farmer (PB #3)

The bathroom of the beach house left nothing to be desired. The two vanities had brown porcelain water basins on top of a white-and-brown granite countertop. All the colors throughout the beach house, along with the expensive furniture, had been chosen very carefully by the owner. At first, Samantha felt the summer rental was too expensive for the budget she had put together, but when she saw it online, she fell in love with it. Law school had been expensive also, but working as a waitress for six years had helped her save money for tuition. She had counted every penny while she was there and never indulged in anything that fell out of her budget, but now was a time to celebrate. *A little, anyway,* she thought.

Her summer vacation was coming to an end, and in a couple of days, she had her new career starting at the Law Firm of Penn and Barnes. She never imagined she would ever get hired at such a prestigious law firm, but Sam also never believed she would make it through law school either, especially starting her law degree at the age of thirty-four.

The end of May and the first part of June were spent at the beach, tanning by day and partying at night at the local beachside bars with people she met either at the beach or through her dating app. Sam, as she liked to be called, found many new friends at Pensacola Beach, some of whom were nothing more than a new girlfriend she would spend the day at the beach with or go shopping with in one of the many souvenir shops lining the boardwalk. But others, of the male persuasion, were nothing more than a nightly distraction. At first, she felt guilty for her copious sexual choices during the first few weeks, but after three years of nothing but studying legal briefs with people ten years younger than herself, it was time to enjoy life.

Sam looked herself over in the bathroom mirror once more. Her blonde hair fell straight down over her shoulders and down the middle of her back. The red spaghetti strap mini-dress was very revealing. It showed way too much cleavage and was too short and nearly showed too much down there as well. Normally, Sam wouldn't wear anything like it, nor would she have bought it for herself, but he had bought it for her, and she wanted to please him. He had bought her lots of things during their time together. She thought he was too perfect when she had first read the bio he had posted on the dating app. He was six foot one and 205 lbs., with dark hair and a muscular build. He was thirty-seven, and most importantly, he was single.

From their first date, William was fantastic in every way possible. He opened doors for her, complimented her on everything she wore, surprised her with small gifts, and brought her roses at least once a week. The only thing that made Sam uncomfortable about William was his insistence on paying for everything. Whenever the two of them went shopping, William bought her gifts, like new shoes, manicures, and even pedicures. He never allowed Sam to pay for anything when he was around, and William never complained about the money he spent on her. He also said the right things and did everything else right in the bedroom. Sam thought William could read her mind when it came to knowing what she wanted and how she wanted it. *He's perfect, right?* she thought to herself.

The future for Sam and William was uncertain, but Sam believed he could be the one. He never mentioned the future, nor did he hint to anything about it. William was more focused on the now rather than the later. She had called her sister Cindy, in New Jersey, for advice, and Cindy told her not to approach the subject unless he brought it up.

Sam sat on the bed and placed her foot into the high heel shoe and strapped it around her ankle, then did the same for the other foot. The shoes were red and matched the dress perfectly, along with the red polish on her toenails. William had surprised her that morning with a spa day and roses. When the limousine arrived that morning, William was there with roses and kisses. She arrived at the spa and realized he had picked everything out, including the color of polish for her toenails. Throughout the day, she thought he had something big planned. She didn't think he was going to pop the question because it was too soon, but maybe he wanted to keep things going between the two of them after the summer was over.

Maybe tonight he will say something about our future, Sam thought to herself as she shut the bedroom light off and headed downstairs, where William was waiting for her.

William heard Sam making her way down the stairs. He was excited and nervous at the same time. He enjoyed what he had come to refer to as the matrimony phase of his relationships. *But I enjoy the divorce even more,* William thought to himself. The evening was going to be one he would remember and fantasize about for the rest of his life and one she would not live through.

As Sam made her way down the stairs, William stood at the bottom and watched her take each step seductively. She was beautiful, and he was glad he had found her online. Out of all the women he had killed, Sam would be the one he would miss the most. *She's a favorite,* he thought. If he were not the man he was, maybe there could have been a chance for the two of them. But for him, that could never be. No one could ever love a serial killer, nor could a serial killer genuinely love someone else more than himself.

"How do I look?" Sam said as she spun around in front of William.

He watched and smiled as she leaned on the railing, allowing the back of the dress to rise slightly and expose the bottom of her buttocks.

"Beautiful and flawless as usual," he answered as he pulled a single rose out from behind his back.

"Another rose?" she asked as she walked toward him. "You spoil me." She leaned in, took the rose from his hand, and kissed his lips softly. She placed her arms around his neck and pulled herself up onto his waist. William grabbed her buttocks and held her there while the two kissed passionately.

"This rose is special," William said as he let her back down to the ground.

"Special how?"

"Because I chose this one from among all the others for you. Just as you chose me from among the others," he answered and kissed her once more.

Sam felt a tear coming to her eye, and she forced herself to think of something else. She quickly changed the subject. "Where are you taking me tonight?"

"Someplace special for dinner. Then we're going back to my place." *Where I might kill you tonight.*

"Your place? Why your place?"

"Because I've got something planned for you there."

"So I guess we're eating at someplace close to Pensacola Beach, since we're going to your place afterward," Sam concluded out loud.

"Probably."

"Should I bring an overnight bag?"

"Yes," he answered. *But you probably won't need it.* He smiled at her.

Sam made her way back upstairs to retrieve some clothes for her overnight stay while William sat on the couch and thought about his plans for the evening. More than once, he changed his mind about killing her, and as she returned downstairs a few minutes later, he still had second thoughts about what he was going to do later.

"Are you ready?"

"Yes," William answered as he took her bag from her and headed for the door.

"Thank you."

"You're welcome. Don't forget your rose," William said from the open door as he pointed back at the rose.

"Oh yeah." Sam grabbed the rose off the table, then hastily walked out the door, with William following close behind.

William opened the car door for Sam and held it while she sat in the passenger seat. She allowed her dress to inch up her thighs, exposing her red silk panties to William. Sam was in the mood to tease her lover, and she felt her lover was in the mood to be teased.

"Nice," he remarked and smiled mischievously. He dropped her bag into the back seat and then sat inside the convertible sports car.

"Can you put the top up?" she asked.

"Yes. We don't want your beautiful hair destroyed by the wind, now do we? Besides, I plan on showing you off tonight," William explained as he pressed the button that engaged the top to close.

"No, we don't. You can destroy it later," she replied flirtatiously as she reached over and rubbed his thigh. He put the car into drive and pulled out onto the street.

The Red Fish and Oyster Bar was nearly empty. William had made reservations for the two of them in advance, and he had asked to be seated in the back corner when they arrived. William never took Sam to the same restaurant twice, and he never sat in the open where people could stare at him while he ate his meal. At first, Sam thought William's dinner behavior was odd, but after dating William for a few weeks, she discovered she enjoyed trying new and expensive restaurants up and down the panhandle from Gulf Shores, Alabama, to Panama City, Florida.

"What would you like for dinner?" William asked.

"Can we start with my favorite?"

"Absolutely," William stated as the waiter approached.

The waiter, a short and very plump man wearing a short black vest, black pants, and a white long sleeve shirt, approached their table. He was polite and asked the couple if he could start them off with a wine or an appetizer of their choice. William was always the gentlemen and ordered for them both.

"We'll start with oysters Rockefeller as an appetizer, along with a bottle of your best white wine to accompany the oysters," William told the waiter.

"Excellent, sir," the waiter replied and walked away as another man, similarly dressed, approached and filled their water glasses.

William and Sam sat there through dinner, flirting back and forth under the table. They both enjoyed the yellowfin tuna with wine. When the waiter returned to clear their dishes, he asked if they would like dessert. Sam was hesitant, but William encouraged her to splurge and enjoy whatever dessert her heart desired.

"I'll look fat if I eat something so heavy," Sam whispered.

"You could never. I think you should have the crème brûlée. I know you really enjoy it," William said and leaned over to kiss her.

The dinner ended with the two of them sharing the crème brûlée while they finished the bottle of wine. William held Sam's hand and walked her to the car, where he opened the door and kissed her wantonly before she got inside.

"I love you," she whispered in his ear.

"And I, you," he whispered back.

When the two arrived at William's beach house, he continued to treat her like a queen all the way to the bedroom.

"Is there anything you would like me to do tonight?" William asked as he removed his shirt, exposing his physically fit torso.

"You know what I really like," she said softly. She placed her arms around his neck, kissed his lips, and pushed him down to his knees in front of her.

William lifted her dress above her hips and pulled her panties off as he kissed her bare skin around her bikini line.

"What do you want me to do?" he asked between kisses as he ran his hand between her legs."

"Oh, William, just do it. You know what I want you to do," She pulled her dress off over her head and fell backward onto the bed.

William moved across the floor on his knees until his head was comfortably between her legs. Sam grabbed the back of his head and pulled him in closer with one hand while she gripped the footboard of the bed with the other.

"Yes, baby, that's it!" She whispered as she grinded her hips and pulled him into her harder.

William stayed there until Sam pushed him away. She sat up and placed her hands on his waist and removed his pants. Sam grabbed him by the buttocks and pulled him into her mouth. William placed his hands on her head and pulled her into him as he pushed his hips forward.

"Fuck me now," she ordered as she stood and then bent over, using her hands to balance herself on the bed.

William wasted no time. He grabbed her by her hips and maneuvered himself until he was inside her from behind.

"Yes, just like that!" she screamed.

William moved in and out of her quickly as she screamed in ecstasy. After a few minutes, he slowed his thrusts and pushed her farther onto the bed. With one hand, William guided her to the center of the bed, and with the other, he retrieved the garrote from beneath the mattress. He took his position behind her once more and moved in and out very slowly as he reached under her and caressed her breast with his left hand.

"Does that feel good?" she asked.

"Yes." He placed the garrote around her neck and pulled it tightly.

"What are you doing?" she screamed. "No, William, I don't like that."

William kept tightening the garrote as Sam fought to move away from him. When she fell limp and passed out, he loosened the strangulation device. He then pushed her legs apart and entered her once more. After a few moments, Sam regained consciousness. She felt William on top of her back, moving in and out of her.

"Stop!" she screamed.

William kept going as she fought to crawl out from under him. He was close to finishing when he tightened the garrote once more.

How could I let something like this happen? Sam thought to herself as William screamed out in orgasm. Sam felt her head dropping to the mattress and then the room turned dark.

William kissed her cheek. He lay beside her and looked into her eyes as he caressed her cheek. "Flawless," he whispered.

Chapter 16
Out Of Tune

Newt continued to share the information he had compiled on the victims. During his briefing, some people excused themselves from the room and never returned. It was a typical behavior Jaxson experienced in other cases involving multiple victims. For some people, the newness of a serial killer investigation was wearing off, and the boredom of not getting any new information to make an arrest was taking its toll. If the killer was identified and an arrest was made, then everyone involved could celebrate in closing the case. Jaxson had learned that law enforcement professionals enjoyed the celebration of solving a serial murder case. Still, no one wanted to be part of or have their name attached to an unsolvable serial murder case. Jaxson knew locating a serial killer was not an easy task, and many cases of serial murder went unsolved for years.

Newt finished his briefing and opened himself up for questions. Stefanie looked around the room and saw that she, Jaxson, and the coroner were the only ones left in the room.

"Why don't you sit with us at the table? I don't think the others are coming back," Stefanie said and, with her left hand, invited Newt to sit in the chair next to her.

"Why is everyone leaving?" Newt asked as he took a seat.

"How many homicides have you worked, Newt?" Jaxson asked without looking up from his notebook.

"Ten to twelve, why?"

Jaxson looked up at the young detective and asked, "How long did it take you to close your longest case and to make an arrest?"

"I had three that took over six months and one still unsolved," Newt admitted quietly.

"Well, we have seven unsolved homicides with no known suspect or anything that could connect someone as a suspect yet. No one wants their name associated with a case this big in case it goes unsolved," Jaxson explained.

"So what do we do now?" Newt asked, his tone resembling that of a terminally ill patient who was just told they only had a few weeks to live.

"We forge on! Just because others are giving up doesn't mean we are," Stefanie said encouragingly.

"Newt, I'm glad they're gone. I never liked large parties. The three of us can work on this case. What do you have in this bag of yours?" Jaxson asked and pointed at Newt's shoulder bag. He seemed to carry it everywhere he went.

"Everything on each victim," Newt replied as he reached down and pulled files out of the bag.

Jaxson was surprised to see that Newt had a duplicate file on every victim. Somehow Newt had collected all the information possible on each and every victim. The files appeared to be complete, to say the least.

"How do you have all this information on each victim? We haven't even completed the autopsies on all of them," Jaxson said, surprised, as he thumbed through a few of the files.

"When we exhumed the bodies and discovered the licenses and other identification cards with each one, I began gathering the information. I wrote all the search warrants the first night and got them to the on-call judge at four o'clock in the morning. By the way, judges don't like being awoken early in the morning. The judge signed all the warrants, and I had the sheriff's help in calling in our computer forensic detectives, who were able to get me the first two victims' social media, cell phone, and other personal information right away. It's how I had Abigail's information ready for you the first day. This other stuff came trickling in, and it still is each day. I think each one is almost complete," Newt said and sat back his chair.

"Detective Waterman, you are a very dedicated professional. When this case is solved, you deserve all the praise people are going to throw your way," Jaxson proclaimed as he reached down and started to look through Samantha Farmer's file.

Newt smiled at the acknowledgment from the FBI profiler. He began looking through the duplicate file, while Stefanie looked over his shoulder.

The file didn't have much of anything different than the others. Jaxson deduced Samantha Farmer had come to Pensacola before starting her new career as a lawyer at a large law firm. It was the Law Firm of Penn and Barnes that had reported her missing when she failed to arrive for a new job with the firm. Samantha's family was almost nonexistent, and no one she knew could be located for questioning. It was then Jaxson had a suspicion. He stood and started moving the files around.

"What are you doing, Jaxson?" Stefanie asked.

"Wait, just give me a minute." Jaxson laid the files in two different categories. He then stood back and looked at them on the table.

"What is it, Jaxson?" Newt asked.

"When I first arrived, I went under the beach house and made an observation regarding the placement of each grave. Four graves were lined up next to each other along the easterly side of the beach house, directly in front of one of the beach house support piers. The other three graves were lined up next to each other along the southern side of the beach house, directly in front of one of the support piers, just like the other four," Jaxson explained.

"I made the same observation and wrote it in my notes when we excavated the graves," Stefanie remarked. She reached down and went through her own bag, looking for her notes.

"Yes, but when I returned later, I found markings on each support pier," Jaxson explained. He handed his notepad with the markings on them to Stefanie and Newt.

"What does 'Ø,' 'S,' and 'K' mean?" Newt asked.

"Wait. There's more," Jaxson answered and explained his theory once more.

"Okay, if we assume the other victims are the people in the identifications, then thus far, Bethany Porter and Brook Evans were found under the support piers marked 'S' and 'K.' Abigail Johnson and Samantha Farmer were found under the support piers marked with the 'Ø,' and Trina Tyler is the third victim who was found under the 'Ø' marking."

"I'm still not following as to what all that tells you," Newt confessed as he looked at the files.

"I'm betting Trina Tyler was murdered with a garrote," Jaxson stated with confidence while placing his finger on the Tyler file.

Dr. Kendrick, who had been sitting in the room quietly, stood and looked over at the three of them. "I'll be back in a moment," the doctor advised and walked out of the room.

Jaxson, Stefanie, and Newt waited patiently for Dr. Kendrick to return. After what seemed to be an eternity, the doctor returned. He stood there, looked at the three of them, and took a deep breath before speaking.

"Trina Tyler, or PB Number Six, appears to have been killed with the use of a garrote that measures the same diameter as the garrote discovered under PB Number Seven. Now, this is a presumption, and I cannot confirm it until I complete the full autopsy," Dr. Kendrick explained.

"What does that mean to you, Jaxson?" Stefanie asked.

"I think three victims were killed with a garrote, and four were killed by manual strangulation, and..." Jaxson paused.

"And?" Newt asked excitedly, encouraging the agent to continue.

"And I think we're dealing with two different killers."

Jaxson left Stefanie and Newt in the parking lot of the coroner's office. He drove back toward Pensacola Beach with unanswered questions still running through his mind.

What do the markings mean? Who is SKO? Wait! 'Ø' 'S' 'K' or 'S' 'K' 'Ø'? Are there two killers or just one?

Billy stayed on the beach, watching Taylor's beach house from a distance. He pondered every conceivable way on how to get into the house after everyone went to sleep. He desperately needed the FBI agent's bag that he was sure held the drone photos. One photo of Billy wasn't enough evidence by itself, but another one to compare it to was more than circumstantial in an investigation. Billy was getting nervous.

I could kill the deputy out front and the one across the street very quietly. Then I could go in and kill that bitch and her FBI man while they slept. Retrieve the drone photos and leave. I'd be done with it all: Pensacola, the FBI, and that asshole I call a friend, Billy thought to himself as he sat behind a large sand dune, out of sight of the residence.

Billy was still planning on how to get the FBI's photos when his cell phone vibrated in his pocket. He leaned back, reached in his pocket, pulled the phone out, and looked at the number.

"What the fuck does he want now?" Billy mumbled unhappily before answering the call.

"What?" Billy answered in low, aggravated voice.

"I'm in town this week. I want to meet with you," his friend said.

"Why?" Billy asked.

"I've been thinking, and I think I've left you hanging out on your own. I want to help you get the photos from the FBI agent, and the other one that was taken of you as well."

"How?" Billy asked. He thought it was odd his longtime friend had now changed his tune and was willing to help.

"I have a plan. Can we meet at your parents' cabin on Coldwater Creek? I don't think we should be seen at your place in town together."

"Yeah, call me when you get here, and we can meet." Billy was hesitant but agreed to meet with his old friend, at the cabin where they had spent many happy years in the past.

"We're in this together," Billy's friend replied before hanging up.

Billy sat there quietly, still holding his cell phone behind the sand dune, thinking about the phone call. He was happy his old friend had had a change of heart, but still, he questioned why. Billy began thinking about the good times he and Will had together over the years and was still thinking about them when the headlights of Agent Locke's car lit up Taylor's driveway. Billy watched as Jaxson exited the car, carrying the bag Billy desperately wanted to get his hands on.

Jaxson walked up the steps to the front door, and when he reached the top, he stopped and stood in front of the door. He didn't know what to do.

Jaxson contemplated for a moment. *Should I knock or just walk inside? I don't have a key, but my stuff is inside. Knock, right?*

Taylor was in the kitchen when she heard someone knocking on the door. She rushed over and looked out the glass window and saw Jaxson standing there. She quickly opened the door and looked at him, slightly confused. "Why did you knock on the door?"

"I really don't know. I don't have a key, and I didn't know if the door was locked. I know my stuff is here, but it's your house and…"

"You don't need to knock. You're a guest here. You can come and go as you please. I'll get you a key. Now come in and kiss me." Taylor reached out, grabbed his arm, pulled him inside, and kissed him passionately.

Jaxson dropped his bag to the floor and placed his arms around her. The kiss felt good, her body felt good, and the relationship felt good. He ran his arms down her back and lightly over her buttocks. Taylor was wearing a T-shirt and yoga pants that fit perfectly.

"I hope you're hungry," she said quietly as she rubbed the back of his head.

"I am. What did you order for dinner?" Jaxson asked.

"What?" Taylor responded, surprised.

"I meant…"

"I know what you meant. I know how to cook, and for your information, I made pork chops." Taylor turned and walked back into the kitchen, pretending to be mad at her houseguest.

Jaxson followed Taylor into the kitchen and helped her set the table, with a smile on his face.

Billy lost sight of Jaxson after he walked up the stairs to the front porch. He maneuvered around the beach house toward the back and watched as the two of them moved about the kitchen. He thought about his earlier phone call and decided it would be better to wait for his old friend Will to come out to help resolve the problem, rather than doing things on his own. Billy checked to make sure he had his phone in his pocket. He then secured his pistol in his waistband and made his way back toward his truck as the sun slowly drifted toward the Gulf of Mexico in the western sky.

"Did you find anything new today?" Taylor asked as she got up to refill their glasses. She and Jaxson had sat in the dining room to eat their dinner. The dinner conversation was centered on anything and everything except the investigation until Taylor got up from the table.

Jaxson looked up from his empty plate and paused before answering. He didn't know what to say—or what he could say, for that matter.

Taylor looked over from the kitchen and saw the blank look on his face. "I didn't mean to—"

"No, we may have," Jaxson said quickly. He decided Taylor was someone he could trust, and besides, he had already shared some information with her when they'd had dinner with the others.

"Jaxson, if you can't talk about it, I understand."

"No, it's okay. I think we discovered something."

"Really! Like what?" Taylor asked as she carried the two glasses of tea back into the dining room.

"Well—"

"Why don't you put your plate in the kitchen and I'll meet you in the living room with our tea? It's more comfortable in there," Taylor said as she started for the living room.

Jaxson dropped off his empty plate in the kitchen and walked into the living room. There, he found Taylor sitting on the right side of the couch. The lights were dimmed, and soft music resonated from the wall speakers around the room. Taylor had placed the tea glasses next to each other on coasters on the coffee table. Taylor's placement of the glasses hinted to Jaxson that she was inviting him to sit in the center of the couch, next to her.

Jaxson sat in the center as expected. He could smell her alluring perfume. He wanted to take her in his arms and kiss her full lips. Taylor had positioned her body toward Jaxson. She brought her legs up onto the couch and leaned in close to him. She then took her left hand and rubbed the back of his neck just below his hairline. Jaxson was taken in by it all, and before he knew it, he was lowering his head, giving her full access to the back of his head and neck. The woman was intoxicating.

"Does that feel good?" she asked softly, continuing to massage him.

"Wonderful," Jaxson whispered.

"Good. Lean forward," Taylor instructed as she raised herself up on her knees to massage his neck and shoulders from the side. Her breasts rested on his shoulder, and then she kissed his neck. It was all too much.

Jaxson turned toward her and took her in his arms. He lifted her off the couch and laid her back down under him. She looked up at his bright-blue eyes while running her hands along his muscular arms and back.

"I like this," Jaxson admitted as he ran his hand down her side.

"Me too."

The events of the day and the question Taylor had asked a few minutes ago were part of the past, and now they were consumed by the present, in each other's arms.

Will walked out onto the deck of the restaurant and gazed at the moon out over the water, while he drank his expensive whiskey from the crystal glass. He thought about the phone call with Billy. He had come to the conclusion Billy needed his help. Will knew the two of them were intertwined and one could not survive without the other. If Billy were captured by the police, then Will would eventually be discovered, even if Billy kept his mouth shut. There was too much history between the two of them.

"Are you ready to go?" Olivia asked from the door leading to the deck of the restaurant. Olivia Harris had accompanied Will to dinner this evening, after he had called her when he arrived in town. She and Will had attended many banquets and parties and spent countless nights together over the years. The two met in high school and had remained friendly over the years, to say the least. Olivia worked for the county assessor's office, where she earned a lot less than what she felt she deserved. She also spent more than she earned.

Whenever Will would come to town, he would call Olivia, and the two of them would spend time together. Will was always generous with his money, and on more than one occasion, he had helped her financially by paying off one or more of her debts. It was her opinion that the financial assistance was nothing for Will, but it helped her out a great deal. Besides, Olivia never felt bad for taking the money Will gave her. She figured it never came close to repaying her for what he liked to do to her sexually. After a night with Will, Olivia had to take time off from work, and on more than one occasion, Olivia spent weeks concealing the bruises around her neck and face.

"Yes, I am," Will answered and drank the rest of his whiskey. He took Olivia by the arm and escorted her toward the door. The two briefly stopped and listened to the orchestra performing on the small stage before walking out.

"The orchestra is horrible," Will whispered to his date.

"Yes, they're bad, and the violinist needs to make some adjustments," Olivia said as they walked out of the restaurant and into the parking lot.

Chapter 17
Mornings

Jaxson awoke to find Taylor lying next to him. She was still peacefully sleeping. He got out of bed and quietly walked around to her side. He stood there for a minute, watching her, then leaned over and kissed her cheek without waking her. He returned to his own room, showered, dressed, and headed for the door. When he reached the end of the hallway, he was surprised to find Taylor standing there, wearing nothing but his shirt from the previous day and holding a cup of coffee.

"Were you trying to leave without saying good-bye?" she asked as she leaned forward and kissed him.

"No. You looked so peaceful; I didn't want to disturb you." Jaxson dropped his bag to the floor before taking the coffee cup from her hand.

"You've could've woken me. Who knows, it might have been fun," she said as she unbuttoned the only button keeping her shirt closed. She then reached up around Jaxson's neck and kissed him again.

"Oh my! I do wish I could stay, but I can't. I have got to go, but I'll be back tonight."

"What would you like for dinner?" Taylor asked as she slowly backed away, allowing Jaxson to get a full view of her.

"Why don't you order us some food, and I'll pick it up on my way back over here this evening?" Jaxson suggested, looking into her eyes. He was intentionally trying to avoid looking down at her desirable body.

"That sounds like a plan, but you may need this." She reached toward the table next to the door and picked up a house key.

"Thank you," Jaxson replied, taking the key from her hand. He then kissed her once more, opened the door, got in his rental car, and started for the coroner's office.

Will got up before Olivia. He had already showered, dressed, and was standing in front of her dresser mirror when she finally woke.

Olivia heard Will moving about her bedroom, but she lay there, not moving. Olivia wasn't afraid to move; it just hurt her to do so. Will had hurt her more than usual. He seemed to be angry about something and had decided to take it out on her.

"I'll call you later," Will said softly from the bedroom door.

"Okay," Olivia replied flatly. She managed to get up and walk to the dresser to look at her bruised face and body.

"I left some money on the nightstand and—"

"And you'll put more into my bank account later, right?" Olivia asked, interrupting him.

"How much?" Will asked as he walked back into the room and stood behind her. He lightly caressed her shoulders with his hands and kissed her bruised neck.

"I don't know, Will! How much do you think this is worth? I'll have to take a medical leave of absence from work. A doctor will need to write me a letter, excusing me. You know I can't afford to miss work. You really hurt me this time. Why did you punch me? I really thought you were going to kill me last night. When I passed out… I… I… I didn't think I was going to…" Olivia tried to answer but started crying.

"I could never do that to you. You know me more than anyone alive," Will said, reassuring her after pulling her into him. She continued to cry as he stood there, holding her naked, beaten body.

"Okay, I—"

"I'll tell you what. I'm putting ten grand in your bank account in a few minutes. Then I'll drop off another fifty grand that you can deposit on your own throughout the year."

"All right," Olivia said in agreement and then turned and walked into her bathroom to shower.

"I'm sorry."

"I know you are," Olivia replied as Will walked out of the bedroom.

Taylor poured herself a cup of coffee, sat in front of her computer to check her emails, and there it was. In the back of her mind, she knew Natalie's family would accept the offer, but she, herself, wasn't ready to accept anything concerning her missing friend. Taylor let out a slight sigh, picked up her phone, and dialed his number.

"Hello," Jeff said after answering the call.

"Jeff, congratulations, it looks like we have a deal," Taylor announced unexcitedly.

"Really? That's fantastic news! When do you think we can close?"

"I can get the documents over to title today if—"

"If… I can get the money wired to the title company. Right?" Jeff asked.

"Yes, actually," Taylor answered.

"I'll have my bank wire the funds after you let me know the title company has the contract. When the title company is ready to close, you and I will be too," Jeff stated.

"We still have to wait until the sheriff's office releases the house."

"Yeah, I figured. Can you check to see when they think that will be? Maybe you can ask your FBI friend."

"I can, and I will," Taylor replied to a very pleased Jeff Carlisle.

"I look forward to closing. I have to take care of something right now, and I need to go, but I'll see you later," Jeff said and then hung up.

Taylor sat there, thinking about her friend and the good times they had spent together, before getting up and going into her room to shower.

Detective Martinez woke to the sound of the alarm going off next to his bed. He reached over and quickly shut it off. Martinez lay there for a moment, thinking about his wife, his kids, and his career. Everything was falling apart, and he didn't know what to do. The detective was tired of moving from one hotel to another. He was disgusted with the lies and the people he was associating with, but most of all, he was disgusted with himself and his own criminal activity. Martinez knew he was wrong for getting involved with them, but the money was overwhelming. He knew he should have just said no to the offer, but he didn't. Now, everything was falling apart. *Agent Jaxson Locke was right about me,* Martinez thought to himself.

"Are you awake?" the man sitting in the chair next to Martinez's bed asked, surprising the detective.

"What the fuck are you doing here?" Martinez yelled as he sat up in the bed and looked at the nightstand for his pistol.

"It's not there. I laid it on the dresser over there," the man said confidently as he stood from his chair.

"What's going on? Why are you here? I was going to call you later today," Martinez explained nervously after seeing a pistol in the man's waistband.

The man was angry with the detective. He believed Detective Martinez was dodging him and not doing as he was paid to do.

"I give you a hundred grand to get you out of debt. You had one small job. What do you do? You gamble it away. Gamblers like you always think they'll win the next race, the next baseball game, or the next card game. You don't ever fucking win! You just get deeper and deeper in debt, and you leave me exposed!"

"I know, but we can work this out. I'm getting it this week," Martinez said.

"When this week?"

"Tomorrow," Martinez answered as he turned toward the man and placed his feet on the floor.

"Tomorrow. I'm afraid that's too late," the man said, right before he placed the garrote over the detective's head and quickly tightened it.

Martinez was able to get one hand between the garrote and his neck, but it was useless. The man twisted the garrote tighter and tighter as Martinez struggled to free himself. It was only a matter of minutes before Martinez's body went limp and his free arm dropped to his side. The man held the garrote in place and continued to tighten it until he saw the pinky finger of Detective Martinez snap off and roll down his chest onto the floor.

The man stood, removed the garrote, and left the room. He

placed the room's Do Not Disturb sign on the knob, walked into the parking lot, casually got into his expensive car, and drove away.

Stefanie was drinking her morning coffee, listening to the local news, and looking out her hotel room window toward the beautiful view of the rising sun. She had gotten up early and had some time to herself before getting to the coroner's office. Stefanie was still enjoying the view when she saw the man who had beaten up Detective Martinez the previous morning as he walked to a car in the parking lot.

"I guess he's looking for a round two," Stefanie said to herself before turning around and walking to the table to get her bag. Before walking out the door, she paused, turned around, and walked back to the bed to use the remote to turn off the television. When Stefanie got to her car, she looked around the parking lot but did not see the man or Detective Martinez. She tossed her bag in the back seat, got inside, and left for the coroner's office.

Jaxson was already sitting in the autopsy room in his usual seat when Newt and Stefanie arrived. He was thinking about what Taylor was going to have him pick up for dinner this evening when Newt and Stefanie came over and sat next to him.

"Why are you smiling?" Stefanie asked her FBI friend.

"I didn't realize I was," Jaxson replied.

"I didn't see Detective Martinez in the parking lot or the lobby," Newt said to the two of them as he placed his bag next to his chair.

"Probably won't show up either," Stefanie said sarcastically as she cleaned off her glasses.

"Why not?" Jaxson and Newt asked in unison.

"His friend from yesterday was there at the hotel looking for him."

"Really?" the two men said in unison once more.

"Yes, really," Stefanie answered as she placed her glasses back on her face.

Jaxson and Newt looked at each other as Dr. Kendrick and his assistant entered the room with another body.

"Are we ready to proceed? Is everyone here?" Dr. Kendrick asked.

"I think everyone who needs to be here is here and ready," Newt answered.

"Good, then let's get started," Dr. Kendrick said as he and his assistant lifted the sheet covering the body. The pathologist went directly into his regular routine.

"The body is a thirty-eight-year-old female, found buried in beach sand. The body is currently identified with toe tags and coroner's band on the left ankle as Natalie Adams. The body is an unembalmed, refrigerated, adult Caucasian female. The body weighs one hundred twenty-five pounds and measures sixty-four inches and is well built and fully nourished. The body was originally identified as Jane Doe PB Number Five but has been positively identified as Natalie Adams through dental records by the Escambia County Coroner's Office. DDS Leon Melton, a recognized forensic odontologist, compared the dental records of Natalie Adams to PB Number Five and confirmed they were the same."

Jaxson sat there and heard nothing Dr. Kendrick had said, except that the woman laid out in front of him was Taylor's friend Natalie Adams. He and Taylor had avoided the topic of Natalie since he moved into Taylor's house. When he returned this evening, they wouldn't be able to avoid it any longer. Jaxson figured they both knew this time was coming, but neither wanted to acknowledge it.

The trained FBI agent listened to the doctor explain how Natalie had multiple facial fractures and how she was manually strangled from the front. For some unknown reason, FBI Agent Jaxson Locke, who had sat through numerous autopsies, had a sick feeling in the pit of his stomach for the first time. He cleared his throat, swallowed, and got up and walked to the water fountain to get a drink. Stefanie and Newt watched him walk away and looked at each other, surprised.

"Agent Locke, should we take a break?" Dr. Kendrick asked.

"No. Let's keep going," Jaxson answered from the fountain, where he remained until the autopsy was completed. He then joined the rest of them in the conference room, where Newt began his briefing on what he had learned about Natalie Adams.

NATALIE ADAMS (PB #5)

Natalie rushed around the beach house, looking for her shoes. Will had bought the expensive red pumps in Paris, and she desperately wanted to impress him. *There they are!* She spotted the pink-and-red box under her beautiful California king. Natalie was filled with exhilaration about what was in store for her and Will. She wanted everything to go just right for the evening with him. The warm summer months they spent together had flown by in a flash. Will, initially, wasn't a part of her summer getaway, but when they met, he became the plan.

It was about five years ago when Natalie gave up on the idea of ever finding a husband who could handle her busy schedule. Natalie was a self-made businesswoman. She conducted her business around the world throughout the year. Natalie's business was centered on commercial real estate, and she was very successful at it, even against experienced men who seemed to dominate the arena of commercial real estate. At thirty-eight, she had ten commercial properties she owned outright. The properties she owned netted her nearly two million a year in revenue. Her other deals for her private investors brought in another million, in a good year.

It was at the end of last year when the busy Natalie decided to purchase her dream vacation home. Natalie wanted a place of her own, a place she could escape to when she needed a break, a place on a beach somewhere. It had to be a place that made her feel safe, comfortable, and at home.

It was in February three years ago when Natalie saw the marketing flyer for the beach house online. Immediately, she knew she wanted to see it. The Venetian-Italian-style villa was a luxury beach house sitting right on the water with views of Pensacola's white sandy beaches and the Gulf of Mexico. Natalie immediately called Oceanview Realty in Pensacola and spoke to Taylor Long, the listing agent, and made plans to view the home.

Two days later, Natalie was standing on the porch of the Italian villa at 1616 Ariola Drive. Once she walked inside, she knew she had to have it. The home was obviously staged by an interior decorator who knew how to market and decorate. The furniture, the sculptures, and the colors accented the Italian theme throughout the luxury home. Natalie made her offer right then and there. Her cash offer was over the asking price, but it included all the furnishings as well. After the purchase, she flew out between business trips one to two times a month. She became close friends with Taylor Long and, at times, invited Taylor in as a partner on some of her own private commercial real estate deals.

This particular summer, Natalie had called Taylor in advance, and the two of them planned to spend the entire summer sitting in the sun, drinking copious amounts of alcohol, chasing after much-younger men, and traveling around the coastal islands shopping. When Natalie arrived, she and Taylor started the summer just as they had planned. Taylor even moved into Natalie's beach house, and the two of them did exactly what they had planned until Taylor received a call from her mother, Carla, who explained she had injured her back and needed Taylor's help.

Taylor had promised to return before the end of the summer so they could continue their *Never Winter* vacation, as they liked to call it. A week later, after Taylor left, Natalie met Will, a successful internet business owner, at one of the local beach clubs. She wasn't looking for a man that night, but she also wasn't going to ignore a handsome suitor if he happened to be there. Will was there alone, and he had saved Natalie from an annoying creeper who seemed to follow her around the club. When the creeper approached her, he made an offensive remark about Natalie's large breasts, which Will overheard. Will stepped in and defended her against the rude man. When the other man continued with his foul language and became a little too handsy with Natalie, Will punched him in the face, grabbed Natalie by the arm, and ran her out of the club.

Natalie, to say the least, had been impressed with Will. Never in her life had she ever had a man defend her or rescue her like that before. *My hero,* she had told Taylor over the phone the next day. From that day forward, the two were inseparable. He even traveled with Natalie to Paris when she had to go there in July for a week. The two flew there on a private jet that belonged to one of her investors. They went to the Eiffel Tower in Paris and toured the beautiful city together. When they returned to Pensacola, Natalie began imagining a life with Will. He was the perfect man. He took care of her, and on Sunday mornings, he brought her breakfast in bed, along with one single red rose.

Now, the summer was coming to an end. Taylor was

returning next week, and Natalie wanted to introduce her best friend to her new love. She had called and told Taylor about Will many times over the summer, and she couldn't wait until all three of them were sitting on her balcony, drinking expensive wine as she and Will told Taylor about their adventures over the summer. A month after Natalie met Will, she tried to make arrangements for the three of them to meet, but the day before she and Will were to fly out to see Taylor at her mother's home, Will had to leave town on an emergency.

Natalie smiled as she slipped her feet into the red pumps, adjusted her breasts in the sexy, spaghetti-strap red bodycon, and made her way downstairs to Will. Walking down the hallway, she stopped in front of the full-length mirror to look herself over once more. Again, she adjusted the thin spaghetti straps and positioned her breasts accordingly.

You girls are going to be working overtime tonight, she thought before continuing downstairs to Will.

Will was sitting in one of the deck recliners out on the balcony, listening to the sound of Antonio Vivaldi's *The Four Seasons* being played loudly from the outdoor speakers. *The Four Seasons* was one of his favorite compositions. Natalie never enjoyed the sounds of classical music until she met Will. He introduced her to many of the great classical composers, and he enjoyed educating her on the personal history of the composers and the music they created. Over the few short months she had been with Will, Natalie had created a list of favorite symphonies and composers of her own.

"Are you ready for me?" Natalie asked over the music from behind Will.

"The question is, are you ready for me?" Will said as he stood, using the remote to turn the music down. He turned and faced Natalie, holding a single red rose in his hand.

"What a beautiful rose!" Natalie remarked as she walked to Will, took the rose from his hand, and kissed him softly.

"Not anywhere close to being as beautiful as you are, my love," Will said in return. He kissed her once more, stood back, and admired the stunning woman standing before him.

"You're so sweet, and you say all the right things," Natalie said as she smiled and looked over the handsome man standing in front of her. Will was athletic, tall, and fit, and tonight, he wore a tight white V-neck dress shirt with black pants and black shoes. *The one thing about Will that no one can ever deny is he knows how to dress to impress,* she thought.

"You look wonderful and very dashing this evening as well, *my love*," Natalie said in return. She emphasized the last two words, as this moment was the second time since they had met, that either had used the word love. The first time the word was used had been last night when they were lying in bed together. Will was holding Natalie close to him after they had made passionate love over and over again, while a thunderstorm played a symphony of its own outside.

The words came as a surprise to Natalie when Will had whispered, "I love you," in her ear and pulled her closer to him.

Natalie, taken in by the moment, turned and faced him. She held him tighter and said the same three words back. "I love you."

I really do believe I love him, she thought as the two stood there looking at each other.

"We better get going," Will said. He moved toward her and placed his hand around her tiny waist, then gently turned her to walk with him back inside the beach house.

"Where are you taking me?" she asked.

"Someplace really nice."

"Are you going to tell me, or is it going to be a surprise?"

"I've made reservations at Outriggers, over on Pensacola Bay," Will answered.

"I've heard about that place. It just opened up a few months ago. I heard you have to make reservations a month in advance."

"A week or so in advance but not a month," Will said as the two walked out to his car.

Natalie sat in the passenger seat as Will drove the car along Via De Luna Drive with the top down, while Henryk Górecki's *Symphony of Sorrowful Songs* blared from the car's expensive speakers. Natalie always enjoyed sitting in the passenger seat so she could see everything without having to concentrate on traffic. As they approached the bridge connecting Pensacola Beach to Gulf Breeze, Natalie looked to her left toward Little Sabine Bay. She watched as people moved about on their boats as the sun rested close to the water in the west.

"Can you tell me about this symphony?" Natalie asked. "It sounds beautiful yet so sad at the same time."

"Yes, I can. It was composed by Henryk Górecki, a Polish composer, and it's known as the *Symphony of Sorrowful Songs*."

"What is she singing?"

"The composition has a solo soprano, who sings three parts. The first part is from the second half of the fifteenth century. It's a Polish lament of Mary, mother of Jesus. The second part was written on the wall of a Gestapo cell during World War II. The third part is a Silesian folk song, of a mother searching for her son who was killed by the Germans in the Silesian uprisings between 1919 and 1921."

"Really?"

"Yes. The first and third verses are from the perspective of a parent who has lost a child. The second verse is from the perspective of a child separated from a parent. All of which are centered around the issue of war."

"How sad."

"Exactly. Hence the title, *Symphony of Sorrowful Songs*." Will reached over and held Natalie's hand.

Natalie smiled at him and then looked to her right at Pensacola Bay as they crossed Three Mile Bridge from Gulf Breeze to Pensacola.

A short time later, they arrived at Outriggers. The couple was seated in the back of the restaurant that provided a view of Pensacola Bay. The darkness over the bay was littered with small lights from the various watercraft that either sat still or causelessly cruised through the flat glassy water. Natalie enjoyed a lobster tail with a side of shrimp scampi and cheddar mashed potatoes. Will chose steak with a baked potato, and they both drank from a bottle of white wine.

Natalie was sitting next to Will, looking at the bay and waiting for the waiter to return with the bill, when she felt Will reach over and rub her thigh. She turned and looked at him and saw the all-too-familiar lustful look in his eyes. She placed her hand over his and moved it up between her legs and then leaned in and kissed him passionately.

"Take me home," she whispered.

It wasn't long before they were back at the beach house. When they went inside, Will picked up the remote for the home entertainment system and selected the *Symphony of Sorrowful Songs* once more. He walked over to Natalie, placed his hands on either side of her neck, and kissed her soft lips. Natalie used her hands and pulled her dress down to her hips. She then reached down and unfastened Will's pants and allowed them to fall to the floor. Will kissed her once more, and used his hands to guide her down to her knees in front of him.

Natalie complied and pleasured Will as he stood there cradling the back of her head. After a few minutes, she stood back up, pulled her dress down over her hips, and dropped it to the floor while Will removed his shirt. She kissed him and pulled her naked body against his. Without warning, he lifted her into his arms and carried her upstairs to the bedroom, where he gently laid her on the bed. He positioned himself on top of her and kissed her as he entered her. Natalie moaned in pleasure, reached around his waist, and spread her legs wider.

"It feels wonderful!" she said as Will ran his hands along

her body. Will moved in and out of her slowly at first and then faster as Natalie moved her body in response to his thrusts. "Just like that!" she screamed.

Will moved his hands from under Natalie and lifted her legs in the air, then quickly took them away and placed them around her neck before Natalie knew what was happening. He squeezed her throat as his thrusts became faster.

"No, Will. You're hurting me." She pleaded as she pulled at his wrist.

Will stopped and removed his hands from her neck.

"That hurts. Please don't do that," she pleaded.

Will smiled, and with a closed fist, he hit her in the face.

Natalie screamed and begged him to stop, but Will held her there with his other hand while continuing to beat her with the other until she was unconscious. He then finished what he had started by reentering her and placing his hands around her neck until he felt the bones snapping under pressure.

After Will finished, he stood next to the bed and stared at Natalie's lifeless body while listening to the final verse of the *Symphony of Sorrowful Songs*.

"You were right. It is beautiful yet so sad at the same time."

Chapter 18
My Friend

Jaxson left Stefanie and Newt in the parking lot of the coroner's office after Natalie's autopsy. Stefanie invited both Newt and Jaxson to dinner with her and Lori. Jaxson would have preferred to go to dinner and spent the evening laughing and having a good time with friends, but tonight, that would not be the case. Jaxson knew tonight would be spent comforting a grieving Taylor Long.

Taylor had texted Jaxson earlier in the day with the address and name of the restaurant she had ordered their dinner from. As he followed the GPS to the restaurant, he thought about how he would tell Taylor about Natalie. The agent imagined the different ways he could tell her and then he imagined how she would react. No matter how Taylor responded, Jaxson figured he had the entire weekend to stay with her. The team of investigators had decided to take the weekend off. They all concluded they needed a break from the case.

Before long, Jaxson was turning into the parking lot of Sonny's Seaside Seafood. He walked inside, gave the clerk his name, and took out his wallet. The clerk had the food ready under the counter. He handed it to Jaxson and explained the order had already been paid for, by the person who called in the order. Jaxson simply shook his head, placed his wallet back in his back pocket, and left the restaurant.

Taylor had spent the day preparing the paperwork for the sale of her friend's home. She also sent an email to the sheriff's office, requesting Natalie's beach house be released back to the family so it could be sold. Around noon, Taylor began to feel depressed. At four o'clock, she finished her work, walked out of her home office, and went into the kitchen to order the dinner she had promised Jaxson.

After ordering the food, Taylor freshened up and put on some clean clothes. She then left her bedroom, walked down the hallway, and before she knew it, she was standing in front of the door leading into the room she kept locked. Taylor took the key ring from her pocket, placed the key into the door, and unlocked it. She paused briefly before turning the knob and walking inside. Once she was inside, she stood there and looked at the timeline board she had created for Natalie. Red strings of yarn led to countless yellow square sheets of notepad paper with the words Dead End written on it. Taylor moved closer to the board, and once again, she thought about the different clues she had followed in trying to discover the fate of her friend.

Taylor sat in the large leather chair facing the board and cried as she looked at an old picture. It was of the two of them sitting on her deck, drinking wine.

"That's a really detailed timeline you've put together," Jaxson announced softly from the door.

"I'm sorry. I didn't hear you come in," Taylor said as she wiped her eyes and started to stand.

Jaxson quickly walked into the room, placed his hands lightly around Taylor's arms, and guided her back to her chair. He smiled, kissed her, knelt in front of her, and took her hands into his. Jaxson could see she was upset and missing her friend. He figured it was the right time to tell her about Natalie.

"What is it, Jaxson?"

"Today, we—"

"It was Natalie's day, wasn't it? You saw Natalie, didn't you?" Taylor cried.

"Yes."

"What happened to her? Tell me!" she shouted as she reached up and placed her hands on the side of his face.

"The autopsy performed today led to the positive identification of your friend Natalie Adams, who you reported as missing. Natalie Adams was one of the women who were discovered buried under the residence at 1616 Ariola Drive. Natalie will be ready for burial the week after next." Jaxson spoke slowly, deliberately, and softly and used Natalie's name as much as possible during his explanation. It was a method of reinforcing the reality of the loss to the deceased's loved one, a technique he had learned from an experienced psychologist whom he had come to know during his time in college.

Jaxson took her hands away from his head, placed them in her lap again, and held them there. He didn't say anything more. He waited for Taylor to absorb what he had said and to gather her thoughts.

"She was my friend," Taylor finally said, breaking the silence.

"I know. Tell me about your friend."

Jaxson sat with her for over an hour. He listened to her stories about the incredible adventures she and Natalie had taken together. Eventually, Jaxson and Taylor moved into the living room, where she continued to share her memories of her friend while they ate the dinner he had picked up. At around eleven o'clock, the two retired to the bedroom, where Taylor fell asleep in the comforting arms of her houseguest.

"Are you going to sleep all day?" Taylor asked as she scooted onto the bed next to Jaxson, waking him up from a deep sleep.

"What?" the still half-asleep man asked as he lifted his head from the pillow.

"Oh no, Jaxson!" Taylor placed the coffee cup she was holding onto the nightstand. She walked into the bathroom and quickly came back in with a wet washcloth.

"What's wrong?" Jaxson asked.

"Your head is bleeding," she answered as she held the cloth to the old wound on his head that had come open during the night.

"Really?"

She removed the washcloth and inspected the wound. "Yeah, it's not bad. It looks like one of the stitches came out, but I don't think it's a big deal."

Jaxson took the cloth from her hand and held it against his head. He looked at Taylor as she stood and grabbed the coffee cup once more. Jaxson noticed Taylor was already dressed and apparently packed. Sitting next to the door was a small overnight bag.

"Are you going somewhere?" Jaxson asked as he stood and walked into the bathroom.

"I am. Well, we are!"

"We?"

"Yes, I'm taking you on a trip down the coast to Panama City today. We'll come back through Pensacola Beach tomorrow, then we'll drive over to Orange Beach, Alabama, for dinner. Finally, we'll be back here late Sunday night."

"I don't know—"

"Jaxson, I really appreciate you being here last night and helping me through what I was feeling. Now, I'd like to show my appreciation to you. Also, I'm not the clingy girl who men get worried about early on in a relationship. Not that I'm saying we're in a relationship. I think the two of us just enjoy the other one's company."

Jaxson didn't know what to say. He stood there looking at the beautiful woman in front of him, holding a wet cloth to his head, thinking about it. "Okay, I'm in."

Billy had gotten up early and driven to Taylor's beach house. He was angry that he hadn't heard from Will yet. He needed and wanted his help. Billy sat on a blanket, while a playlist of various classical music resonated through the earphones covering his ears. He pretended to be an average beachgoer and made every attempt to blend in with the others. Occasionally, Billy looked over at Taylor's beach house for any sign of her or the FBI agent. Billy had promised to wait for Will to arrive before doing anything else on his own, but this morning, after not hearing from Will, he changed his mind and decided to see if an opportunity presented itself. Billy was getting more and more impatient as the days passed by. Billy figured all he needed was for the two of them to take a walk on the beach, maybe go to dinner, or anything else that would get them out of the house together.

It wasn't long before Billy watched Taylor Long and Agent Jaxson Locke walk out of the beach house. For a brief moment, Billy got excited and began to gather his belongings, but then he saw the small suitcases—and of course, the bag he was sure carried the drone photos—being placed into the convertible.

"Damn!" Billy said out loud as he started down the dunes toward his truck.

The traffic on the scenic seaside drive from Pensacola to Panama City was light. The couple was about twenty miles into their trip before Taylor looked over at the man sitting next to her. Before they had left the beach house, Taylor asked Jaxson to drive. Before he could refuse, Taylor was already opening the passenger door and sitting down.

Jaxson determined Taylor still needed time to think and to give herself a moment for her mind and body to relax, to accept the fate of her friend. When Jaxson looked over and saw Taylor staring at him, he smiled back, reached over, and took her hand into his as the ocean air whipped around the two of them.

They arrived in Panama City at close to noon, and before going to one of Taylor's other rentals and unpacking, they found a restaurant overlooking the beach and had lunch. Taylor hadn't said much during their drive, so he was surprised when she finally spoke.

"Tell me something about you," Taylor said before taking a bite of her lobster roll.

"What do you want to know?"

"Anything. Do you have a family?"

"Are you asking if I'm married or If I've ever been married?" Jaxson questioned and then took a bite of his own lobster roll.

"No. I know you're not married, nor have you ever been."

"How do you know that?" Jaxson asked suspiciously as he pondered how she had come to the assumption.

"Well, you don't have a ring on, and I didn't see one when I went through your stuff when you left the beach house the other day," Taylor answered and then looked away quickly.

"What?"

"I'm just kidding. I didn't go through your stuff. You should have seen your face," Taylor said as she laughed.

"Funny girl."

"I think I am."

"You are," Jaxson replied as they both laughed out loud together.

"Where do your parents live?"

"My mother lives in Hampton, Virginia, and my father passed away about four years ago," Jaxson answered.

"Do you have any brothers or sisters?"

"I did," Jaxson replied with a change in his tone and looked down at his plate.

Taylor read his body language. She realized her last question was a sensitive subject for him, and she wished to know why.

"I'm sorry. I didn't mean to—"

"It's okay," Jaxson quickly said, interrupting her. He looked away from her and out toward the beach, where families were setting up their beach chairs and blankets on the hot sandy beach.

"How was the lobster roll?" she asked, changing the subject.

"It was delicious."

Billy followed the two of them into Panama City and then watched them from the concealment of his truck while they ate lunch. He was waiting for an opportunity to present itself when he suddenly felt his phone vibrating. He quickly answered it.

"I thought you were going to help me?" Billy asked angrily into the phone.

"I'm here. Where are you?" Will asked.

"I'm in Panama City."

"Why?"

"Because I didn't hear from you, so I decided to follow the agent and Taylor here. Isn't that where you met Bethany Porter two years ago?" Billy asked sarcastically.

"Yeah."

"Now, what do you want me to do?" Billy asked.

"Stay with them and keep me informed, but don't do anything stupid," Will stated and hung up.

"Fuck you!" Billy uttered and tossed the phone into the seat.

Will had driven to Pensacola Beach and sat in front of 1616 Ariola Drive, looking at the empty house. He then called Billy. At first, he was angry with Billy for following the agent and Taylor Long, but then when he learned they were in Panama City, he needed to know why. He was worried the FBI agent was onto him, so he decided he needed to take additional safeguards.

The clouds moved in unexpectedly by the time Jaxson and Taylor reached the beach house. Their original plan was to sit by the pool and then go out to dinner. Jaxson was looking out the sliding glass door at the dark purple skies. They had let loose a torrential downpour of rain over the entire area, while flashes of lightning streaked across the sky. Jaxson was looking out of the window at the storm as it continued to rage, so he didn't hear Taylor walk up behind him until she spoke.

"How does it look?"

"I don't think we're going to be sitting by the pool today," Jaxson said without turning around.

"I guess we'll just have to stay in then," Taylor said softly.

Jaxson turned around slowly and saw Taylor standing behind him, naked and holding a bottle of wine. He smiled and walked toward her. He took her in his arms and kissed her hard, then picked her up and carried her into the bedroom.

The two of them stayed in the beach house and only got out of the bed to answer the door for the delivery man who brought them their dinner.

Newt was asleep when he was awakened by the ringing of his cell phone on the nightstand beside him. He quickly sat up and answered it.

"Detective Waterman here," Newt said into the receiver. "Yeah, I got it. I'll head that way right now." He hung up and placed his phone back onto the nightstand. He sat there quietly with a puzzled look on his face.

"Is everything okay?" Lori asked from the other side of the bed as she sat up. She and Newt had gone out the previous evening and ended up staying at her place.

"No, it's not. Detective Martinez has been murdered."

Jaxson was sitting in the dining room, drinking his morning coffee and waiting for Taylor to come out of the bedroom so they could head to Destin, when his cell phone rang.

"Hello," Jaxson said into the phone.

"Agent Locke, how are you doing this morning?" SKO asked.

"I'm fine, and you?" Jaxson answered as he hurried into the kitchen to retrieve his notepad and a pen.

"I'm good. How's Taylor? Are the two of you enjoying each other's company?"

"Yes, we are. Thanks for asking," Jaxson answered. He figured the time for subtleties was over and being frank with SKO was the best plan.

"How's the rest of the team doing? Have you gotten any more leads?"

"They're good, and no, not really. Did you call to provide some additional information that could help us in finding you or your friend?"

"Friend? Whatever do you mean, Agent Locke?"

"You know exactly what I mean. Why did the two of you kill the girls? Why did you bring me here?" Jaxson asked just as Taylor walked into the room.

"Maybe I wanted you to meet Taylor Long. Maybe I'm a very talented matchmaker. Maybe I just wanted to see if you are good enough," SKO answered, taunting the FBI agent.

"Good enough for what?"

"Not what, who," SKO responded, correcting Jaxson.

"Who? What do you mean by who?"

"That's enough for now. You and Taylor enjoy your day together."

"Wait!" Jaxson yelled into the phone, but it was too late. SKO was gone.

Taylor waited for Jaxson to put the phone down before saying anything to him. She sensed his phone call was important. "Are you okay?" Taylor asked as she poured a cup of coffee for herself.

"Yes, are you ready?" Jaxson asked, though he still seemed distracted by the phone call.

"I'll drive today. You can relax."

Newt wasn't allowed into the crime scene at the hotel room. All he knew was that Detective Martinez had been choked to death with a garrote. The Pensacola Police Department had taken control of the investigation. It was standard procedure for when someone from another agency was murdered. He stood outside and waited to speak to the lead detective. He was standing next to a cruiser when he heard someone calling his name.

"Newt!" Stefanie yelled from behind the police tape.

"Yeah," he answered and hurried to her. "What are you doing here?"

"I'm staying here," Stefanie answered.

"That's right. Oh, shit! Get in my car," Newt said and bent down. He dipped under the tape, took Stefanie by the arm, and walked her to his car.

"What's going on? What are you doing?" Stefanie asked nervously.

Newt helped Stefanie into the passenger seat. "Someone killed Detective Martinez. The killer could be watching right now." He got into the driver's seat and sped out of the parking lot.

"Okay, but why take me away?"

"You saw Martinez get assaulted in the parking lot. Then you saw the same man Friday morning in the parking lot. Martinez was killed with a garrote. It could have been one of our killers, and you are the only one who knows what he looks like."

"Oh my!"

Chapter 19
Martinez Is Dead

Jaxson and Taylor backed out of the driveway, and Taylor was about to turn left when Jaxson stopped her.

"Wait! Can we go by this address?" Jaxson asked as he pointed to his notepad.

"You want to see 16999 Front Beach Road?" Taylor asked.

"Yes."

"Can I ask why?"

"Yeah, it's the beach house one of the victims rented."

"Sure, let me put it in the car's navigation." Taylor leaned over and input the address.

Newt took Stefanie to Lori's hotel and dropped her off. He then returned to the crime scene at the hotel. He had a plainclothes detective go to Stefanie's old room to have her belongings taken to Lori's. Newt had decided to keep the identity of the possible witness a secret until he knew more about the murder of Detective Martinez. There was one person he still needed to tell about Martinez's murder, but Newt wanted to wait until he had more details before he called Jaxson.

Taylor followed the car's navigation system, and within twenty minutes, she and Jaxson were pulling up in front of 16999 Front Beach Road. The beach house was a large home, painted blue with yellow trim. Jaxson got out of the car and stood there looking at the house. It was just another one of the many expensive beach houses lining Front Beach Road with views overlooking the gulf.

"What are you looking for?" Taylor asked as she walked over to Jaxson and stood beside him.

"I don't know. I just got this gut feeling I'm missing something right in front of me."

"Like what?"

"I don't know."

"Well, the beach house is beautiful. I bet it gets a lot of vacationers. Clear Sky Realty Vacation Rentals is probably making a nice profit with this one," Taylor commented as she looked around.

"How do you know that?" Jaxson asked.

"Right there," Taylor answered as she pointed at the Clear Sky Realty Vacation Rentals sign erected in the front yard next to the street.

"Oh."

"That one is a rental, those a few houses down are rentals, and the one across the street is too," Taylor explained.

Jaxson looked around at all the different companies advertising their rentals. From what he could tell, over half of them on the street were vacation homes.

"Do any beach house owners actually live in these full

time?" Jaxson asked, looking around at all the homes with rental signs in front of them.

"Well, I live in mine and some of my friends live in theirs, but most of us all own other homes we rent out to vacationers."

"I see."

"Are you ready?" Taylor asked as she walked back to the driver's side of the car and sat in the seat.

"Yeah."

Billy was still following the couple after they left Panama City. He had stayed far behind them to ensure he was not noticed. Besides, he had a feeling as to where they were going when they left the other beach house earlier in the day. Now, it looked like they were heading back to Pensacola Beach. Billy felt it was time to update Will.

"Yeah," Will said, answering the phone. He had just put his shirt and pants on and was getting ready to leave for the day when the phone rang.

"They went to your old girlfriend's beach rental," Billy stated.

"Why? What did they do there?" Will asked.

"I don't know. They just stood outside, looking around."

"That's it? Nothing else?"

"No. Taylor just pointed at all the other rentals on the street. What do you think about that?"

"I don't know," Will replied quietly.

"I do. It means they're getting close."

"No, it doesn't," Will said and hung up the phone.

Jaxson and Taylor arrived back in Pensacola shortly before three o'clock. The sun was shining, and the beaches were lined with locals and vacationers out enjoying the day. Jaxson was reviewing the case and browsing the drone photos on his laptop but paused a moment to look around the area from the passenger seat. The pictures of people on his computer weren't going anywhere. They could wait. He didn't know how to explain it, nor could he put his finger on it, but he knew everything seemed perfect at this very minute. Maybe it was the beautiful woman sitting next to him. He looked over at her and smiled.

"Something wrong?" Taylor asked. Taylor had been driving and listening to the radio for most of the drive. Her passenger had been busy looking through his extensive collection of victim files for most of the drive. Now, he was on his laptop. She knew Jaxson was preoccupied with the case and wasn't up for conversation, but still, she wanted the man's attention.

"No, I'm just thinking how much I'm enjoying the moment."

"It doesn't seem that way. You've been going over those files for most of the trip. Now, you're looking through your laptop."

"You're right," Jaxson said in agreement. He closed the laptop, put it back into his bag, and leaned over to kiss his chauffeur when they stopped for a red light.

"How much farther?" he asked.

"Less than an hour. It's a short drive through Pensacola and then we'll be back along the coast," Taylor answered and then kissed him again before the light turned green.

"Well, isn't this nice?" Billy asked himself as he watched the couple's public display of affection from a few cars back. "Where are you going now?"

Newt stayed at the hotel until the coroner arrived and removed the body of Detective Martinez. He then spoke to the lead Detective, Peter Carter, from the Pensacola Police Department. Detective Carter explained that he believed Martinez knew his attacker based on his observations of the crime scene. He also confirmed a garrote had been used and that the murder itself appeared to be very violent.

Newt decided not to say anything to Detective Carter about Stefanie Mack being a possible witness. He did, however, suggest he might have some information for him later on. Newt didn't want to divulge anything that could put Stefanie in danger. He figured if the killer had contacts, like Martinez, within the sheriff's office, then the killer could also have contacts within the police department.

Newt thanked Detective Carter for the information and got into his car to call Jaxson, but his cell phone rang before he could dial Jaxson's number.

"Hello."

"Detective Waterman, this is Buck Miller. I'm returning your call from last week."

"Yes, Mr. Miller, I understand you have some of Jodie Lawrence's belongings at the city building there in Orange Beach."

"Yeah, we emptied her locker and kept her stuff here, but no one ever came for it."

"Yes, I know," Newt replied as he watched the coroner's van pull out of the parking lot with Detective Martinez inside it.

"Are you going to come by and get it?"

"I'll send someone over tomorrow morning to pick it up."

"Okay, I'll have it at my office in the city building."

"Thank you, Mr. Miller, and I'm sorry it's taken so long to get someone out there," Newt said, offering an apology.

Jaxson and Taylor entered Orange Beach, Alabama, at a little after four o'clock. Jaxson talked the entire way with Taylor interrupting him a few times to direct his attention to the different points of interest along their route. Jaxson was enjoying himself, but for the first time in his life, he didn't know where he was or where he was going. All Jaxson knew was he was in a car with a beautiful woman he was getting to know and that he was going somewhere with her but didn't know where, both figuratively and literally. The two of them held hands and flirted with each other along the way.

The vibrating of Jaxson's cell phone interrupted their conversation about a popular bar located on the state line between Florida and Alabama.

"Hello… Newt, how are you? … You've got to be kidding me! … No, I can return tonight if I need to. Taylor and I are in Orange Beach right now… I can do that. Yes, let's push it back until tomorrow afternoon… Find out what you can about Martinez, and I'll pick up the belongings and meet you at the coroner's office at one tomorrow… Find a safe place for them."

"What's going on?" Taylor asked, interrupting Jaxson's phone call.

"Just a minute, Newt," Jaxson said and directed his attention toward Taylor. "Someone killed Martinez, and my friend may have seen the killer. Martinez's killer and our serial killer could be the same person. Newt's trying to find a safe place to take her and her friend until we can figure this out."

"Take them to one four six Fort Pickens Road. I own the penthouse condo there. No one can access the building without the code to the front door. The combination for the door to the building is one one nine five. The penthouse is at the top, and the combination to the door is nine five one one. They'll be safe there," Taylor explained as she continued to drive.

"Are you sure?" Jaxson asked.

"Yes, I think you guys are close to finding Natalie's killer, and I want to help in any way I can."

"Okay, thank you," Jaxson said as he reached out and held Taylor's hand.

"Newt, take Stefanie and Lori to one four six Fort Pickens Road. Stay with them. I want to keep them safe until we figure this out. Don't share this with anyone. I need time to think. I'll text you the rest of the information on how to get inside the penthouse."

"Where are you two going?" Billy mumbled as he continued to follow the couple into Alabama. He was getting nervous. If they went by the beach house in Panama City, then they might be heading to Jodie's rental in Orange Beach. In Billy's mind, he was sure they were putting things together, and it wouldn't be long before they had what they needed.

Billy picked up his phone and called Will.

"What now?" Will asked when he answered the phone.

"I think they're going to Jodie's rental now. I've decided to put an end to this when I get a chance," Billy proclaimed. Billy decided he wasn't taking orders from Will anymore.

"Don't do anything stupid! They may not know anything!" Will yelled over the phone.

"I'm doing whatever I need to do," Billy uttered before ending the call.

"What's the plan?" Taylor asked.

"Well, we can drive back to your place tonight and come back tomorrow morning, or we can stay the night here. I need to go by the city building in the morning and pick up one of the victim's belongings. Newt arranged for someone to meet me there," Jaxson explained.

"Why don't we just stay here tonight? I have extra clothes in my bag."

"So do I, but do you know where we can stay on such short notice?" Jaxson inquired comically to the vacation rental owner sitting next to him.

"Really, Jaxson?"

"I didn't know if you had a place over here or not but thought you probably might."

"I have four, but the three nice ones are rented right now. So, we'll have to stay in the less-expensive rental."

"Okay, does it have an air conditioner?" Jaxson asked in a manner suggesting he was still in a mood to tease her.

"Yes, we'll have AC, but if you want to get in the pool, you'll have to walk from the beach house to the community pool in the neighborhood."

"Great! It sounds like we'll be slumming it tonight," Jaxson said and started laughing.

"Whatever, Jaxson."

Newt picked Stefanie and Lori up and drove them to the address he was given by Jaxson. The three of them entered the high-rise, climbed onto the elevator, and took it to the penthouse suite at the top. When they entered the penthouse foyer, they gaped at the shiny tile floors, exquisite porcelain water features on the walls, and a view that went for miles over the bay.

"Is the sheriff's office putting us up here?" Stefanie asked.

"No. It's Taylor Long's place. I mean, it's one of her rentals anyway," Newt answered as he walked around the living room, admiring the furnishings.

"Oh, there isn't somewhere else we can stay?" Stefanie asked.

"Not right now. I think you two need to stay here for now, at least until Jaxson gets back from Orange Beach," Newt suggested.

"Oh, let's stay here, for a little while anyway," Lori blurted, admiring the view and pool outside.

"Okay, I guess it'll be okay for now." Stefanie reluctantly agreed as she picked up her suitcase and walked to one of the bedrooms. She really didn't want to stay in a place owned by Taylor Long. It made Stefanie feel uncomfortable.

"You're staying too, right? I mean, we should have an armed guard protecting us," Lori said, hinting to Newt that she wanted him to stay.

"Yes, I'm staying. I'll stay on the couch," Newt replied. He didn't know if Stefanie knew he and Lori had spent the night together.

"No you won't. Lori would rather you stayed with her in her room," Stefanie announced before she shut her bedroom door.

Newt looked at Lori in surprise.

"What can I say? We've been friends for a long time. We tell each other everything," Loir admitted.

Taylor's beach house on Orange Beach was anything but slumming. Like the other beach houses Taylor owned, it was immaculate, expensive, and comfortable to say the least. Jaxson was sitting on a barstool at the large granite counter in the kitchen, looking through the drone photos once more while he waited for Taylor to freshen up. There were hundreds of people on the beach the day Jaxson arrived, waiting to get a look at what was going on under the beach house. Everyone in the photos seemed to be dressed appropriately. They all seemed to be at the beach to enjoy the day, and there didn't appear to be anyone out of place, except for one individual who looked to be surprised when the drone flew over him taking pictures.

The man wore a T-shirt and shorts. At first glance, he appeared to be normal, as far as beachgoers go, but the look on his face was one of surprise.

"He's attractive. Who is he?" Taylor asked after she walked up behind the distracted agent.

"I don't know," Jaxson answered.

"Is he a suspect?"

"Probably not. I paid a drone operator to take some overhead photos of the crime scene and the crowd of people when I arrived. This guy was caught in one of the images the drone operator captured with his camera."

"Well, if you decide to dump me, I'll have to see if I can find him."

"Yeah? Where would you start looking?" Jaxson asked.

"Let me see." Taylor playfully nudged Jaxson aside so she could see the image of the handsome man on the screen more clearly.

"Okay," Jaxson stated and backed up so she could get a better look at the screen.

Taylor studied the image for a few seconds. She focused on one specific area on the photo and then blew it up so she could see it better. Taylor then backed away, walked to the coffee pot, and poured herself a cup. She didn't say anything, just stood there with a smirk on her face.

Jaxson was perplexed. He waited, but still she said nothing. He saw the logo on the man's shirt earlier and knew Taylor was focusing her attention on it, but he decided to let Taylor enjoy herself. Jaxson was enjoying the playful behavior between the two of them.

"Okay, okay. I give up." Jaxson threw his hands in the air and leaned back as if he were surrendering.

"Good. Well, I would start by driving over to the Legacy Classical Academy of Pensacola, where I would show his picture around to see if anyone knew who he was," Taylor explained proudly after she walked back over and stood next to the FBI agent.

"Really? Why?" Jaxson asked, already knowing the answer to his question.

"Because of that," Taylor stated as she pointed out the Legacy Classical Academy of Pensacola logo on the man's T-shirt. "It's a private school for kids who are gifted in the performing arts."

Jaxson was impressed with Taylor's investigative skills. Although, he had already determined Taylor wasn't just a former beauty model. She was an intelligent woman. The timeline board she had created for Natalie in her spare room proved she could think logically. He smiled at her and then leaned over and kissed her.

"I would start there too."

"Good. Where are we going tonight?" Taylor asked.

"I'd like to go to 3383 Washington Avenue."

"What's there?"

"The beach house Jodie Lawrence rented. She's the victim who will be autopsied tomorrow. Her belongings are the ones we're picking up tomorrow morning."

"All right. Let's go, but I get to choose the place for dinner," Taylor said as she headed for the front door.

"Deal." Jaxson closed his laptop and placed it into his bag, threw it over his shoulder, and followed her out.

Jodie's beach rental was adequate at best. It was a one-bedroom rental with less than six hundred square feet of living space inside. It looked to have been built in the 1950s. Jaxson walked around the outside of the old rental without saying anything. Taylor followed close behind, wondering what he was thinking.

"Interesting," he remarked as he stood and stared at the back of the home.

"What?" Taylor asked.

"How much do you think Summer Stays Vacation Rentals gets for this place a month?"

"A lot less than most of my rentals and a lot less than the one we saw in Panama City. Most companies have rentals that fit most people's budget. The company just advertises them differently," Taylor replied.

Billy walked around Jodie's beach rental and made his way to the side. He used nearby houses to conceal his movement. Billy then ducked down and walked over a large sand dune. He made sure to stay low and out of sight. When Billy crested the dune, facing the back of the beach house, he pulled his .45 from his waistband and took aim.

"Can I help you?" a man asked, standing at the open back door.

Jaxson and Taylor were surprised when the back door of the beach house opened. When they turned around, they saw a huge man, who appeared to be angry at discovering two people trespassing.

Billy dropped back behind the dune and quickly walked to his truck. He knew shooting two people was dangerous, but three at once was just impossible. Besides, there could have been more people inside the beach house.

"Too many unknowns," Billy mumbled as he climbed back inside the truck and drove back out to the main road.

Jaxson explained who he and Taylor were to the irate man and left the area. The two of them drove to dinner and returned to their beach house shortly before ten o'clock, then retired to bed soon after.

Chapter 20
Pictures

Jaxson and Taylor were up early. They ate breakfast at the Orange Beach Sunset Diner, and at nine o'clock, they were sitting in the lobby of the City of Orange Beach city building, waiting to see Buck Miller. The lobby was small. There was one row of three seats in front of an old coffee table with two chairs at opposite ends. The table held countless realtor brochures, vacation flyers, and tourist attraction coupons.

"Do you think there are any good realtors in that magazine on the table?" Jaxson asked as he reached over and picked up the area realtor magazine off the table.

"Yeah, on page nine there's one. She's smart, she knows the area, and she's like super-hot," Taylor mused as Jaxson turned the pages to Taylor's ad on page nine. He looked down at the ad and her professional photo accompanying the advertisement. It made Jaxson smile.

"What?" Taylor asked, seeing his reaction to her ad.

"It's not what I imagined."

"What did you expect?"

"I expected to see you standing there with your arms crossed, wearing a sports coat with your company logo on it.

Not you on the beach dressed casually in front of your own beach house," Jaxson admitted.

"Stereotypes! I didn't take you to be someone who stereotyped others," Taylor stated while rolling her eyes.

"I don't, but look at the rest of the ads." Jaxson flipped through the other pages that advertised realtors who were posing just as he expected.

"I get it. I just don't want to be like the others. I actually had one photo taken like that but decided against it," Taylor said and sat in the chair with her arms crossed over her stomach.

The two laughed as he continued to look through the magazine. A few minutes later, a man walked out of a door behind the receptionist's counter. He was carrying a box that he laid down on the counter. Jaxson placed the magazine back down on the coffee table and stood to address the man.

"Are you Buck Miller?" Jaxson asked as he approached the counter.

"Yes, are you with the sheriff's office?"

"Actually, I'm Agent Locke with the FBI. I'm working with the sheriff's office and Detective Waterman," Jaxson explained as he displayed his credentials.

Buck looked at the identification Jaxson displayed and then back up at the agent. He slid the box out toward Jaxson.

"There's not much in it. We took it out of Jodie's locker after she didn't come back after a month." Buck looked down at the counter. Jaxson and Taylor could see Buck was saddened by the loss of Jodie Lawrence.

"Did you know her well?" Taylor asked.

"Yes and no. Jodie worked for me, and she did a great job. I was going to offer her a full-time position after the summer. She was a good person and a dedicated employee. Everyone around here knew Jodie was going to get the full-time position. We were just waiting to surprise her at the annual end-of-the-summer office party, but she…"

"Did you ever meet anyone she was seeing, or did she ever mention someone she was seeing.?" Jaxson asked before the man got lost in his emotions.

Buck cleared his throat. "No. Well, Jodie did say she was seeing someone named Billy. Some local guy."

"How do you know Billy was local?" Jaxson asked as Taylor quietly and slowly looked through the box.

"She and I had to work together a few times. I would tell her about my wife and kids, and she told me she was divorced, had a son, and that she met a guy who worked on shrimp boats, or maybe it was fishing boats," Buck explained, trying to recall the memory.

"Is there anything else you can remember?" Jaxson asked as he wrote in his notepad.

"Not that I can think of."

"Thank you for your time." Jaxson reached out and shook Buck's hand.

"If you need anything else, just call me," Buck offered before walking back through the door.

Billy stood across the parking lot and watched as the FBI agent and Taylor Long walked out of the city building. The fact they were at the city building was concerning, but when they came out carrying the box, his level of concern rose even higher. Billy knew the box contained a photo of him. The picture Jodie had hanging in her locker. The picture she took of him while he was sleeping. The photo she confessed to taking weeks before he had killed her. He tried to get the photo a few days later, but getting into the city building wasn't as easy as he thought it would have been.

Billy needed Jodi's photo of him, along with the drone

photos. Now, things were desperate, which made him angry.

JODIE LAWRENCE (PB #4)

Jodie made her way around the beach house, cleaning anything and everything. She wanted to make sure she got her security deposit back from the rental agency. For Jodie, money was pretty tight, and every penny counted. She had taken the summer job with the city of Orange Beach in Alabama. Throughout the week, she cut grass and pulled weeds for the city. On the weekends, she sat on the beach of Wolf Bay or the shores of the Gulf of Mexico next to Billy. She had arrived in Orange Beach, Alabama, from Salt Lake City, Utah, after she was hired for the summer position.

Jodie had hoped to stay on working for the city through the winter months, but she hadn't heard yet if she had gotten the one and only position, they had available. She felt she had worked hard over the summer for the city. She never called in sick, always stayed longer if needed, and treated everyone very politely. But still, Jodie figured she may have to move on at the end of the month and figured she would start cleaning now instead of waiting. *Besides, I got to find another place less expensive anyway, even if I do get the job,* she told herself.

The beach rental Jodie rented was expensive. She'd had to think twice about finding something else for the four months that she was going to be in Orange Beach, working for the city. For many people, three thousand a month for a rental wasn't very much money, but to Jodie, it was expensive. She had saved all winter for this trip. With the money she would make working for the city and the money in her savings, she thought she could swing it. She knew she could ride her bike to work and to the grocery store that was also close to the beach rental. She had ten grand in the bank and was making twenty-seven hundred a month. The city didn't pay much, but it provided her the opportunity to make money. At the same time, she experienced the beach-living lifestyle and the people of the South, and she decided to move there permanently.

Jodie wanted to leave Salt Lake City for good. She was thirty-eight with no education, no job skills, and one divorced husband who never looked back after he left her and their son, Ryan, for another woman. Jodie and Walter were high-school sweethearts, and at the young age of sixteen, Jodie had found herself pregnant with Ryan. Then at the age of thirty-four, she found herself alone after Ryan joined the army. For the next four years, Jodie bounced from one dead-end job to the next. While working for a florist two years ago, she saw an advertisement for Orange Beach and wondered if living near the ocean was the life for her.

When Jodie first arrived in Orange Beach, she worked very hard, showed up early, and got to know what was expected of her by the city. Within a month, she had a routine down and found herself comfortable, which was when she met Billy. Billy worked on various ships around the area, either fishing or shrimping. He was thirty-seven, fit, good looking, and single. She had met him one day when she was picking up trash, along a sidewalk people took to get to one of the many public beaches. Billy met her in the worst way possible. She was covered in dirt and sweat. He wore board shorts, a T-shirt advertising a local bar, and flip-flops. He was carrying a paddleboard, and as he tried to pass her, he pretended he couldn't get by with her blocking the sidewalk. *Which I wasn't doing!* she thought as she hurried about, cleaning.

The connection between the two of them was nothing more than a chance meeting that had blossomed into a summer of love for Jodie. Billy always arrived on time, spoke to her kindly, and never ever told her she looked bad or that she embarrassed him—all of which were things Walter had done and said over the years. Billy was the first man Jodie had allowed to enter her life since the divorce. She had waited for Ryan to leave home before dating again. Never in a million years would she have thought she could find someone to love her and accept her the way she was.

Jodie had already moved some of her personal things to the trunk of her car. Some items of value, she took to her locker at the city building. Jodie was never one to procrastinate, so after she was satisfied that the beach house was clean for the time being, she rushed off and prepared herself for the evening. She showered, dried her hair, tied it back in a ponytail, and applied a small amount of makeup. She painted her fingernails and toes with a red polish that matched the outfit. Finally, she went into the bedroom and found the dress and shoes Billy had bought for her.

The dress was red, tight, and short. She usually would not have picked it out for herself, but she wanted to make Billy happy. Jodie didn't know what to expect from Billy, but he did tell her he had something big planned. In her mind, Jodie wanted and hoped that Billy was going to ask her to move in with him. *Maybe he wants me to stay with him just as much as I want to stay with him,* she thought. She heard Billy come into the beach house and then announce he was there. She looked in the mirror once more, smelled the roses next to the bed, crossed her fingers, and made a wish.

Jodie walked into the tiny living room and found Billy standing there, holding a rose for her. He wore blue jeans and a light blue T-shirt that Jodie thought fit him well, and instead of flip-flops, he wore a pair of white tennis shoes. Billy was quiet, kind, and simple. Yes, simple. Nothing over the top, easygoing, and easy to please. *Frozen pizzas were good for dinner, evenings at home instead of evenings out were great, and he never criticized me for not wearing makeup every day,* she thought to herself as she admired the man standing in front of her.

Billy watched as Jodie entered the room. The dress and shoes she wore were something Jodie normally wouldn't wear. The makeup, the painted fingernails and toenails, were all over the top for her. He could see she was slightly uncomfortable. The look on her face told Billy she needed reassurance from him.

"I…"

"I think you look fantastic! I'm blown away," Billy said as he moved closer to her.

"Really? I was worried. I don't wear things like this normally. I don't think I've ever worn anything this revealing," she explained as she looked down at herself.

Billy put his arms around her and kissed her. He then pulled back while still holding her and smiled. Jodie returned the smile and pulled away.

"I know you gave me money for a manicure and pedicure, but I figured I could do it all myself and save you the money," Jodie explained as she took money from her purse and handed it to him.

Billy took the money from her hand and walked over to sat on the couch. He shook his head from side to side as he placed the money in his wallet.

"Are you upset with me?" she asked with concern.

"No. I've just never had anyone woman like you who cared more about me than herself," he explained.

"Well, they should have. You're a good man. By the way, how does the dress look?" she asked as she slowly spun around in front of him.

"You look amazing! Are you wearing panties?" he asked.

"Yes. Can you see the panty lines?" Jodie asked as she looked down around her waist.

"Yes. Come here."

Jodie moved closer to Billy until she was standing in front of him once more. He knelt down, then looked up and smiled at her as he lifted the tight dress up over her waist and pulled her panties down around her ankles.

"Billy! I don't know if I can do that in public," Jodie said unconvincingly.

"You'll be just fine," Billy replied as he pulled her dress back down. He stood and kissed her once more.

"I've never gone out in public without underwear on, and now, on top of everything else, I'm not wearing anything to cover myself except this thin dress."

"It'll be fine."

"What if the restaurant is cold? My nipples will stick out, and everyone will see."

"Then I'll enjoy the evening even more." Billy moved closer to her and kissed her once more while pulling the top of her dress down. He bent down and softly kissed her nipples.

"Billy, don't do that! You're going to make them stick out," Jodie exclaimed but did nothing to stop him or pull away. Finally, after a moment, he lifted his head and kissed her lips again.

"All right, let's go now," Jodie said as she backed away and pulled her dress back over her breasts.

Billy walked her out to his truck and opened the door for her. She started to get inside but saw another rose sitting on the seat. Jodie picked it up and turned and smiled at him. She then kissed him and climbed into the truck. Billy's truck was built in the seventies, but he had restored it himself and took care of it. It was black, lifted slightly, and had the best sound system Jodie had ever heard. Billy's truck looked like all the other ones in Pensacola. The only thing separated it from the others was the man driving it.

Once they started down the road, Billy reached over and grabbed Jodie by the thigh. He then pulled her to the center of the seat next to him. Jodie smiled and placed her head on his shoulder as he turned the music on.

"Who are we going to listen to tonight?" Jodie asked.

"Johann Sebastian Bach's Brandenburg Concerto No. 3 in G Major," Billy answered.

Jodie considered herself the type of person who listened to anything, as long as she enjoyed the sound. She had never really listened to classical music until Billy came into her life. At first, he had kept his love of classical music from Jodie, but one day she caught him listening to it as he worked in the beach house. At first, he seemed embarrassed, but eventually, he confessed to her that he enjoyed listening to the great classical composers.

The two traveled from Orange Beach, Alabama, into Perdido Key, Florida. From Perdido Key to the restaurant, the drive took about forty-five minutes. Still, before long, they were crossing Three Mile Bridge, and a short time later, they were on Pensacola Beach. Billy pulled into the parking lot of Charter's Seafood and Oyster Bar and parked.

Billy stepped out of his truck, and Jodie scooted across the seat to exit on the driver's side as well. He took her hand and proudly walked her into the restaurant, where the two were quickly seated in the back. Jodie was excited but felt slightly out of place with the other dinner guests, who appeared to be wealthy and dressed in more elegant clothes.

Jodie leaned across the table toward Billy. "Honey, can we afford this place? It looks expensive," Jodie said quietly.

"Baby, it's fine. Besides, it's a special night for us."

"If you say so." Jodie loved the way Billy's Southern accent came out every time he called her baby.

"I've got a surprise for you."

"I can't wait," she said excitedly.

Billy ordered the steamer special, which consisted of fresh shrimp, blue crab, scallops, potatoes, and corn. Jodie ordered the fried snapper with fries. They both washed it down with a domestic beer and then shared banana pudding.

"We could have made this at home for a lot less than what we're paying for it here," Jodie whispered.

"Baby, please let me spoil you tonight."

"All right. What's next then?"

"Are you ready to go?" he asked.

"I am if you are."

"I am," Billy said and stood.

Jodie got up, and the two of them headed for the door after Billy left cash on the table to pay for the meal. When they got back in the truck, Billy pulled out of the parking lot, and instead of heading back toward Orange Beach, he turned left and started down Via De Luna Drive.

"Where're we going?" Jodie asked.

"That's the other surprise. A friend of mine is letting us use his beach house for the night. It sits right on the Gulf side," Billy answered.

"How wonderful!" Jodie said and leaned over to kiss Billy's check.

After a short drive, the old truck was pulling into the driveway of 1616 Ariola Drive.

"It's beautiful!" Jodie said as she hurriedly opened the passenger door and jumped out. She stood there for a moment and looked at the Italian-villa-themed beach house. She walked to the side and went around back and saw the waves crashing on the shore.

"Let's go inside!" Billy yelled from the front.

"Okay," Jodie said as she ran back.

Billy used the combination he was given and opened the front door. He let Jodie go in before him. She was still giddy with excitement and hurried inside. The lights were already on, and Jodie stood in the center of the living room, amazed at the sheer beauty of the home.

"Billy, I don't think I've ever seen anything like this in my life. I can't believe we're staying here."

Billy walked up behind Jodie and wrapped his arms around her waist. He kissed her neck and then moved his hands up her stomach to her breast. Jodie turned to face him and cupped her hands around his face. He could see a tear beginning to stream down her face.

"What's wrong?" he asked.

"I'm just happy," she admitted and kissed him.

Billy took her by the hand and walked her upstairs to the bedroom. When they walked inside, Jodie saw the rose petals spread out over the bed. She released his hand and walked to the edge. She pulled her dress down, stepped out of it, and turned to face him.

"What are you waiting for?" she asked.

Billy removed his clothes and walked toward her. He kissed her and gently laid her back onto the comforter. Jodie placed her legs up on the edge of the bed, giving Billy full access. He knew what she wanted, and he immediately pleasured her. Jodie reached down with both hands, placed them behind his head, and started grinding herself against his face. It didn't take long before Jodie was squirming in ecstasy and screamed out in pleasure.

Billy lifted her and moved her farther onto the bed, then crawled on top of her. He and placed a pillow under her lower back and moved to in between her legs. His movements were slow but steady, and soon Jodie was pushing her hips up and down each time Billy moved in and out. Before long, Billy's hips were moving faster and faster as he got closer to finishing.

Jodie felt he was getting closer, and it excited her. She moved her hips faster as well. "Are you getting close?" she asked.

Billy didn't answer. He looked up toward the ceiling and then suddenly back down at Jodie as he placed his hands around her throat. He squeezed hard as she fought to stop him.

"NO!" she screamed as she beat her hands against his chest and scratched at his face and arms.

Billy did not release his grip. He squeezed her throat harder and harder until he felt her windpipe collapse and the bones in her neck snap. When Jodie stopped moving, Billy reentered her and finished. He then stood, walked into the bathroom, and climbed into the shower. After he finished washing himself off, he dried off and walked back into the bedroom where Jodie's dead body still lay on the California king. Her eyes were still open. Billy sat on the bed next to her for a moment. He then got up, covered her face with his towel, and got dressed. When he finished dressing, he started to walk out of the room but stopped. He then turned and walked back to the bed. He removed the towel from her face, leaned over, and kissed her once more.

"You were the best!"

<h1>Chapter 21
Upside Down</h1>

Jaxson and Taylor left the Orange Beach city building at ten o'clock and headed back to Pensacola. Taylor was driving while Jaxson looked through Jodie's box containing her personal property. Taylor occasionally looked over when Jaxson pulled something new from the box. There were countless photos of her son, Ryan, as he grew from a boy into a man serving in the military.

Billy was still following the couple as they drove back toward Pensacola. In his mind, things were looking bad. He knew he had to make a move to recover the photos. Suddenly, Billy had an idea. Taylor had taken a route that would force her to cross over the Hwy 98 bridge just before Lilian Highway.

If I'm going to do something, then that's the time to do it, Billy thought to himself.

Billy looked up the road and saw the bridge. He entered the oncoming westbound lane when it was clear of traffic and passed the one car that had been in front of him. He then moved back into the eastbound lane behind an old sedan. Taylor's sports coupe was directly in front of the sedan. His plan was to pass the sedan and get behind Taylor, where he would swipe her rear left quarter panel, hoping it would send her and the FBI agent over the short guardrail leading to the bridge. From there, he would take care of them if they were still alive.

Jaxson was rummaging through the photos when he pulled one out of a man sleeping. He was an attractive man in his thirties. Taylor looked down at the picture in Jaxson's hand.

"Is that—" Taylor heard the driver behind her honking his horn. She looked up at her rearview mirror and saw the sedan behind her and an older-model truck speeding past it.

"What's he doing?" Taylor watched in the side mirror as the truck caught up with them.

Jaxson looked behind them at the truck and the driver. He double-checked the photo in his hand and then looked back at the driver.

"Drive faster!" Jaxson yelled.

Before Taylor could accelerate, she felt the impact from the side. She tried to control her convertible, but it slid sideways 180 degrees. The truck passed them. The agent briefly saw the driver. It was the man from Jodie's photo, the man from the drone photo, and the man he was looking for.

Taylor tried to control the car by steering the front wheels back to the right, but it was useless. The convertible rolled backward into and then over the guardrail. It flipped over once and came to rest upside down in the ditch.

After the car came to a complete stop, Jaxson looked over at the unconscious Taylor. He released his seatbelt and fell to the ground on his side. He reached up and felt for a pulse in Taylor's neck. Jaxson held his breath for a moment until he located it and then looked down and saw her chest rise and fall with each breath she took. He let out a sigh of relief. Suddenly, he heard someone moving around the car. He quickly reached down and pulled his subcompact 9mm from his ankle holster.

Billy was the first person to reach the upside-down

convertible. He had his .45 in hand, and he stood there listening for any movement from the occupants inside. He slowly made his way to the passenger side of the convertible. He looked around at the other people rushing over to help. Billy had to act quickly. He bent down on one knee and peered inside, where he saw the FBI agent lying on the ground, under the unconscious Taylor.

There on the ground was his photo, right next to the agent's bag that Billy was sure held the drone photos. He slowly reached inside the car toward the bag.

"Can I help you with something?" Jaxson asked with his gun pointed at the surprised Billy.

"What the!" Billy yelled as he lifted his gun in the direction of the FBI agent.

Jaxson fired his subcompact at the killer. Billy returned fire, shooting blindly into the car as he retreated from the onslaught of bullets. Once he was out of the line of fire, Billy grabbed at his wounded chest as he stumbled up the side of the ditch, passing the crowd of people who had ducked when the gunfire started. Billy fell once, picked himself up, and made his way to his truck as fast as his injured body would allow.

Newt was at the penthouse with Stefanie and Lori, eating an early lunch before he and Stefanie left for the coroner's office, when he heard his cell phone vibrating on the countertop. He put his glass of water down and looked at the number. It wasn't one he recognized.

"Hello… This is Detective Waterman… Yes, I know him… Oh my God… I know where it is, and I'm on my way now." Newt placed his phone in his pocket and looked at Stefanie and Lori worriedly.

"What is it, Newt?" Lori asked after she saw the look of concern on his face.

"It's Jaxson, he's…"

"He's what?" Stefanie yelled. Every possible scenario ran through her mind.

"He and Taylor were in a crash, and they've been taken to Baptist Hospital. It looks like someone ran them off the road."

"Are they all right?" Lori asked.

"I don't know, but we should get over there," Newt suggested as he started for the door with the two women behind him.

Billy drove back to his family's cabin on Coldwater Creek and called Will. His longtime childhood friend said he would come out to the cabin and would bring help with him. Billy was tired, confused, and hurting. He sat in the old recliner in the center of the room, looking at the music awards he had received as a child. His mother had hung them proudly around their home. The cabin was modest. It was the only home that his father—an abusive man, a drunk, an uneducated garbage truck driver—could afford for his family. Billy looked over at the small grand piano taking up most of the room. The old piano belonged to his blind mother. Both Billy's parents had died in a boating accident when Billy was twenty years old. It was his mother who had taught the young prodigy how to play and how to enjoy the works of the classical greats. Billy closed his eyes and thought about those happier times with his mother, as a single tear dripped down his cheek.

After a few minutes, Billy gently stood, leaving a large red stain on the recliner. The killer was turning pale and getting colder by the minute. He gathered all the strength he could and walked over to sit on the bench at the piano. He then raised the keyboard cover and began playing Johann Sebastian Bach's "Come, Sweet Death, Come, Blessed Rest. The pianist closed his eyes and played the music from memory.

Will pulled up to the cabin and heard the piano playing inside. He stood there for a moment, listening to his friend playing the old grand. Billy didn't hear Will walk into the cabin and didn't know he was there until he heard the sound of Will's violin. Will joined his fellow musician at precisely the right moment in the symphony. The two prodigies played beautifully together, just as they had done so many times before.

When the final note was played, Billy dropped his hands to his side, looked at the photo of his parents on the counter, and spoke his last words.

"Come, sweet death, come, blessed rest."

Will pulled the pistol from the small of his back and aimed it at the base of his friend's head. The echoing of the shot filled the small cabin as Billy's head fell forward onto the keys of the old grand.

Will stood over his friend and quoted Mozart.

"As death, when we come to consider it closely, is the true goal of our existence, I have formed during the last few years such close relationships with this best and truest friend of mankind that death's image is not only no longer terrifying to me but is indeed very soothing and consoling."

Newt drove fast and used his lights and siren to move through traffic and red lights along the route to the hospital.

Stefanie sat in the backseat, worried about her friend. She tried texting Jaxson numerous times but didn't get a response. Stefanie was concerned. She knew someone had killed Detective Martinez, tried to kill Jaxson earlier, and now someone may have attempted to kill him again, along with Taylor Long.

When they arrived at the hospital, they were directed to the emergency room where they found deputies and FBI agents standing around, waiting to speak to Jaxson and Taylor. In the back of the crowd of uniformed officers, Newt saw someone he recognized; resident FBI agent Travis Baker was standing there speaking to a nurse.

"Agent Baker! Agent Baker!" Newt yelled over the crowd as he moved through the room of uniformed deputies toward Agent Baker.

"Newt, I heard you were working on this case with Agent Locke," Baker stated as he signed some hospital papers.

"How's Jaxson?" Stefanie blurted after she and Lori made their way through the crowd.

"He's fine. Just a little sore. Taylor Long has a concussion and some cuts and bruises. They'll both be fine after some recovery."

"Where are they now?" Newt asked.

"Over here," Baker answered as he motioned at the trio to follow him into a private room.

When they walked into the room, they found Jaxson sitting in a chair next to a bed that Taylor was lying in, holding her hand. Jaxson's face was covered in dried blood, he had cuts along his arms, and when he stood, he winced in pain.

"Are you okay?" Stefanie asked as she moved past the others to get to her friend, whom she hugged tightly.

"I'm okay," Jaxson answered as he held her close.

"How's she doing?" Newt asked.

"I'm fine. I'd like to go home," Taylor said wearily.

"Do you have anyone who can keep an eye on you for a little while?" the emergency room doctor asked as he walked into the room. The doctor had treated both Jaxson and Taylor when they arrived.

Taylor tried to adjust herself and winced. "I think—"

"Yes, we'll watch after her," Stefanie proclaimed before anyone else could say anything. Stefanie had had a change of heart. When she entered the room, she saw Jaxson holding Taylor's hand and realized she needed to get over her jealousy if she wanted to keep her friend.

"Yes, we are fortunate to have a very comfortable penthouse that sleeps ten," Lori said as she patted Taylor's arm.

"Twelve actually," Taylor stated as she looked around at who she determined to be her new friends.

"Okay then, I'll prepare her release papers," the doctor told the group and then walked out of the room. He knew he wouldn't win an argument about admitting Taylor for observation with the company she kept.

"What happened?" Newt asked Jaxson and then looked at Taylor.

"It was one of the killers. Here's his picture," Jaxson replied. The others quickly gathered around him to look at the photograph in his hand. Jaxson then went on and explained what had happened after he and Taylor left the Orange Beach city building.

The group waited until Taylor was released and left the hospital as a group, heading back to Taylor's beach house to pick up some clothes for her and Jaxson before driving to the penthouse. Newt called the coroner's office and advised Dr. Kendrick to go ahead and complete the autopsy on the next victim. Dr. Kendrick agreed to call the detective back if he found anything interesting during his examination.

When they arrived at the penthouse, Taylor leaned back on the sofa gently, with Jaxson's help. Jaxson sat next to her on the edge. He leaned over, kissed her forehead, rubbed her shoulder, and slowly stood back up.

"What's the plan?" Newt asked, standing in front of Stefanie and Lori. All three of them were curious as to Jaxson's thoughts.

"What time is it? I can't find my cell phone."

"It's three o'clock, and I've got your phone right here," Baker said from the kitchen where he was helping himself to something cool to drink.

"You have it?" Jaxson asked.

"Yeah, I've got it. The attending nurse gave it to me when I arrived at the hospital," Baker explained as he handed the phone back to Jaxson. Jaxson was a little perplexed as to why Agent Baker had held on to his cell phone for so long.

"We need to go over to the Legacy Classical Academy of Pensacola and see if they know this guy," Jaxson said proudly. He looked down and smiled at Taylor while holding up the photo of their suspect.

The Legacy Classical Academy of Pensacola was located on the northeast side of Pensacola. Jaxson and Newt made it there before four o'clock and were greeted by a young woman sitting at the receptionist's desk in the front office. The receptionist directed the two of them to sit and wait for Dr. Ling, the school principal, to come out and get them.

"Would you ever want to go to a school like this?" Newt asked as he looked at ballet photos on the wall.

"No, I can't even walk straight most of the time, much less dance."

"I played the guitar for a little while in middle school but put it down to pick up a baseball bat," Newt said.

"Yeah, I played sports too. I never could play an instrument, act, or anything that was considered performing," Jaxson admitted right before a thin, elderly, Asian-American man walked out of a door directly across the room from them.

"I'm Dr. Ling. Can I help you, gentlemen?" Dr. Ling asked as Jaxson and Newt stood to greet the man.

"Yes, I'm Agent Locke, and this is Detective Waterman, and we would like to ask you if you know this man," Jaxson explained as he held the photo out for Dr. Ling to look at.

"That's Billy Clayton. He tutors some of our piano students who are struggling. Is he all right?"

"We think so, but we'd like to speak to him. Do you know where he lives?" Newt asked.

"Yes, we have his address. Claire, can you get Billy's address for these two men? It's probably under William and not Bill," Dr. Ling explained to the receptionist, who began typing on her keyboard.

"How long have you known Billy?" Jaxson asked while they waited for the address.

"Since he was a teenager. At first, Billy came here as a student and then went to college for a little while but dropped out after his parents passed away. When he came back, we hired him as a tutor. He's been here ever since."

"He was a good student?" Jaxson asked.

"He's the best pianist I know."

"Here's his address," Claire announced as she handed Dr. Ling a sheet of paper.

"There are two addresses here. The top one is Billy's current address, and the bottom is the one he lived at when he was a student here," Dr. Ling explained as he handed the paper to Jaxson.

Jaxson and Newt thanked Dr. Ling for his time, left him their business card, and made their way to the door. The two were excited. They were getting close to capturing one of the killers and were sure that Billy's capture would lead them to the other killer as well.

Taylor stayed on the couch in the living room. She had convinced Stefanie and Lori to go out and relax by the pool. Taylor used the time by herself to browse her emails on her phone. She had the usual realtor advertisement emails that she deleted, she answered her rental guest emails, and she came across an email from the title company. The title transfer was ready for Natalie's place, and if the funds were wired quickly from the buyer, the closing could happen by Friday. Taylor took a deep breath and advised the title company to send the closing documents to Natalie's family and their lawyer for them to sign. She then dialed Jeff's number.

"Hello, Taylor, how are you?" Jeff said upon answering the phone.

"I'm good. How are you?"

"Good, just sitting on pins and needles, waiting for your call."

"Well, it looks like everything is ready to close if you can call the title company and have the funds transferred by tomorrow," Taylor replied.

"Consider it done. I'll have it done by nine o'clock tomorrow morning."

"That'll be great."

"I would like to have a toast to celebrate after the closing. I won't take no for an answer. It'll only take a minute, and we can do it when you meet me at the beach house to give me the keys in the afternoon after the title is transferred," Jeff stated.

"All right. I'll meet you there in the afternoon at five o'clock."

"Good, see you then."

Taylor ended the call and sat there for a minute, thinking about everything. She really didn't want to go back inside Natalie's place, and she didn't want to celebrate anything about it. Taylor also didn't want to lead Jeff on. She always felt Jeff wanted to have more than a business relationship with her, and that wasn't something she wanted or wanted to lead him to think.

Chapter 22
Keepsakes

Jaxson and Newt went back to the sheriff's office and made plans with both agencies to start surveillance on Billy's two known addresses. They briefed everyone involved on what they knew about the suspect. Jaxson informed them that he was sure he had shot the suspect at least once, and the blood found at the crash leading away from the convertible later confirmed it. The two agencies devised a plan that would involve a full tactical entry at both locations simultaneously.

After the surveillance was completed at the cabin on Coldwater Creek, it was reported Billy's truck was parked out front. It was decided that since Billy was last seen leaving the crash scene in his truck, Jaxson and Newt needed to be at the cabin during the raids.

It was a forty-five-minute drive from the sheriff's office to Billy's cabin on Coldwater Creek. The tactical team leader, Lieutenant Watkins, briefed everyone on the plan. He then called the team in town to execute the raids. Jaxson and Newt waited in the sheriff's office's command center located a half a mile away from the cabin. The two of them sat inside the converted RV and listened to the tactical teams over the radio.

"Have you ever done a raid yourself?" Newt asked.

"Yeah, unfortunately," Jaxson muttered just loud enough for Newt to hear.

"That doesn't sound like it was a good experience."

"It wasn't. I ended up coming face-to-face with a serial killer, who, by the way, stabbed me."

"No, kidding!" the surprised Newt replied.

The two men abruptly ended their conversation when they heard Lt. Watkin's voice over the radio. "EXECUTE!"

It was quiet inside the command center as the tactical teams made entry. Jaxson and Newt sat there listening to both teams as they entered Billy's homes. It was two minutes into the raid when it was announced that a body had been found in the cabin.

"Sounds like you may have done more than wounded him," Newt said sadly.

"Sounds like it," Jaxson replied and then looked at the radio. The two law enforcement professionals knew that if Billy was dead, then capturing the other killer would be difficult.

Taylor, Stefanie, and Lori ordered dinner and sat on the deck overlooking the bay to eat the lobster rolls that had been delivered. The women discussed everything from where they went to college to their careers and the men they dated. As they talked, Stefanie found herself enjoying Taylor's company. Stefanie concluded she'd had an image of Taylor that wasn't consistent with the person she actually was and maybe Taylor was the right woman for Jaxson.

The conversation eventually turned to the investigation. The three wondered if there could actually be more than one killer. Stefanie supported Jaxson in his theory and further explained how he had proven himself time after time in multiple cases.

"He's actually the best profiler the FBI has right now," Stefanie stated and took the last bite of her lobster roll.

"I don't doubt that. I just wished I knew more about serial killers than I do."

Lori chimed in. "I don't think you do!"

"I agree," Stefanie stated as she got up to gather everyone's empty plates.

"Can you imagine the things he's seen and heard? I wonder how he sleeps at night," Lori said as she stood to help Stefanie.

"I guess he does see a lot of evil things," Taylor replied as she started to stand too.

"Oh no! We got this. You sit there, and we'll come back with some wine. Wine for Lori and me, that is. You're still on restrictions from alcohol, according to your medical release papers," Stefanie stated.

Taylor smiled and sat back down. She returned to thinking about Jaxson, the man she was dating, and what his career with the FBI exposed him to regularly.

It took about twenty minutes for the tactical teams to clear both locations, after which Jaxson and Newt were finally given permission to enter the cabin. When they pulled up to the front, Jaxson saw Billy's pickup sitting there with the damaged right-front fender. He opened the driver's door and looked inside at the blood-soaked seat. He turned back to face the house and followed Newt toward the door. As they walked up the steps and onto the porch, Jaxson noticed the red rose bushes growing wild along the front of the home from one end to the other.

Inside, the cabin was clean and well kept. The furniture

was old but not abused. There were two bedrooms, one bathroom, a small kitchen, and an open living room. The living room wasn't large. There was one couch, two recliners, and a television on the far wall. Next to the living room was a dining room, but there was no table or chairs, only a grand piano with a very dead Billy sitting in front of it, slumped over onto the keys. Above the keys, someone had placed three red roses.

"Looks like you got him but someone else finished him off," Newt said as he walked around the piano and pointed at the gunshot wound in the back of Billy's head.

Jaxson walked over to stand next to Newt to observe the fatal headshot. "I guess so."

"The cabin's clear, and there wasn't anyone at the other address. I'll keep some of my guys around until you're finished with what you need to do here," Lieutenant Watkins explained from the front door before walking away.

Jaxson and Newt worked the crime scene along with the evidence team. Jaxson started his investigation in the bedroom that he believed belonged to William Joseph Clayton, or Billy as he liked to be called. Inside Billy's room were countless awards and trophies on the dresser and walls that Billy had won for his performance as a pianist. There was a picture on the far wall of Billy with another boy and girl playing instruments in the cabin. On another wall was a picture of Billy and the other two children on a stage, standing next to a woman in a red dress holding a dozen red roses next to a piano.

"I guess Billy was some type of hotshot piano player. There's more stuff hanging on the walls in the living room and around the piano," Newt announced from the bedroom door.

"Looks like it," Jaxson called as he sat on the edge of the bed, looking at it all.

"What's wrong?" Newt asked, seeing the puzzled look on Jaxson's face.

"All of these awards and trophies are for first place," Jaxson replied.

"So?"

"When you said you played baseball, did you win every game you played in?"

"No, I didn't," Newt answered.

"Neither did I. I wonder where all the other second, third, and honorable mention awards are."

It was almost midnight when Jaxson finally made it to the other bedroom, which he believed Billy's parents used. Jaxson entered the room and thought it looked as though no one had changed a thing in twenty years. Jaxson opened the drawers and found miscellaneous items that most people kept in their bedroom drawers. When he opened the nightstand on the left side of the bed, he found an old cigar box. The box appeared to be decorated colorfully by a child even though there was nothing written or drawn on it by hand. However, someone had taken the time to attach a message in Braille, and there were different types of colorful textured cloth attached to it.

Jaxson stood from the bed, walked to the foot of it, and looked at the mattress. The right side of the bed was sunken in more than the left. On the nightstand on the right side of the bed, sat a book. A pair of reading glasses was folded next to it. Jaxson then looked at the nightstand on the left. There was no book, reading glasses, or a lamp. "Billy's mother was blind," Jaxson whispered to himself as he looked back down at the keepsake box.

When Jaxson opened it, he found precisely what he thought he would. There were various medals and other awards Billy had received that were not first place. The box was a keepsake for a blind mother who could hold her son's success and feel the realness of it in her hands. Billy's mother saw every award as an accomplishment, but for Billy, nothing but first place was good enough.

Jaxson and Newt left the cabin after Billy's body was taken

away by the coroner's office. They, along with the evidence team, collected and identified countless items of possible evidence. It was five o'clock in the morning when the two men pulled into the parking garage of the condominium. They took the elevator up to the penthouse. Before going to bed, the two men decided to get up at ten o'clock to drive to the coroner's office to meet with everyone, where they would go over the evidence and everything else.

Taylor was sleeping soundly when Jaxson entered the room. He quietly walked into the bathroom and showered before sliding into the bed next to her. Jaxson lay there in the darkness thinking about the case. He was pleased with locating Billy, but there was still another killer on the loose. There were so many unanswered questions that kept the experienced agent awake.

Who's the second killer? Why did he kill Billy? Maybe it was a mercy killing, or maybe it was to keep him quiet. Is he like Billy? They're both white males. Both are between the ages of thirty-five to forty, both are sexually competent, and both are organized killers. How did they come to know each other?

"Damn it," Jaxson remarked loud enough to wake Taylor.

"Jaxson?" Taylor mumbled, half asleep.

"Yeah, it's me. Go back to sleep," Jaxson whispered as he rolled over and pulled her close to him before he fell asleep with Taylor in his arms.

Newt awoke shortly before ten and decided to lay there quietly before starting his day. He was still half asleep, listening to the women in the other room, when he heard his cell phone vibrating on the nightstand to his right. Newt sat up and reached for the phone. The caller ID displayed it was a private call.

"This is Detective Waterman."

"Detective Waterman, this is Detective Lombardi with the New York Police Department. I'm calling you concerning a Wendy Collins."

"Yes, she's a possible witness of mine," Newt replied.

"That's too bad. She and her husband, Richard Collins, were killed a few days ago. I got your number off of her cell phone."

"Really? I called Mrs. Collins the other day, hoping to interview her regarding her friend she reported missing." Newt spun around on the edge of the bed and searched the nightstand for a notepad and pen.

"Do you think your missing person's case can be related?" Detective Lombardi asked.

"I don't know, but can you email me everything you got?"

"Yeah."

Newt gave Detective Lombardi his information. In the living room, he found Jaxson sitting in the kitchen, drinking a cup of coffee surrounded by three beautiful women. Jaxson appeared to be enjoying the attention as he shared old FBI stories with the women.

"Good morning," Lori said, greeting the overworked detective as she handed him a cup of freshly poured coffee.

"Good morning."

"Everything okay?" Jaxson asked. He saw something in Newt's expression that told him something was up.

"Yeah, I'll tell you later."

Jaxson was sitting on the edge of his bed, putting on his shoes, when he felt his phone vibrate in his front pocket. The caller was calling from a private number. Jaxson knew who it was, so he reached for his notepad and answered the call.

"This is Agent Locke."

"Agent Locke, how was your evening?" SKO asked in an even-mannered voice.

"Busy, but I think you already knew that," Jaxson replied in the same tone.

"I did! So, tell me what you learned about Billy."

"Why don't you tell me what you know about Billy?" Jaxson quickly said back. The agent wanted to set the playing field this time.

"Fine, same rules as before?" SKO asked.

"Sure."

"Okay, shall we keep score this time? Some people like to keep score," SKO proclaimed with more excitement in his voice.

"Is that something you and Billy did?" Jaxson asked as he took notes.

"Billy liked to keep score," SKO replied.

"I can see that."

"Now, what did you learn about Billy?" SKO asked, figuring it was his turn to ask a question.

"I learned Billy played the piano, and he needed to be the best."

"Oh yes, all those trophies and awards on the wall for first place. Most people don't like to lose. Some people just can't stand being runner-up or second best."

"What are the roses about?" Jaxson questioned.

"His mother grew them around the home. A rose was something a blind woman could feel and smell. Children often give their mother flowers. Haven't you ever given your mother flowers before?"

"Yes, and you?" Jaxson asked quickly as he continued to write in the notepad.

"I believe it was my turn to ask a question, Agent Locke," SKO replied.

"Actually, I believe you asked if I ever had given my mother flowers before. I answered you and then asked my next question," Jaxson explained. He knew SKO's question was more rhetorical than an actual question. Still, Jaxson wanted to see how SKO would respond to the assertion.

"That I did, and you're correct. I've given my mother flowers on many occasions," SKO answered in a slightly irritated tone that Jaxson picked up on.

"Now, what else have you learned, Agent Locke?"

"I believe that's a clarifying question," Jaxson replied with confidence. He knew he had caught the man off guard.

"Fine, then our conversation is over!" SKO proclaimed and ended the call angrily.

Jaxson let his cell phone drop to the bed while he continued to write in his notepad. The phone call was a win in his mind. When he finished with what he was writing, he picked the phone back up and tried to call his supervisor. The phone rang once and was sent to voicemail. Jaxson was irritated to say the least. This was the third time this week that his call was forwarded to voicemail. None of his emails to his supervisor had been returned since he had arrived in Pensacola either.

Jaxson sat in the passenger seat, still thinking about the phone call and still wondering why his supervisor wasn't responding to him. His only contact with anyone in the bureau was Agent Baker. Jaxson was looking out the passenger window when he felt Newt tapping his arm.

"Yeah," Jaxson blurted as he turned to face the detective.

"I was about to tell you about a phone call I received from a detective in New York this morning, but it looked like you were in your own little world just now."

"I was, but I'm back now. Why did a detective from New York call you?"

"Well, last week I was doing some follow-up on the cases, and I called the woman who reported Trina Tyler missing. I left her a message to call me back, but she never did," Newt explained.

"Okay, and now?"

"Someone killed her and her husband."

"Really! How?" Jaxson asked with more interest in his voice.

"They were shot on the sidewalk in front of their home. I got this email before we left. It has the report attached."

Jaxson took Newt's cell phone and read over the NYPD report on the way to the coroner's office. When they arrived, Jaxson handed the phone back to Newt and started to get out of the car.

"What do you think?" Newt asked, hoping Jaxson had some insight.

"I really don't know," Jaxson answered flatly. The FBI agent had so many things running through his mind, he couldn't focus on one thing without something else coming up. He felt as though everything to do with the case was fluid and moving in different directions, and all of it was still open for interpretation.

"Not what I was hoping for, but on a positive note, I've got a sketch artist going out to the penthouse later today. Maybe Stefanie can describe the man she saw beating up Detective Martinez in the hotel parking lot." Newt was hopeful that Stefanie had had a good look at the possible killer and that she could describe him to the sketch artist.

Chapter 23
The Last Victim

Jaxson and Newt sat quietly in a crowded meeting room at the City of Pensacola's administration building. Newt had received a phone call informing him their meeting was moved from the coroner's office to the administration building. It was clear that locating Billy had stirred the interest of everyone who believed they had an iron in the fire. The sheriff, the police chief, someone from the governor's office, attorneys from the DA's office, and just about everyone in between had shown up for the briefing and autopsy results for the last two victims. The only people missing from the room were the media and the general public, who had gathered outside waiting patiently for an interview.

"This is crazy," Jaxson whispered to Newt.

"No kidding. It's a circus."

"When they call you up, try to avoid giving out too much information," Jaxson said quietly.

"Why?" Newt asked suspiciously.

"We only have one killer. We still have another one out there, and he could be sitting in this room," Jaxson answered.

Agent Baker was the first to stand at the podium to brief

everyone about what he, the other entry team, and evidence technicians had discovered inside Billy's home in town. Agent Baker presented photos of the inside of Billy's residence, photos that hung on the wall, and miscellaneous items they had discovered in his drawers and closets.

"We haven't gone through all of the evidence. We plan on doing that over the next couple of days," Agent Baker announced after his last slide was presented.

"Is it safe to say that the man responsible for the deaths of the women found under the beach house has been located and he is now deceased?" Sheriff Thomas asked from his seat in the front row. Sheriff Thomas was in uniform, and he was apparently preparing himself to answer questions from the press after the briefing.

"I believe Agent Locke and Detective Newt are more prepared to answer that question," Agent Baker answered as he looked at Jaxson and Newt for help.

Newt didn't get up. He quickly looked over at Jaxson and waited for his lead.

Seeing the expression on Newt's face, Jaxson promptly stood and walked toward the front of the audience with Newt close behind him. Agent Baker nodded at the two men and made his way to the back of the room.

"Well, Agent Locke?" Sheriff Thomas asked.

"Well, we got one of them," Jaxson answered after thinking about it for a moment. At first it was quiet but then suddenly the attendees began speaking all at once.

"What happened with that whole thing about not sharing too much?" Newt asked sarcastically.

"I didn't know what else to say," Jaxson admitted.

Sheriff Thomas turned and faced the crowd. "Just a minute!" When everyone stopped talking, the sheriff turned back toward Jaxson and Newt. "What do you mean when you say one of them?" the sheriff asked slowly.

"We believe we're dealing with two serial killers. The man we located last night, William Joseph Clayton, or Billy as he's commonly known, was found deceased."

"Yes, and we understand you shot him when he ran you off the road, correct?" Sheriff Thomas asked.

"I did shoot him, but Billy later died in the cabin of an apparent gunshot wound to the back of his head." Jaxson watched as the others in the room conversed with each other again and tried to ask questions over each other.

"Quiet!" Sheriff Thomas yelled over the chatter in the room. He looked back at the FBI agent and his detective. The sheriff stood there for a moment with his hands resting on his hips, thinking about what to do, then walked over and stood next to Jaxson and Newt.

"No one is to speak to anyone outside of this room about what they heard here today. The only people I want in this room right now are these two men here, the chief of police, and the coroner. Now clear the room," Sheriff Thomas ordered.

After the room was cleared, Sheriff Thomas looked at Jaxson and Newt. He was angry because he felt he had been kept in the dark. Now, he wanted answers, and he was looking straight at the two men he felt had those answers.

"Why am I just learning about this other killer now?" Sheriff Thomas asked, looking directly at Detective Waterman.

"Well, we thought it best to gather information before we confirmed there was another killer," Newt answered nervously.

"Yes, it was a theory before, but after discovering Billy last night and the fatal gunshot wound to the back of his head, it's more than a theory now," Jaxson stated.

"What about the murder of Detective Martinez? Do you think Billy or his partner killed him?" Chief Packer asked. The Pensacola police chief had been quiet up until now, but he had questions too.

"We don't know, but I've got a police sketch artist speaking with a possible witness," Newt answered.

"A witness! What witness?" the chief asked in a disgruntled tone.

Jaxson and Newt looked at each other like two kids who had just got caught with their hands in the cookie jar. Newt had forgotten he kept Stefanie under wraps until he and Jaxson knew more about the case.

"Well…" Jaxson said and began to explain everything.

Stefanie sat in front of the sketch artist as she tried to recall the man she saw beating Detective Martinez in the parking lot. John Willard sat in front of his easel and asked clarifying questions as his hand moved back and forth across the canvas. Lori sat quietly behind the artist and watched as he created an image from Stefanie's description. Taylor spent her time working on the paperwork involving the sale of Natalie's beach house in the privacy of one of the penthouse bedrooms.

Taylor had received an email from the sheriff's office releasing Natalie's beach house back to the family. It was followed by an email from the title company confirming the buyer's funds had been received for the purchase. Taylor arranged to go by in the morning to sign the closing documents, then picked up her phone and called Jeff.

"Hello, Taylor," Jeff said after seeing Taylor's name appear on his phone's screen.

"Hi, Jeff. It looks like everything is ready for tomorrow. I just spoke to the title company, and they have all the documents and are ready to close tomorrow," Taylor explained.

"Yeah, I got the email from the title company a few minutes

ago. Don't forget to meet me at the house at five o'clock for a celebration toast," Jeff announced happily.

"About that—"

"I won't take no for an answer. If you can't do it tomorrow, then I insist on buying you dinner this weekend," Jeff stated.

Taylor didn't want to do dinner and knew Jeff wouldn't stop until they met to celebrate the closing. After a second of weighing the options to herself, she responded to the persistent Jeff.

"Okay, I'll meet you at the house at five o'clock to toast the closing," Taylor said in the happiest tone she could present at the moment.

"Great! I'll see you tomorrow," Jeff confirmed and then hung up.

Taylor sat on the edge of the bed and started to think about her friend once more when suddenly she heard Lori calling for her from the other room.

Jaxson and Newt explained everything they knew, including Jaxson's theories. When they were finished, they sat there and waited for either the sheriff or the chief of police to respond.

"I think we need to think about this for a little while," Sheriff Thomas stated.

"I agree," Chief Packer said in agreement.

"What do we do now?" Newt asked.

"How about I tell everyone about what I learned during the autopsy?" Dr. Kendrick asked from the side of the room.

"I think that's a good idea," Jaxson replied.

Dr. Kendrick stood in front of the people who were allowed to remain in the room and began his briefing. The doctor started with Jodie Lawrence's autopsy, which revealed she had not been beaten and not killed with the use of the garrote. Still, she had been strangled manually from the front. There were some questions from the sheriff and police chief, but Jaxson and Newt thought it was best not to ask any questions, for now anyway.

Dr. Kendrick then described his autopsy on Trina Tyler that he had completed early that morning.

TRINA TYLER (PB #6)

Trina found the furnishings of the beach house to be mediocre at best. Either the owners or the person they had hired to decorate it forgot a few things that a sophisticated person needed during an extended summer vacation at the beach. Trina believed that for the price she was paying, it was merely adequate, and that was exactly how she was going to describe it in her review after her vacation was over. She believed the living room had too much furniture, which made it difficult to maneuver around the house. The recliner squeaked when she sat in it to rock back and forth, and it was irritating when she tried to read a book. The kitchen was designed for someone more interested in how it looked than functionality. *It caters to women, as if a man would be prohibited from making dinner for themselves, which is precisely how most of society has been conditioned to view the topic.*

Trina had spent the last six months, before her vacation, critiquing and editing five cookbooks, three fashion advice books, and two how-to books written by ten different ghostwriters for ten various celebrities who thought they were the go-to person on those topics. The only way she made it through those long months was that she knew this summer was the break she needed and that she was going to take it no matter how many hours she had to work. She hadn't taken any vacation in the past four years from her publishing company, but they had promised her time off when those last ten books were completed. There was just too much needing to be done with them. Most authors thought their writing was perfect and none of them required any proofreading, editing, or any other changes at all.

Who uses the word ain't anyway? she thought to herself. *Everyone in Fort Walton Beach is who!"*

Trina had chosen Fort Walton Beach as her summer destination, and after three months in the rental overlooking the beach, she was glad she had. She spent days reading books that she had not had the opportunity to read in over ten years. The long, hot days were spent sitting on the beach, under an umbrella that protected her fair skin from the harmful summer sun. Trina had spent the last ten years alone. She only ventured out to date once or twice a year but never found the right man. It was last year when she visited her parents and saw how happy they were together, and she decided she needed someone in her own life to grow old with. *After all, that's what people do. Grow old with someone and die,* she told herself. On the advice of a friend, she went online and joined a dating app. It took her over a month to finally connect with someone she thought she could tolerate.

Who would've thought there were so many people who didn't know how to use proper grammar when describing themselves? Or used a penis picture to entice a woman, as if it were something a decent, educated woman would find attractive? Trina thought, looking at herself in the mirror that sat above the dresser as she prepared for her date with William.

William was on vacation as well, and he, too, needed the break. There were many things she and William had in common. He also was an editor, but not like her though. William did freelance work for independent authors who tried to market themselves and self-publish online. *No money there!* she whispered to herself as she continued to get ready for their evening together. The two also shared an interest in reading the classics of literature. The most notable aspect of William was that he was dependent on Trina. After all, he was staying at a friend's beach house for free, and of course, he was in between jobs and always seemed to be waiting to get paid from one of those independent authors.

Trina liked that he was tall, muscular, and dressed the way she wanted him to dress. William also brought her coffee in the morning, along with a red rose. He didn't seem to mind that she paid for everything and that on some occasions, she berated him in front of strangers when she thought he was failing at a simple task.

"How else is he going to learn if someone doesn't correct him?" she had asked her friend, Wendy Collins, from the publishing company. Wendy had shown up unexpectedly on her way to Mexico. *Who cares if William was upset about Wendy just showing up and surprising them? Wendy was her friend, not his, and Wendy could join them for dinner anytime,* Trina thought as she continued to get ready.

She didn't particularly care for the dress, the high heel shoes, or the red toenail polish William had applied to her toes earlier in the day. Still, she felt he deserved a treat tonight. Trina was more comfortable in loose clothes, not that she couldn't pull off the strapless red dress he had picked out for her. She just wasn't comfortable in it. She had the breasts to hold it up and the backside to fill it out, but those were things men desired from women along with cooking, cleaning, and pampering, all of which she refused to do. Besides, Trina wanted William to go back to New York with her permanently in a few weeks. She had grown accustomed to him waiting on her every whim, not to mention the foot massages he gave her three to four times a week.

Trina walked out of the bedroom and started downstairs, where she had William waiting for her. She stopped halfway down the stairs and looked at the handrail that was chipped. *That's a good place for someone to cut their hand. I'll be adding that to my review,* she thought. William was sitting in the leather chair in the living room, where he sat patiently for his dinner date. He wore tan slacks, a light-brown shirt, and tie with a sports coat. His shoes were new and tight. Everything was new and bought for him by Trina, who'd insisted he wear it for their dinner date this evening.

Trina had expressed her desire to speak with William this evening about something important. She hoped the topic would be something the two of them would end up celebrating. As she made her way down the stairs, she flirted with William by blowing kisses at him while pulling her dress up ever so slightly. Trina was uncomfortable with flirting but knew it was something men enjoyed. She usually would not be caught dead acting or dressing this way, but tonight, she wanted William to agree to come back with her to New York, and she had prepared herself to do whatever was necessary to make sure he agreed.

William smiled at Trina as she made her way downstairs. He wanted to laugh out loud at her poor attempt at flirting. William thought Trina was beautiful with a model's desirable curvy figure, but she had a feminist mind, and that was something he disliked. The months he had spent with her were excruciating, to say the least. She, among all his victims, was the one who needed killing the most.

Trina had berated William in public for small mistakes, insulted him on his choice of clothes in front of others, and was, in his opinion anyway, just a mean person down to her very cold and ugly heart. William fantasized about her death more than the others, and on many occasions, he thought about killing her before tonight. William desperately wanted to choke the life out of her. He deserved an Academy Award for his performance over the last few months. *There have been so many times I wanted to tell her she was full of shit, followed by a punch in her man-hating mouth,* he thought as she walked over and kissed him.

"I hope I didn't keep you waiting," Trina said.

"No, besides, you're worth the wait," William replied. *What a performance!* he thought.

"Now, did you make the reservations at The King Fish Bar and Grill like I told you to?" Trina asked.

"Yes, dear."

"What about my car? Is it washed and cleaned out?" she asked.

"Yes. I made all the arrangements that you wrote down for me this morning," William answered.

"Look at me, William. You haven't complimented me on my outfit yet."

"I'm sorry. I'm just excited about this evening." *Because I finally get you to kill you,* he thought to himself once more.

"Well, what do you think? I know this is something men want women to wear. I did it for you."

"I know. It's just that I'm at a loss for words. The dress and how you look in it is amazing. I really want to take you upstairs and have my way with you," William blurted.

"Don't be vulgar! I know men view women as objects, but I'm a person with feelings."

"Yes, and I should watch what I say and how I say it. But I do have something for you."

"Really? What is it?" she asked excitedly.

William went to the coffee table and picked up the single rose he had lying there. He then walked back to her and held it out in front of her.

"Out of all the men in the world, you could have chosen someone else much more desirable than me. Therefore, I spent the better part of the day going from one florist to another in search of the perfect rose for you."

Trina smiled as she reached out for the rose. She titled her head and placed her other hand on the side of his head. "It's a beautiful rose, but not quite perfect. See how some of the petals fold over to the side?" Trina asked as she held the rose in front of his face.

"Yes, I see it," William despairingly agreed.

"Now, are we ready to go?" She discarded the rose by tossing it onto the sofa. She then stood there, waiting for William to open the door for her.

William stood behind her, staring at her curvy figure. *Just do it!* he told himself.

"William, the door?"

"Of course," William said as he pulled the garrote from his pocket and then threw it over her head. He pulled her to the couch, where he tightened the ligature around her neck until she passed out. He released the pressure on the garrote and lifted her dress, exposing her backside to him, and then quickly pulled her dress down, away from her breasts. William dropped his pants to the floor and proceeded to have intercourse with her from behind. When Trina regained consciousness, she placed her hands toward her back to stop him.

"Please don't, William!" she begged.

William pushed her hands back in front of her and tightened the ligature again, causing Trina to pass out again. After a few moments, Trina came around again and felt him inside of her. This time, she didn't fight or resist him in any way. She just lay there and waited for him to finish. When Trina thought he was about to climax, she felt the ligature tighten once more around her throat. Once again, she felt herself drifting off into unconsciousness.

"WILL…"

When William finished, he lay on top of her back and rested quietly. After a few minutes, he released the tension on the garrote, removed it from her neck, and kissed her cheek.

"I didn't want it to be like this. I wanted to have a beautiful evening, but you ruined it," William said as he pulled his pants up and walked toward the bathroom to clean himself up. When he flipped the light on in the bathroom, he turned once more toward the lifeless Trina.

"And the rose was perfect!"

CHAPTER 24
HYPNOSIS

The drive back to the penthouse was quiet. Newt drove while Jaxson reviewed Agent Baker's photos of the items recovered from Billy's home in town. Before leaving the administration building, both men gave their word to the sheriff and the police chief that they would keep them in the loop, no matter what the theory or discovery was, from now on concerning the investigations.

"I'll probably be working back in the jail when this is all over," Newt said as they drove over the bridge leading them back to Pensacola Beach.

"Not if we solve this," Jaxson replied.

"Do you think we can?"

"Yeah, I do. I feel that solving this case is right here in front of us, but we're missing it," Jaxson admitted.

Jaxson and Newt surprised the others when they showed up at the penthouse earlier than anyone expected. John, the sketch artist, had already left but gave the rendering he had completed of Detective Martinez's killer to Stefanie. The women looked at the two men and knew they'd had a rough day. Jaxson was about to say something to them when he heard the voice of Sheriff Thomas resonating from the television. Jaxson and Newt walked over and stood in front of the large television on the wall. Everyone in the penthouse watched as Sheriff Thomas gave an update to the news media on the investigation from behind a podium.

"We believe we have located someone responsible for the murder of the victims found on Pensacola Beach. We are still conducting the investigation and hope to have more information to pass along soon. Please remember this is an ongoing investigation and we are not at liberty to share a lot of information at this time. I'm now ready for your questions," Sheriff Thomas announced.

"WOW! He read what you wrote verbatim," Newt said, looking at Jaxson.

"It protects him. The sheriff doesn't mention there's another killer, nor does he deny it. When we locate the second killer, the sheriff can address the media again. Then he can say that in the interest of justice, he couldn't say anything about a second killer earlier."

"Earlier, like right now!" Lori stated as she pointed at the television.

"Yes, like right now," Jaxson confirmed.

"What do we do now?" Newt asked.

"How about we eat some dinner while we review everything on that large dinner table?" Jaxson suggested as he pointed at the dining room table in the other room.

"That sounds like a plan," Newt said in agreement.

Will drove to Billy's cabin but passed by without stopping. Police were still there protecting the scene. He then drove to Olivia's house and parked in her driveway. He wanted to tie up loose ends, and Olivia was a loose end that needed tying up before it was too late. He got out of the car, pushed the driver seat forward to remove a black gym bag from the back seat, and walked up the sidewalk to knock on the door. After a moment of waiting, Will thought she was not going to answer. He turned and started to leave when he heard the door open.

"I don't want to do anything tonight," Olivia stated.

"I didn't think so, but I thought I should come over and talk to you anyway."

"Do you know about Billy?" Olivia asked as she started to cry.

"Yes," Will answered sadly, slowly moving into the house. He dropped the bag to the floor, shut the door behind him, and embraced his old friend.

The penthouse was full of conversations as everyone attempted to provide insight into the case. The group had examined the sketch of Martinez's killer, but no one recognized him. Eventually, their food was delivered, and they all sat on the deck, enjoying their brief break from the case. Agent Baker came by to help and had something to eat with them. Before long, they were back at it.

"Who's this?" Baker asked as he picked up the sketch sitting on the counter next to the refrigerator.

"Oh, that's the man Stefanie saw beating Detective Martinez in the parking lot. None of us recognize him. I'll take the sketch to the police department tomorrow and drop it off with the investigating detective. Hopefully, he'll have some luck in identifying the man," Newt explained as he flipped through one of the victim files.

"No need to do that. I know who he is," Baker announced to the stunned group. They all stopped what they were doing and sat in silence, waiting for Travis to continue.

Will sat on the sofa next to Olivia with his arm around her shoulder. The two drank red wine while they reminisced over memories of high school. Will, Billy, and Olivia had been friends since first grade. The three had experienced many firsts together. They performed in front of strangers for the first time. They traveled out of state for their first competition. They even lost their virginity together. Olivia was the boys' girlfriend, and she was shared by the two of them. Olivia was the only thing in their lives they didn't compete over. Olivia thought she knew all of Will's and Billy's secrets, but she did not.

"I wasn't able to put the money in your account," Will admitted as he looked into his friend's beautiful but bruised eyes.

"I know, but I figure you're good for it," she replied softly.

"I am good for it." Will leaned forward and kissed her cheek before massaging her back and neck. "You have a beautiful neckline."

"Thank you."

"Who is he?" Lori asked after waiting for what she believed was an eternity for Agent Travis Baker to answer.

"He looks like Victor Oblonsky."

"Who's Victor Oblonsky?" Taylor asked.

"He's a Russian immigrant who is involved in anything and everything along the Florida coastline. We've been after him for a long time. He's one of the top guys in the Russian Mafia, and he's known for using a garrote to kill his enemies. We just haven't been able to pin anything on him," Agent Baker admitted as he continued to look over the sketch.

"Are you sure it's him?" Jaxson asked.

"Yes, he's just missing the scar along his right cheek where someone tried to cut his throat one night, right about here," Baker said, pointing at the man's cheek.

"I guess you got something on him now. Me," Stefanie said with disappointment.

Olivia and Will ended up in her bed after they finished a bottle of wine. For the first time in a long time, Will made love to her. There was no choking or beating. Will was kind and gentle with her, just the way he and Billy were the first time they shared her in the cabin so many years ago.

"Did you know Billy was killing those women?" Olivia asked, even though she already knew the answer. She wanted to hear it from him.

"I knew."

"Did you help him?"

"I did more than help," Will answered after a moment of silence.

Olivia wanted to ask why, but she resisted the urge. She just lay there on her side with her back toward Will. Suddenly, she felt his hands on her back. He rolled her over to face him and slowly placed his body on top of hers. He kissed her, running his hand down her breast, to her buttocks, and back up to her neck. He then placed his hand around her neck and looked into her eyes.

"Don't, Will."

It was getting late, and the group decided to put things away until the next morning. Jaxson sat next to Taylor on one couch, and Newt and Lori sat together on another while Stefanie reclined in an oversized leather chair. All of them were tired and feeling beaten. Agent Baker had left and had taken the sketch with him. Baker interviewed Stefanie before leaving and informed them he would take the investigation away from the local police and lead the investigation into Victor Oblonsky with the full support of the FBI.

"Did you ever meet the guy Natalie was dating?" Lori asked, breaking the silence in the room.

"No. I spoke to Natalie once when he was over at her place, but I never really met him," Taylor admitted nonchalantly.

Jaxson quickly sat up and looked at Taylor. She just revealed something she had never mentioned to him before.

"What?" Taylor asked after seeing Jaxson's surprised expression.

"You never told me that," Jaxson replied.

"I didn't think about it until just now. Is it important?"

"What can you tell me about the phone call?" Jaxson asked as he sat on the edge of the couch, looking at Taylor intently.

"I don't know. What do you want to know?" Taylor was worried she may have held something back that could have helped with the investigation.

"Did you hear his voice? Was there anything going on in the background? Did she mention what they were doing?"

Jaxson asked excitedly while the others sat up and waited for Taylor to answer.

"I don't know. I really don't know!" Taylor replied and started to tear up.

Jaxson saw Taylor's panicked reaction and realized he had overstepped and was pressuring her. He quickly backed off while reassuring her the phone call wasn't that important. Still, he wanted her to try to remember everything about it. Taylor tried, but she couldn't concentrate with everyone watching her.

"I'm trying to remember, but I can't," Taylor admitted after a few minutes.

"It's okay. I have an idea if you're willing to try it," Jaxson replied.

"I'll do anything!"

Jaxson moved Taylor to the recliner and placed a kitchen chair next to it for him to sit in. He had everyone else leave the room.

"Are you going to hypnotize her?" Newt asked before he left the room.

"No. I'm just going to make her comfortable, relax her, and talk to her."

"Sounds a lot like hypnosis," Newt said before he left the room.

Jaxson closed all the doors leading to the living room and had Taylor recline into a comfortable position in the chair. He then took the seat beside her.

"Are you going to hypnotize me?" she asked.

"No. This is a concentration exercise, and all I want you to do is concentrate on my voice and relax."

"Okay," Taylor responded softly and slightly leaned back.

"Taylor, lie back further, close your eyes, and imagine sitting on the deck next to your pool after a long day at work. The sun has gone down, the wind is blowing slightly, and you can hear the water in the pool lapping against the sides. You're tired and want to rest. As you listen to my voice, you are getting more and more drowsy and want to go to sleep, but you won't. Taylor, do you understand?"

"Yes," she answered softly.

"Taylor, can you tell me about Natalie and the phone call you had with her when you were away, helping your mother?"

"Yes."

"When you spoke to Natalie that day, did she tell you what she was doing?"

"She was with him, and they were about to have dinner. Natalie was drinking a glass of 1959 Rosa Dulce. She sounded happy," Taylor answered.

"Did Natalie like that type of wine?"

"Yes, but he brought it."

"Can you hear anyone else with her?"

"No, only the music," Taylor replied. She squinted her eyes as if she were trying to hear the music once again.

"Taylor, what kind of music do you hear?"

"The classical kind."

"Do you recognize it?"

"No, but I think I've heard it before."

"What else can you hear?" Jaxson asked.

"A violin."

"A violin," Jaxson repeated.

"Yes, but it's louder. I think he's playing it along with the music. Wait, he is playing it. Natalie told me he was playing it."

"Taylor, what else do you hear?"

"Nothing except Natalie. She sounds so happy. I miss her so much," Taylor stated as she started to cry.

"Taylor, you're okay, and I need you to listen to my voice now. You're not tired anymore, and in a moment, you'll open your eyes and talk to me."

"Okay."

"When you open your eyes, you'll realize you've done

everything possible to help Natalie and that there's nothing you could have done to save her."

"All right."

"Okay, I'm going to count to ten, and when I get to the number ten, you'll open your eyes and see me sitting next to you. You'll feel warm and safe."

When Jaxson reached ten, Taylor sat up and looked at the man sitting beside her, and suddenly she felt warm and safe.

Will woke in bed next to Olivia. He rolled over and placed his hand on her shoulder. She was still and felt cold. He got out of bed, covered her up, and walked into the bathroom to shower. Will allowed the warm water to run down his back for a few minutes. His time was coming to an end. He half expected the police to come rushing into the bedroom last night to arrest him. Will knew he was on borrowed time, and it wouldn't be long before the FBI and the police connected him to Billy. He dried off and wiped the condensation from the mirror.

"The game is tied. It can't end in a tie!" Will said as he looked at his reflection.

Will was sitting at the foot of her bed, putting on his shoes, when he felt Olivia moving in the bed behind him. He stood and walked to her side of the bed and sat next to her. He ran his hand across her face and through her hair. She smiled at him and caressed his hand. He then leaned over and kissed her cheek.

"You've always been a good friend to me—to Billy and me… I'm leaving a bag there with fifty grand in it. There are also papers inside it that you'll need to sign. I created a trust account for you. You'll never have to work again."

"Why? Wait! What are you doing, Will?" Olivia asked as she sat up in bed.

"Something I should've done for you a long time ago," he answered before kissing her on the forehead and rushing out of the house.

Will got into his car, backed out of the driveway, and took out his cell phone.

Jaxson got out of bed early and sat in the dining room to look over the case files once more and drink a cup of coffee. He knew there was something there, but he couldn't put his finger on it. He turned on his computer and went through the images Agent Baker and the evidence technicians had taken at Billy's house in town. He moved from one photo to the next, and after about ten images, he saw something that stopped him cold. There in image 421 labeled "Bedroom #1 Northside Nightstand Top Drawer" was a sheet of paper. On the paper was written:

S

1111111111111111111= 18

K

1111111111111111111= 18

"Eighteen to eighteen. The game is tied," Jaxson mumbled. He startled when his cell phone rang, and once again, it was from an unknown caller.

"Hello," Jaxson said after taking the call.

"Agent Locke? How are you this morning?" SKO asked.

"I'm well, and you?"

"I'm good too. Have you learned anything new?"

"I've learned that the game is tied," Jaxson answered and then waited for a response.

"So it is. What's your next move?"

"I don't know, but I thought I'd catch the other killer.

Do you have any suggestions on where I should look?" Jaxson asked sarcastically.

"Why don't you look for commonalities?"

"Commonalities?"

"Yes, Agent Locke. People, places, and things. Serial killers and victims have things that are in common. You need to find the commonalities in this case, and when you do, you'll solve it," SKO answered and hung up.

Jaxson was sitting there looking at his cell phone when Taylor entered the room. She came up behind him and kissed his cheek and rubbed his shoulders.

"You all right?" she asked.

"Yeah, just thinking."

"I have to sign some paperwork today, but I'll be free at lunch if you'd like to meet," Taylor suggested.

"I'd like that."

"Good, I'll text you the address when I'm heading over. I'll meet you there," Taylor replied as she walked out.

Chapter 25
Commonalities

Jaxson, Newt, Stefanie, and Lori spent the morning reviewing the case files over and over again, looking for anything that could help them identify the second killer. Jaxson felt there had to be something identifying the second killer hidden within the seven victim files, but he didn't know where.

"What are we missing?" Newt asked after throwing the Bethany Porter file back onto the table out of frustration.

"I don't know, but it seems there should be something here that helps," Stefanie stated.

"I wish I could've given you more about the roses," Lori said from the chair at the end of the table.

"I know there is something here. We just need to find it!" Jaxson snapped.

"Well, what do you know? To be an absolute, I mean." Lori stood from her chair with her hands on her hips.

Newt turned toward Lori. "What?"

"When I'm looking at a species of flower, plant, or anything else, I group them together into the knowns and unknowns. Each group has something in common within those two groups."

"In common or commonalities!" Jaxson quickly separated the files.

Newt moved back away from the table to give the excited Jaxson room to work. "What are you doing?"

"We've been looking over each file separately trying to find something to identify the second killer. What we've not been doing is grouping the victims together to locate a commonality between them. I want to create a list of everything each victim has in common with the other."

"Okay, but I already completed the victimology for each one," Newt stated.

"Yes, you did, but we were reviewing each victim individually. Let's combine them and identify what they have in common," Jaxson replied.

"Is there anything we can do?" Stefanie asked.

"Yes, actually there is. I'd like the two of you to review the evidence photos from both of Billy's addresses. I want you looking for anything that stands out," Jaxson instructed.

"The knowns and unknowns," Lori blurted.

"Exactly!" Jaxson said.

"Okay! We can do that."

Jaxson and Newt each took a file on each of the seven victims. Jaxson had the copies, and Newt had the originals. Their plan was to go through the files and separate everything into categories. There were categories for the autopsy, social media, family, and the people who reported them missing. They created other categories for anything else that didn't fit into one of the others.

The four of them worked diligently on their assigned tasks for about two hours. It was nearly eleven o'clock when Stefanie found something in the photos. She noticed that on a wall in the cabin, there was a photo of Billy and two other children. There was also a photo of Billy and possibly the same two children on his bedroom wall at the address in town.

"Jaxson, look at this." Stefanie stood with the laptop in hand and walked to the FBI agent.

"What is it?" he asked.

"This photo from the cabin of Billy and two other children—"

"I saw that when we went in the cabin, but I don't know who they are. What are you thinking?" Jaxson asked.

"Well, it seems they could be the same two children in this photo that was found at Billy's address in town. They're just a little older. Maybe they went to school with Billy. Look, the other two are holding violins."

"You're right. What if all three attended the Legacy Classical Academy of Pensacola? I bet Dr. Ling could tell us who they are. Newt!" Jaxson yelled.

"I'm already on it," Newt said with his cell phone against his ear.

Beach Taco was a small restaurant that overlooked Casino Beach. Jaxson sat there admiring the beautiful emerald water as it pounded wave after wave onto the white sandy beach. Vacationers sat on chairs, blankets, and towels, soaking up as much sun as they could before the end of their summer vacation. Jaxson found the directions to the restaurant easy to follow. Taylor had texted him the address and the directions to the restaurant at a little after the noon hour. He wanted to keep working on the case, but he also needed a break and, of course, some private time with Taylor. This was something he was looking forward to doing as well. The two of them hadn't spent as much time together as Jaxson would have liked, but it was difficult with everything going on. Not to mention the added number of people who were now around them twenty-fours a day.

"Come here often?" Taylor asked as she walked up behind the surprised Jaxson.

"No, not really. What about you?" Jaxson stood, pulled Taylor into him, and kissed her deeply. He knew it wasn't professional, but he missed her.

"No, but I'll come by more often if that's the welcome I get," Taylor said and sat in the seat next to his.

"I just wanted to make sure we're good," Jaxson said, looking into her eyes.

"Good? Good, how?" Taylor asked in a flirtatious and teasing manner.

"Well, with everything going on, you and I seem to have taken a break, or rather, we haven't gotten to spend much time together. I mean, after the crash, it seems we've both been going ninety miles an hour in different directions."

"We're good. As long as you're good with me," Taylor confessed happily.

"I'm good with you."

"Then we're good." She reached over and affectionately rubbed his back.

The two enjoyed fish tacos while listening to eighties rock playing from the speakers overhead. Jaxson updated her on the case and what the team was working on. Taylor explained to Jaxson that she had to return to the title company after lunch and re-sign some paperwork. Jeff had changed the name of the trust on the title paperwork, so now everything needed to be re-signed by Natalie's family, the lawyers, and herself.

"How long will re-signing everything take?" Jaxson asked.

"Most everything is done electronically. If Natalie's family signs quickly and gets it back to the attorney and he signs it right away, then it shouldn't take more than an hour or two," she explained and drank the last bit of her tea.

"How about you and I try to get away tonight? If nothing comes out of what we're working on, then let's do something."

Jaxson put money in the folder that held their lunch bill and then laid it back down on the table.

"Like what?"

"I don't know. What would you like to do?" he asked.

"I'd like to go back to Orange Beach, and stay in one of my other rentals, and have my way with you," Taylor answered quietly before leaning in and kissing him.

"Okay, then let's do it. It's close enough that if something does come up, I can get back here in a hurry and—"

"Shoot! I forgot that I have to meet with Jeff at Natalie's place for a toast. He wants to celebrate the closing, and I told him I would," Taylor explained.

"Really? Celebrating with another man, are you?" Jaxson asked comically, pretending to be jealous.

"It's not like that. Realtors do this all the time. I'm not into him. Trust me! We can leave right afterward though."

"I do trust you. What time do you think we can get out of here?"

"You can come over to my place around five. I'll meet Jeff and come back over, and we can leave from my place."

Jaxson happily agreed. "Sounds like a plan."

Jaxson left Taylor and returned to the penthouse a short time later. He found the rest of the team still going over the case files. There was an empty pizza box and half-empty liter of cola sitting on the counter.

"How was lunch?" Newt asked before placing his last bite of pizza into his mouth.

"It was good. I had fish tacos."

"Ooh! That sounds good," Stefanie admitted.

"It was. Did you guys come up with anything?" Jaxson

asked as he walked to the dining room table. It was covered in piles of paperwork from the case files.

"No, I'm waiting to hear back from Dr. Ling. I emailed his secretary about the photos we found and included mine and your cell phone numbers for him to call," Newt explained.

"Good, hopefully he'll call soon." Jaxson stood in front of his stacks of different categories concerning each victim. He picked up the social media pile. "How is it that all of you women attracted these two men? How did they find you?" Jaxson mumbled to himself as he sat down and began reading.

Taylor was reviewing the last few documents in the title company's closing room at a little after four o'clock. She had been waiting for over two hours for Natalie's family's attorney to send the paperwork back with their new signatures on them. The only thing Taylor found odd with the documents was the name Jeff was using on the trust that he had created at the last minute.

"Maybe it's his mother's name," Taylor mumbled right before Karen Smith, the title company's closer, walked in.

"Is everything there?" Karen asked.

"Yes, it looks like it. I just finished going over everything and signed in my spot."

"Good. Jeff Carlisle already signed all his documents. Congratulations, you've closed another one, and I have your check right here." Karen handed over the envelope with Taylor's commission check inside.

"Thanks," Taylor replied somberly. Normally, she would be thrilled at a closing where she earned a large commission, but not this time. Taylor had mixed emotions about the real estate deal. On one hand, she was happy to be ending this chapter in her life, but on the other, it was the chapter where Natalie was no longer a part of the story.

Jaxson continued to review the files in the dining room of Taylor's house. He was waiting for her to return so they could leave on their overnight trip. He had told the others he and Taylor were going away for the evening but would be back the next day after lunch. Newt and Jaxson agreed to call each other if either of them heard from Dr. Ling. At a quarter to five, he heard Taylor walk in the front door of the beach house. He laid the file down and quickly walked into the living room. Taylor hurried across the floor to him and kissed him just as he had done to her at lunch.

"Miss me?" she whispered.

"Yes."

"What now?" she asked as she ran her hand down his chest and around his waist.

"You tell me."

"I've got to walk over and see Jeff for a few minutes and then I'll be back." Taylor sighed and then went into the dining room to drop her copy of the closing documents onto the table next to the case files.

"Okay, but hurry. You still have to pack," Jaxson said to remind her.

"Why don't you pack my things for me? Grab something out of my top dresser drawer for me to wear later tonight," she suggested as she moved back toward the front door.

"Like what?"

"Whatever you like, honey. Surprise me!" Taylor said flirtatiously before she stepped out the front door.

Taylor walked to 1616 Ariola Drive and used her old key to get in. Once inside, she took her time walking around the large beach house one more time. She walked into every room, and in each one, she found a memory of Natalie. In the master bedroom, Taylor found the small sculpture of two naked lovers intertwined with each other, sitting on a waist-high column in the corner of the room. Natalie had purchased the large statue in Paris and brought it back with her on the plane instead of having it shipped. Taylor never liked the sculpture, but Natalie did, and somehow it always found its way into their conversations about men, women, and love. Natalie had even named the two lovers.

"Well, Ricky and Taylor, it's time to move on!" Taylor stated and laughed out loud. She always thought it was funny that Natalie had named the woman Taylor and the man Ricky, after a good-looking waiter they saw in Panama City. Taylor was still looking around when she heard Jeff pull up outside. She hurried downstairs and found Jeff in the kitchen, opening a bottle of wine.

Jaxson removed his holster from his ankle and placed it on the counter along with his wallet, phone, and the change from his pocket. He wanted to shower and change clothes before they left but decided to put things away first. He was picking up the files and placing them in his bag when he looked down at the closing documents Taylor had brought inside. A name on the closing documents caught his eye. Jaxson reached down and started to pick it up when his cell phone rang.

"Hello, this is Agent Locke," Jaxson said to the unknown caller as he sat down and pulled the files back out of his bag.

"Agent Locke, this Dr. Ling from the Legacy Classical Academy."

"Yes, thank you for calling me. Did you get a chance to review the photos Detective Waterman sent over?"

"I did, and I know who the children are in the photo."

"Really, who are they?" Jaxson flipped through the files, quickly removing one specific document from each one.

"The guy on the left is Billy, the girl in the middle is Olivia, and the guy on the right is Will. Strings, Keys, and O-Lively as they were known here at school," Dr. Ling explained.

"Strings and Keys. What do you mean by Strings and Keys?" Jaxson asked.

"Well, Will played the violin, and Billy played the piano. String and Keys," Dr. Ling answered.

"Is there anything else you can tell me about them?"

"The three of them were thick as thieves. All three hung out at Billy's place. Will's mother died when he was born, and Olivia's parents were nonexistent most of the time, so Billy's mom was kind of a mother to all of them."

"What about their fathers?" Jaxson asked.

"Billy's dad was not a kind man, and many of us here thought that he beat Billy. Will's father was the same. I think he blamed Will for his mother's death and took it out on him. Olivia, well, her parents were alcoholics and drug users, so they never came around much. Those three kids worshiped Billy's mother. She came to every one of their recitals, and they presented her with roses each and every time."

"Would Mrs. Clayton dress up for their recitals?" Jaxson asked, already knowing the answer.

"Yes. Sara Clayton wore a different red dress every time. She was both elegant and laid-back. She was blind, but she was a music lover, and she played both the piano and violin better than most sighted musicians."

"Do you know how I can find Will, Dr. Ling?" Jaxson asked.

Taylor could tell Jeff was excited about the closing and seeing her as well. He wore a great suit, smelled nice, and was in good spirits. The wine, she was sure, was expensive. Taylor knew Jeff wanted more of her than a real estate deal.

"It's time to celebrate!" Jeff proudly proclaimed as he pulled the cork from the bottle and looked at Taylor.

"It is," Taylor said in return but with less enthusiasm.

"I think we should let this breathe for a little while before we drink it," Jeff suggested and placed the bottle down after pouring two glasses. He walked to the in-house stereo system and connected his phone to it.

"When was the last time you got to see this place?" Taylor asked.

"When your friend outbid me for it," Jeff stated with a bit of resentment in his voice.

"Oh, yes. I remember when I showed it to you. Now, if I remember correctly, you decided to wait on making an offer because you thought I overpriced it. You know, you could've bought it that weekend, but you waited, and it gave Natalie time to make her offer. I called you and told you that if you wanted to make an offer, you needed to bring your highest and best offer."

"I know. I did too, but it was a hundred K less than Natalie's offer," Jeff remarked regrettably.

"What are your plans for the place?"

"I don't know, but I think we'll redecorate," Jeff said after selecting music from his phone's playlist.

"What are you going to change?" Taylor was disappointed.

She had always liked how the home was decorated and didn't want to see it remodeled.

"Well, I'll get rid of the furniture first of all and that awful looking sex sculpture in the master bedroom—"

"What's this music?" Taylor asked, the sounds of classical music resonating through the house's speakers.

"It's *Beethoven's 5th Symphony in C Minor*. Do you like it?"

The music was familiar to Taylor. It was the same music she had heard over the phone, playing in the background, when she spoke to Natalie, when Natalie was with Will.

How does he know about the sculpture? Taylor asked herself.

"Here's your glass of wine. I think you'll like it. It's a 1959 Rosa Dulce," Jeff explained as he walked toward Taylor, holding the glasses.

Jaxson waited for Dr. Ling to answer, but he already knew where to find Will. He picked up the closing packet and compared the buyer's real estate company logo to the ones on the leasing documents that some of the victims had signed. Jaxson had discovered that some victims signed a lease with a different real estate company, but all of those companies fell under one larger real estate investment company, Carlisle Real Estate Investments.

"You can find Will around town, but he doesn't go by Will anymore. He uses his first name now, Jefferson or Jeff. Yes, Jefferson William Carlisle. He's a big shot real estate guy now," Dr. Ling said right before Jaxson hung up the phone and ran out of the beach house. He dialed Newt's number as he desperately raced toward 1616 Ariola Drive.

Taylor wanted to run, but she was afraid. Jeff was standing between her and the door, holding the wine glasses.

"You know, Jeff, my friend is waiting for me to come back so that we can go on a trip." Taylor reached for a glass of wine. She took it from Jeff's hand and held it up. "Congratulations on your purchase," she said and then drank the entire glass down. She didn't know what else to do, so she began to ramble as she maneuvered around the island counter toward the front door.

"I think your mother will love the house, and I'd love to see it after you redecorate it and—"

"What gave me away?" Jeff asked as he placed his wine glass down.

"What do you mean, Will?" Taylor asked nervously.

He quickly moved in front of her. "That's what I mean. You just called me Will."

"I—"

Will reached back and punched her in the jaw, sending her backward onto the tile floor.

"You know, you were the one who got away. I came here for you, not Natalie, but you left town and I ended up with Natalie," Will stated as he straddled the dazed Taylor and grabbed her by her hair. He pulled her head up and punched her over and over again in the face.

Taylor screamed and tried to stop him, but Will continued to hit her until her body went limp. He let go of her hair and allowed her head to drop to the hard floor beneath her.

"I've wanted you for so long," Will said excitedly as he reached under Taylor's skirt and ripped her panties away. "Now, I'll have you!"

"No, you won't!" Jaxson yelled as he ran toward the surprised Will. Jaxson delivered one blow with a clutched fist to just behind Will's left ear at the base of his skull. The impact forced Will to the side and off of Taylor. Jaxson slipped on Taylor's blood but quickly recovered at about the same time as Will. Will was hurt, but he wasn't finished. Jaxson grabbed him and delivered one fist after another into the killer's face, forcing him backward with every crushing blow. Will fought back and caught Jaxson in the left eye with a lucky punch. The impact blinded him in his eye for a moment, so he backed up to refocus.

A moment was all Will needed. He grabbed the bottle of wine on the counter and brought it down onto Jaxson's already-injured head.

Jaxson stumbled backward. He stood there for a second as blood dripped down his forehead, but through his blurred vision, he saw Will pull a gun from his own back. "No!" Jaxson yelled as he rushed forward. He grabbed Will by the waist and forced him backward as he reached for the gun. Jaxson was able to grab Will's wrist, but it wasn't enough. Will fired one shot. Jaxson yelled out in pain as the bullet tore through his shoulder.

The pain was intense, and as Jaxson continued to struggle with Will, he looked over at Taylor, who was still lying on the floor motionless in a growing puddle of blood. Jaxson knew he had to push through the pain if there was any chance for her to survive.

"What now, HERO?" Will yelled as he turned the gun toward Jaxson once more.

Jaxson looked behind the killer and saw the sliding glass door that led out to the deck over the driveway. With everything he could muster, Jaxson threw his body weight against the killer, forcing him backward toward the glass.

Will tried to stop him, but he was no match for the determined FBI agent. Within seconds, the two men crashed through the sliding glass door. Their momentum carried them across the balcony, over the handrail, and onto the concrete driveway below.

Jaxson was disoriented, so it took him a moment to collect himself. He rolled over and found Will lying a few feet away, with part of the handrail sticking upward through the center of his torso. Will coughed and gasped for air. Slowly and very carefully, Jaxson sat up onto his knees.

"We're not done," Will grunted through labored breaths.

"What?" Jaxson asked as he turned to find Will pointing the gun at him.

Suddenly, there were three quick flashes of light. Jaxson watched as Will dropped his gun and fell backward onto the driveway. He then turned back toward where the flashes of light came from and saw Newt standing there with his gun in his hand. Stefanie and Lori were seated in the car next to him.

"Thank you," Jaxson said before he fell forward onto the driveway once more.

"Jaxson!"

Epilogue

Jaxson spent four days in the hospital following minor surgery before he was released. Taylor spent two days in the hospital after a plastic surgeon realigned her nose and closed the cuts in her face above her eyes. The two of them then spent the next few days recuperating at Taylor's beach house.

The news of Jefferson William Carlisle spread across the world, and everyone was surprised to learn that a man worth millions of dollars was a serial killer. News outlets surrounded the beach house at 1616 Ariola Drive once again for a few days. Carlisle's other beach properties along the coastline from North Carolina to Texas, where other victims had been discovered, were just as busy with local and national news agencies.

The game between William and Billy had ended in a tie, with neither man winning. The losers of their game were the victims and their families. Jaxson was placed on medical leave until he could be released back to full duty. He took advantage of the leave and decided to spend it in Pensacola with his new girlfriend.

It was a few Saturdays later when Taylor decided that everyone needed to celebrate and enjoy a good old Southern seafood boil at the beach house where Jaxson had first stayed. It was currently occupied by Newt, Lori, and Stefanie. Everyone involved in the investigation was invited. Agent Baker and his family showed up, Sheriff Thomas and the police chief made an appearance, and Deputy Bo Turner, Dr. Kendrick, and his assistant, Wally, came by to eat as well. It seemed that everyone was pleased with the work they had done in capturing not one but two serial killers.

Agent Baker explained that during the investigation into Detective Martinez's murder, he discovered Martinez was in deep with the Russians. Martinez had taken money from the Oblonsky family in exchange for destroying evidence. The only problem was Martinez never destroyed the evidence. Baker informed Stefanie that her name was being withheld, for now, while federal prosecutors built their case against members of the Oblonsky criminal organization.

Jaxson and Newt were standing on the deck over the driveway, enjoying a beer, when they looked over and saw a moving truck pull up to 1616 Ariola Drive.

"I can't believe this," Newt said as he watched the moving truck back into the driveway.

"Neither can I," Jaxson replied.

"Jaxson, you got to keep the arm at ninety degrees if you want it to heal right," Stefanie said as she and Taylor walked out onto the deck to join the two men.

"What's going on over there?" Lori asked after she walked out of the house behind the other two women, carrying three glasses of wine.

"Looks like I'm getting a new neighbor," Taylor mumbled out of the side of her injured mouth as she and Stefanie took a glass from Lori.

"Why would she move there?" Stefanie asked with a suspicious look on her face.

"It's the place that keeps her connected to the two most important men she's ever loved," Jaxson answered as he and the others watched Olivia Harris on her deck, looking over at them.

"The Olivia Harris Living Trust, a trust with a house and ten million dollars in it. All left to her, legally, by one Jefferson William Carlisle," Newt stated.

"I don't think we'll be friends," Taylor announced as best as she could. The comment made everyone laugh.

Jaxson raised his glass in the air and proposed a toast. "To friends!"

Everyone repeated the toast and touched glasses. The party ended at around midnight, and Jaxson and Taylor walked back to her beach house and went to bed.

Jaxson awoke to find Taylor lying next to him. He couldn't sleep, and after an hour, he found himself still awake, lying on his back and looking up at the ceiling fan as it spun quietly. His thoughts drifted back and forth over various aspects of the case. The experienced profiler still had questions. The biggest was why Will had called him and why he'd brought him to Pensacola.

"Did he want to get caught?" Jaxson asked himself before he got up and walked into the other bedroom, leaving Taylor lying peacefully in the bed.

Jaxson entered the other room, took the victim's files out of his bag, and looked at each one once more. "It all doesn't fit," Jaxson mumbled as he took out the autopsy photo of each victim and placed them on the bed.

"Wait!" he whispered as he placed the girls in rows according to their injuries. He then stood back and looked at each row. He took out a pen and three sheets of notepad paper and wrote an S, a K, and a Ø on them, then placed them next to each row of victims.

He determined that Will, S, killed Bethany Porter and Natalie Adams and used his fist in an uncontrollable rage to beat them severely. Billy, K, killed Brook Evans and Jodie Lawrence without rage. Then there was Abigail Johnson, Samantha Farmer, and Trina Tyler, who were all killed with a garrote from behind and buried under the Ø mark.

"Those three victims weren't part of Will and Billy's game. There weren't two killers; there were three!" Jaxson declared as he looked at his cell phone vibrating on the nightstand. He bent over and picked it up, looked at the caller ID, and saw it was from an unknown number.

"Why did you bring me here, and why did you kill those three women?" Jaxson asked after answering the phone.

"Good, you figured it out. I was getting worried that you weren't the profiler I was hoping you would be," SKO announced proudly.

"Why do this?"

"Because every side in a game needs an opponent. Good versus evil. The Nazis versus the Allies. Will versus Billy. You and I, Agent Locke! You are my opponent."

"I won't play your game," Jaxson declared.

"Not yet, but you will. I need to train you a little more before you and I actually meet on the playing field."

"What are you talking about?"

"You aren't ready for me yet, but you will be when I get done training you."

"How do you suppose you will train me?" Jaxson asked, starting to get angry.

"I'm going to help you capture some serial killers," SKO stated proudly.

"What's your real name?"

"SKO."

"Why the letters SKO?" Jaxson asked in a tone that let the man know he was getting irritated with his game.

"It's an acronym. Can you guess what it stands for, Agent Locke?"

Jaxson took a second before answering. "Serial Killer Offender," Jaxson finally answered.

"Good job. That's my name. Now, the people in charge of you, your superiors as they like to be called, are going to tell you some things about me. All of which are true, by the way. So prepare yourself."

"Like what?" Jaxson inquired of his self-proclaimed tutor.

"I'll let them cover that. I hope you and Taylor enjoy your time off at the beach together. I'll be in touch. Good-bye, Agent Locke."

Jaxson hung up the phone and thought about SKO. He looked at his phone and saw there was a reminder to check his voice memos on his phone. The odd part was that Jaxson had never set up a reminder to check his voice memos. He swiped his phone to the memo app and saw there was a voice memo recorded the day that Billy ran Taylor and him off the road.

Jaxson pressed play.

THE MAN

FROM

MEDAN

AGENT JAXSON LOCKE FBI MYSTERY THRILLER SERIES BOOK 4

PROLOGUE

The Ourang Medan left the Chinese port of Dalian on May 25, 1947, on its way to Johnston Island in the Pacific Ocean. The atoll was under the control of the United States of America. It was located over nine hundred miles from the Hawaiian Islands. The crew of the Ourang was unnerved because of the mysterious cargo that had been loaded by men in military uniforms. The crew was not allowed to be aboard or to handle the shipment themselves when it was loaded. Fadhlan, the ship's executive officer, was Indonesian by birth. He was raised in England after the start of World War II, and he, like the ship's captain, was new to the vessel and its crew of Indonesians. Captain Meyer was a German man who, like Fadhlan, spoke English. Fadhlan was explicitly hired for his English-speaking skills. He had been directed to assist Captain Meyer with giving orders to the Indonesian crew members.

Since the departure from the Chinese port, rumors swirled around the ship. Some members of the crew believed the ship's cargo contained the remains of Chinese men, women, and children who had been experimented on by a Japanese secret military organization, Unit 731. Most rumors supported the 731 rumor or added to it in some fashion. Some crew members believed the ship was carrying chemical and biological weapons that Unit 731 had created and used on civilians during the war. The ship was out to sea for five days when a fire broke out in the ship's galley. The fire was quickly extinguished, but the next day, another fire started in the ship's engine room that killed three crew members. It didn't take long before the crew began to believe that the ship was cursed along with its cargo. The crew spoke in private in small circles around the ship.

Captain Meyer had approached Fadhlan and asked him directly what the crew was talking about. The captain had observed some men gathering in groups as they whispered outside the entrance to the cargo doors that led to their mysterious cargo. When Fadhlan told him what was being said, he ordered Fadhlan to inform the crew that they were carrying ammunition, brass, and small arms and nothing more. Fadhlan relayed the message to the crew, who accepted their captain's answer for the time being, but still some men had their suspicions.

The ship had been at sea for twenty days before they reached the outskirts of the Marshall Islands. Once more, after replenishing the ship's supplies, the crew's rumors began again. Some of the crew members observed what they believed to be a submarine off the port side of the ship the day they left the Marshall Islands. Once more, Fadhlan told the crew their cargo was nothing more than military equipment and it needed to be delivered to the United States military on Johnston Island. That evening, two men were walking on the deck of the Ourang when they passed by one of the doors leading into the cargo area. They stopped abruptly after noticing an odd smell from the cargo area. Immediately they called for Fadhlan, who rushed to their location.

§

On June 7, 1947 at 11:00 pm, two ships passing by the Marshall

Islands, the City of Baltimore and the Silver Star, both picked up a chilling SOS message from the Ourang Medan.

"SOS from Ourang Medan. We float. All officers including the captain dead in chartroom and on the bridge. Probably the whole of crew dead." One more message followed shortly after: *"I die."*

Captain Morris and his crew of the Silver Star were the first to reach the Ourang Medan. When they arrived, they boarded the ship and every crew member they found was dead. They were found in the chartroom, the bridge, and scattered around the decks of the ship. Every man was found in a position of fright with his mouth gaping open wide as if each one saw something that literally scared them to death. One member of the Silver Star told Captain Morris that when he boarded the ship, the crew members seemed to be silently screaming as they lay dead. The crew of the Silver Star immediately tied onto the Ourang Medan and pulled it toward port.

Fadhlan, who was sitting in the radio room, was still alive. He had sent the SOS message, and after he heard the crew of the Silver Star leaving the Ourang Medan, he stumbled out onto the deck. He tried to take a deep breath in the night ocean air, but his lungs burned. He staggered farther toward the starboard side of the ship and looked out at the open water of the Pacific Ocean. Off in the distance, he observed a projectile skimming just below the surface of the water toward the Ourang Medan.

Fadhlan looked down and recognized the image of a torpedo just before it struck the Ourang. The explosion sent Fadhlan over the side rail into the ocean. As he slowly sank deeper into the depths below, he watched as two more torpedoes barreled into the ship. Two more explosions echoed through the water. Fadhlan went unconscious but not before seeing the Ourang Medan sink into the dark depths of the Pacific Ocean next to him.

About the Author

Michael grew up in Pensacola, Florida, where he spent the summer months as a youth at the beach, tubing down the river or splashing around in a pool near his grandmother's home. After graduating from high school, he joined the US Army and served in the Military Police Corps. After nearly seven and a half years, Michael left the military. He took a position at the Colorado Springs Police Department, where he served the community for ten years. An injury on duty forced him into early retirement from policing. Currently, Michael is the Department Chair of the Criminal Justice Department at a local community college. Michael earned a Bachelor of Science in Sociology with an emphasis in Criminology from Colorado State University and a Master of Criminal Justice from the University of Colorado.

Michael started his writing career as a ghostwriter for a publisher of textbooks. Eventually, he co-authored a textbook. Michael has always had the desire to write fiction. Through the encouragement of his family and friends, Michael started writing mystery fiction and hasn't stopped. Michael's wife, Stefanie, still catches him daydreaming as he drives down the highway thinking about different stories. The facial expressions that he makes reveal to her that somewhere in his mind, he's reviewing a chapter, scene, or dialogue between characters for a new book.